# SMOKE

# HOUSE

*& Other Stories*

MATTHEW G. REES

## Praise for Matthew G. Rees's story collection *Keyhole* published by Three Impostors www.threeimpostors.co.uk

'...*a superb collection... the stories reminded me of Aickman, of M.R. James and of Ramsey Campbell... in the most complimentary sense.*'
Stephen Volk, author and BAFTA-winning screenwriter

'*Rees is fully in control of that particular gift of authors of fantastic stories, which consists of placing banal objects in situations where they are at the same time innocent and threatening... On other occasions, his stories are wonderfully weird and funny at the same time.*'
Guido Eekhaut, award-winning author of *Absinthe*

'*In turns elusive, eerie, delicately unsettling and quietly devastating... his story arcs cast their strange net over the reader.*'
Carly Holmes, prize-winning writer

'*A tour de force.*'
Sally Spedding, poet and author

'*This is a hugely recommended collection that marks Rees out as a writer capable of spinning tales of vibrant imagination and who is unafraid to peer into strange places.*'
Wyrd Britain

'*His great stories are refreshingly different, he paints a startling and detailed portrait of a world slightly askew, and he knows how to cast a spell with a sentence.*'
The Short Story

'*Matthew G. Rees is an author whose name was new to me, but is now noted. Further work from him will receive a warm welcome!*'
John Howard in *Wormwood*

'*...beautiful writing throughout... wonderfully accomplished.*'
Wales Arts Review

'*A stunning debut from a major new talent... superbly crafted and extraordinary tales.*'
AmeriCymru

# SMOKE HOUSE
## & Other Stories

## by

# MATTHEW G. REES

A WORK OF FICTION

PERIODDE PRESS

# Author's Note

The stories that follow are works of my imagination. No similarity is intended or should be inferred with any place, publication, person, institution or thing – alive or dead.

Those seeking blood-soaked horror will not find it here. That genre of fiction has never been my line. The supernatural, the strange and the sinister lie much closer to my heart. But there *will* be blood at times, of course.

Most of these stories make their debut here. Some are from sources no longer accessible and some have been updated.

In *Keyhole*, my earlier collection published by Three Impostors press in 2019, the stories were set in Wales and its borderland with England, known as the Marches.

Here, as well as Wales and England, the settings include America, Russia and, very briefly, France. These are, of course, no more than notional backdrops; none of the stories – fiction from first to last – should be connected with any specific location.

Certain of the stories are obviously meant as 'entertainment'. Others perhaps have a more serious intent. Dark as some of them may sometimes be, I hope that readers will find them rewarding, likewise the photographs taken on my travels. These have no direct link with the stories, and nothing should be inferred from their inclusion. They are here because the subjects, I believe, are interesting.

While editing these tales, I found myself calling to mind some lines written by Arthur Machen in his memoir *The London Adventure*, published almost a century ago:

> *'secret and severed people who have fallen out of the great noisy march of the high road for one reason or another, and so dwell apart'*

Machen was describing a particular part of the English capital and its inhabitants. My sense is that his words chime with the people and places in the pages that follow – characters and communities that are separate from us, though not greatly distant.

Wander from our own worn tracks and we might find them. Who knows?

Matthew G. Rees

For more about Matthew G. Rees visit
www.matthewgrees.com

# Stories

# Dead Wood

THE willows were of some literary significance.

A young girl, no more than ten, approached me in the soft darkness of a mid-summer night as I considered how I might best destroy them.

'What are you doing?' she called from behind me.

'I'm… checking the trees,' I said, swinging round.

The girl was in her nightdress. She had a grey rabbit in her arms, which she was petting.

'Why?' she asked.

'They need to be checked, sometimes,' I said.

'I'm checking Roger,' she said, and she stroked back the ears of the rabbit.

'That's good,' I said.

Lights came on in the downstairs of the house at the top of the garden. A woman's voice called, 'Martha! Are you out there?'

The girl walked away, talking to the rabbit.

For a moment she turned back to me, then she ran on.

I gathered my things and went to the jetty at the bottom

of the garden. I slipped the moorings of the boat that I'd tethered there, then drifted downstream, in the moonlight.

When I think of it now, it still surprises me that hers – Martha's… the child's – was the only interruption that I suffered in all that strange, long, *cruel* year.

It seemed no one ever thought (or wanted) to connect the fresh stumps of six old oaks in a Norfolk park with a copper beech sliced and diced on a Gloucestershire green. Or the savage splintering of a fine spinney in the Scottish borders with the felling of five plane trees – in lovely full-leaf – in a North London street.

The police attributed my 'work' to vandals, thieves, bungling contractors.

But it was me, always me.

When I finally laid waste to the willows, it made the newspapers and television, as you may recall.

Headlines branded it an outrage, an atrocity, the deed of a maniac.

I felt insulted, outraged by their outrage.

I considered calling a press conference, to explain myself… my work… at which I'd 'reveal all': how and why I'd been hired: the stimulus for my slaughter, in so far as I'd been briefed: the dinner party at the fine house by the river, the slight that a thin-skinned guest thought he'd suffered from another who was present; the insistence of the 'wounded' man that the willows – though the trees and their owners were entirely innocent – be made to 'pay', in some perverse show of his strength.

In spite of my anger, I kept my own counsel and (still possessing *some* sanity) I said and did nothing… publicly, at least.

My… 'situation' is something that we'll come to.

For now, I should perhaps tell you how everything – my killings – began.

I'd been a cab driver. Night shifts. I lost my licence when I lost my temper and a customer lost three teeth. That was when they found me (in the way that people like them do). Before the cabs, the Army: theatres of war… that strangest of phrases… conflicts you'll have heard of, but not actually known, *suffered*, in all their gory glory, unless you were there.

I learned about trees from Ken.

I found him in a forest in Canada. On the internet, I mean, in my local library. He'd made films of himself, cutting down trees.

I'd imagined lumberjacks to be tall, athletic. But Ken was on the dumpy, stumpy side. He had a ginger beard and a shirt in red and black checks. He wore an orange helmet and blue earmuffs.

His skills impressed me, both in terms of his cutting *and* his teaching. After he'd made an incision he'd turn off and lay down his saw and say something like, 'Now I want you to take a good look at this, so you'll remember what it is that I've done'.

He'd point at a birch or a pine to make clear why he'd gone about things in the way that he had. Sometimes he'd place a tape measure against the bark. He didn't promote a particular saw or jacket or ask if I wanted to meet other lumberjacks. It was just Ken, cutting trees. And I appreciated that.

He was concerned a lot for my health and safety (which was something that was new to me). He talked about the importance of always planning an escape route, which he said the American way: *rout*… like clout.

One time he seemed to run pretty quickly towards the camera (which wobbled). But he still declared the job 'a great fall' (while catching his breath).

There were eight films in all. At the end of each of them Ken warned of the importance of cutting with care. Then he said, 'Happy felling, fellers!' and raised his safety helmet.

I came to see him as a friend.

Ken's films had been on the internet for ten years. A counter said they'd been watched by eleven people, none of whom had left any feedback.

So I wrote, 'Thanks, Ken'.

For the next twelve months, I killed trees.

They say you remember your 'first' of everything: girl (or boy), car, cigarette, drink. My first tree was a full-grown cedar in the back garden of a house in a comfortable English suburb.

I climbed her at night in the chill, damp dark.

When I'd set eyes on her, in the day, she was a beauty – stunning, in fact – like (weird as it may sound) some Hollywood actress from a golden age. But now, inescapably, she was a bitch… a geriatric of the kind that refuses to yield. All knees and elbows, mad eyes, wild hair, fighting, kicking, *biting*… thin coverlet clenched to thick-bristled chin.

The rough serrations of her bark and the sharp spikes of vicious sticks that sprouted from her ripped my skin and pierced my palms, never mind the heavy-duty nature of my gloves and overalls. Beneath them, I sensed blood, trickling over me in streams.

Other, longer boughs did their best to send me tumbling from the trunk, pushing and prodding me, bargepole style. Needles – in horrific, dense showers – rained into my eyes as, looking up, I struggled for those parts of her that I might seize and hold.

She had no natural steps, no considerate clefts. Her awful, dark branches reached at awkward angles, held themselves at hostile levels. It was as if they had grown with resistance in mind. With that night in mind.

Past combat told me that the blood that ran from me was fast becoming more than the mere seepage of flesh wounds. My hair grew wet with sweat. My lungs burned.

When I'd clawed far enough, I stopped and sat – *collapsed* might be a better word – in in the collar of two branches, where – gasping – I caught my breath in the cold, vaporous air.

After some moments, I took hold of the rope that I'd looped at my shoulder. I drew it out, in a length, and circled it tight – like a ligature – around the cedar's trunk.

This action seemed to provoke a fresh struggle from the tree, which seemed to shift... physically... and shudder, in the otherwise still and breezeless night. It was as if the cedar was trying to uproot itself. As if, like some prisoner or hostage, she had thoughts of escape – perhaps to the sanctuary of some wood or forest: the safety of her own 'lines'.

Yet I sensed that all of this was for show – one final flourish – and that, like some creature that had been netted, she was becoming subdued.

I threw the ends of the rope down to the lawn.

Having done so, I began my descent.

Near halfway was the ugly, splintered site where the bough that now lay in next door's (deeply offended) garden had broken – its unwelcome separation being the incident that had sparked my intervention.

I looked down at the sheared limb in the ruins of the greenhouse on which it had crashed, atom-bombing the frame, the glass and every plant that had been nurtured in the warm, fertilised soil of the laboratory conditions within. A chaos of canes and chrysanthemums lay either side of the bough's fearsome black form.

Suddenly, my head swam.

I locked my hands on the tree, breathed heavily, held her close... hateful as she was... and steadied my heart's hammering beat.

After some moments, I resumed my route down.

Finally, I jumped to the lawn.

A fox was running on the wet grass, skittering, looking at me.

I picked up the ends of the rope that I'd tossed from the tree. I then walked to the far side of the garden and lashed one end around a steel peg; this I hammered into the lawn with a mallet (having first muffled the head with some rags). I did the same with the other end at a distance from the first.

The presence of the watching fox calmed me.

When I lowered my goggles and ripped my saw to life,

the animal deserted… fled – its nimbleness strangely at odds with the heaviness of everything around us: the houses, the tree, the night.

I angled the saw into the trunk and felt the *clunk* as the teeth connected… *bit.*

The tree seemed to convulse: a spasm surging upwards through my hands and my arms, all the way to my neck and my head.

The saw spat aside bark. Orange dust flew out.

I carved the first notch, driving the saw deep, incising a gap – like an open mouth – in the cedar's side.

I then went around to the opposite side and cut a second wound, this time further, into the tree's heart.

My immersion detached me from the noise of my actions… my concentration effectively muting the saw's whine and drawl.

Satisfied, I drew the saw out and silenced it.

In my peripheral vision, I became aware of lights in nearby houses. But I kept my focus on the tree.

I drove two wedges, at left and right, into the second cut. Then I struck them with the same mallet I'd used on the pegs.

A lament of cracking, groaning, *mournful* sounds came from inside her. They were of the kind that an aged boat built of beams might make at sea.

For a moment, the cedar seemed to hesitate, to waver.

Then, with a moan and an almost gentle *swish* and, finally, a great *crash* that shook the ground and swept me with a resinous gust (the last, blown kiss of a perfumed old lady, a poetic soul might have said), she came down – hard… *dead* – on the lawn.

Now lights were coming on everywhere. A dog was barking; its noise setting off another dog. Somewhere a woman was calling. 'Can you see anything? Tom? Please be careful!'

An English suburb in polite panic.

I headed down an alley to my van, threw in my things, drove.

In the morning, I went to the café. An old guy I'd seen there previously was at the next table, staring into space. Trish, who runs the place, said his name was Neville and that in the night someone had done something dreadful and cut down his tree. Trish said Neville's dad had planted it on the day Neville was born. Why would anyone have done such a thing? What was the world coming to? Trish wanted to know. She glanced at my left hand, which I'd bandaged. 'Been in the wars?' she asked.

When I got home the phone was ringing.

I received my orders for my next target.

'Leave only firewood,' came the command.

Later, when I located it, I had no qualms: a conifer hedge of the soil-leaching, light-blocking kind. Bogus, birdless trees. Green, but dead. Rubbery. Synthetic. Revolting.

I cut straight through them at night.

A mercy killing, I told myself. Even the shelled wastelands of the Somme would have shunned them.

Twenty.

It felt good.

But it wasn't enough.

I worked coast to coast, mountain to valley. A motorcycle courier left packets of cash in Trish's café. She knew nothing, of course.

There were some notable *kills*. In Scotland, I scythed a stand of pines that had a preservation order but were blocking alterations at a high-end golf course. On the south coast of England, I dismembered a fine chestnut that had spread itself into the sea view of a 'personality' often seen on TV. In the Welsh borders, I destroyed an entire orchard of ancient apple trees that had threatened a planned estate of what the agent called 'executive homes'.

I had my subtle side, too. A monkey puzzle tree (*Araucaria araucana*), in the quad of a famous college, began its slow and steady death thanks to the poisoned rods I skewered in its side one half-term. My linkman was the college's head porter. He said the senior dons – how appropriate that word now seems – knew everything. They were hungry to erect some steel-and-glass 'centre', part of an endowment from a billionaire who'd made a fortune mining minerals and selling arms. The porter assured me I had nothing to fear. Developers were the instigators of most of my instructions, of course. They didn't want trees holding up projects, causing a fuss. But some of my sponsors might surprise you. The client who had me cut down a perfectly healthy beech in a Midlands town square was a white-haired spinster aggrieved by the way youths congregated beneath its branches come evening. Despatching it in the early light of one red-skied dawn, I caught sight of her at a window... thrilling at my deed.

My killing became industrial. Chainsaws weren't enough. Through a process of contamination, I erased an entire mile of greenbelt outside one northern city: a single-handed act of destruction that to this day defies belief. The authorities, who had themselves hired me, later re-classified the land as 'spoil', paving the way for an out-of-town stadium and shopping mall with a car park only marginally smaller than the hectares of tar of an airport runway.

I was uncatchable, unstoppable.

Then came the yew. A thousand years old. So ancient it no longer looked like a tree: its girth enormous. Deformed. Mutated. Grown-in on itself. It didn't have bark in any normal sense, but a grotesque hide of coarse ridges, sinister valleys, foul tumours, clenched knots. Its crown squatted absurdly low, as if it had been stamped down by a vengeful sky. Surveying its mounds and sprouts and swellings, I couldn't help but think of poor Merrick, The Elephant Man.

But I had no pity for the yew, and it had no mercy for me. Its loathsome black needles brimmed with poison.

It crouched beside a West Country church of equal antiquity in a yard of flaking headstones lodged at strange angles, like ships run aground.

And yet, for all of the yew's foulness, there were those who saw it as beautiful, venerable and even sacred. Had not our archers at Crécy, Poitiers and Agincourt cut bows from trees just like it?

In the old, grey church, a faded pamphlet spoke of the yew and the Angel of Mons: how the ghostly bowmen of Agincourt rose as one in a Flanders field, five centuries on, to hurl back the Hun and save the lives of beleaguered British soldiers... to whose ranks I had, of course, once belonged.

The vicar – a new man – saw things differently and wanted the yew dead. He was young, a high-flyer: lean, keen and smelling of cologne. The yew stood in the way of his plans for a meeting hall, kitchen and cloakrooms. It stood in the way of *him*. The congregation had split into factions. A special court had been arranged to decide the yew's fate. But this parson was impatient. He wanted to make his mark and move on. There were rectorships, deaneries, bishoprics, waiting to be had. The yew required... an accident.

I left word that I'd return when conditions were favourable.

When, one evening, I saw the isobars tight as a knot on the television news (and a weatherman's worried frown), I knew that it was time.

The wind hurled anything and everything it could seize: litter bins, sods of earth, stones, bricks, roof tiles, fence posts, wire. Branches and, at times, whole uprooted saplings flew through the air like the ordnance of some Satanic artillery. The force of it pummelled my van. I fought the wheel like the besieged skipper of a storm-tossed trawler. Sticks came at my windscreen like tomahawks; pine cones as if they were grenades.

Soon there was no traffic.

The sky blackened and rain of a kind that I had never before seen swept down in waves like arrow-swarms.

Abandoned cars littered my route. Torn cables slithered, hissed and fired sparks across pools that glowed with electric-blue light.

Now trees became my obstacles, falling and blocking my way. It was as if they knew my business. As if they were sacrificing themselves for the yew.

I chainsawed through them, and drove on, amid dark woods that moaned and seethed and wailed.

When I reached the church, the yew glared.

It knew.

Wind blasted the lychgate shut. I heaved it open, dragging after me the chains with which I intended to shackle that hag of a tree.

Flowers from headstones flew into the air. Notices tore away from a board, whirling furiously, like so many startled rooks, disappearing into the night.

Slates crashed from the roof of the old church, shattering on crosses and tombs. Its stained glass meanwhile erupted outwards, as if machine-gunned from within. I dropped my chains by the porch and went back to my van for my saw and my axe.

When I re-entered the yard, my reception party was waiting.

Ken was first to scurry alongside.

'As with every specimen,' he gasped, 'what you have to ask yourself is: do you really need to take down this tree?'

I brushed him away. He gave me a resentful look. His helmet flew into the churning sky. He eyed me sourly, then went after it.

Next came Trish: the blue tabard she wore at work tight against her in the gale. She waved envelopes that were bursting with banknotes.

'All *this* is yours!' she said. 'How many more must die?'

She threw the notes into the air. The wind drove them against stone monuments, spiked them on hedges, swept them into brooks that boiled and laughed.

Next, I saw old Neville. He was clinging to a beam in the porch of the church, as if to the edge of a cliff, or even the edge of the world.

I leaned into the storm and looked at him.

The tempest unlocked his fingers one by one. Then, incredibly, the church bowed outwards and sucked him into its stones... head, chest, waist, the whole of him... as if it were some awful, molten bog.

I reached the yew.

Beneath its swaying branches stood little Martha whose willows I had spared... then slaughtered.

The yew had hold of her hair and was twisting her locks backwards into the foul folds of its trunk.

'You're not checking the tree!' she said, spreading herself against it. 'You're not! You're not!'

The bells of the church began to peal.

It was as if the yew – with the cunning that had seen it survive for centuries – was summoning defenders to its boughs.

Voices made me turn.

Answering the ancient tree's call were the dead of the parish who, even before my eyes, were rising from their graves: smocked farmers and their wives; soldiers in scarlet; a parson, holding down his hat in the headwind.

All arose. They stamped their feet, shook soil from their clothes.

A nurse in a uniform of blue-and-white helped the older, less able corpses to their feet. A teacher called her young charges, who ran to her skirts. Whiskered men mustered in groups. An aproned butcher spoke with a doctor whose Gladstone bag swung in the gale.

A lean man in a top hat and chain of office thrust a furled umbrella into the wind. The indignant dead assembled behind him, bent into the wind and marched – on me.

They drove me back, against the yew, stripping me of my axe and my saw. Their pale, pinched faces pressed inches from mine.

'He wants our tree!' the schoolteacher said.

'Well, he's not having it!' said the lean man with the chain. He thrust the wooden handle of his umbrella under my chin.

'You're not having it! You hear?' joined in the butcher, taking my hair in his fist, like entrails from a block.

Soon they all chorused: 'You're not having it! You're not having it! YOU'RE NOT HAVING IT!'

The children ran back to their graves and returned with soil, which they pelted at my face and my chest.

The women tore off my clothes, so that I became naked. Two soldiers took my arms and held me hard against the yew. Parting the mob, a group overseen by the man with the chain advanced and placed on my head a crown of thorns.

Above me, the yew shook and creaked and groaned. And then… all was blackness.

No earthly signs of me remained. Not a tooth, not a nail, not a hair, not a button, not a lace, not a thread. Not a thing.

Had I been hanged, or gored, or garrotted, or been beaten or burnt, *something* of me – perhaps a finger, maybe my watch… charred and cracked – would have been left.

But there was nothing.

It was as if I'd been swallowed.

Whole.

The problem with the yew has been solved. What I mean to say is that the tree has stayed and the young vicar has… gone. Clippings ground into his fancy leaf tea saw to that. He suffered a little, I suspect: trembled and staggered – as the toxins took hold – then collapsed, turned cold, on the vicarage floor. I can't say for sure but it's possible that his last sight – through his kitchen window, as he fell – was of the churchyard and the yew, which – unlike him – was still standing, of course.

Next, I went in search of the courier whose job it had been to bring me my bounty as the hired hand.

I knocked him from his motorbike in the street near Trish's café. I put a saw to his throat, told him my killing had to stop.

He told me to go to a grey block in a part of town long

conquered by concrete. He said that there I would find Him, the One that I wanted.

My entrance was... spectacular.

Call to mind, if you will, those stalkers, trappers and soldiers of the kind who camouflage themselves with nets, twigs, grass and creams – hiding undetected for days in ditches and fields – and you will, perhaps, have half the picture.

In my case, the foliage was real. Green shoots that sprang from my skull. Tendrils that twisted and turned in place of my tongue. Stalks and stems that swept from my excavated eyes and ears. Leaves that swarmed my torso and limbs. Needles, like scalpels, that flailed from my fingers. A beard of lush moss that clung at my jaw. Each and every inch of me, coppiced, spinneyed, sown.

I found Him, my Controller, Master – call Him what you will – at a desk with a telephone and papers piled high. On a wall were maps punctured with red pins. He was skewering-in yet more.

I went about my work.

An incision to the right of the trunk, a deeper cut to the left, then wedges hammered left and right (just as Ken had taught me).

I detached myself with clinical efficiency from His shouts and His screams, so that, amid the crimson fountains, I would and did avoid any entanglement of limbs.

The fall was a good one.

And where am I now? What is my 'situation'?

Well, sometimes, when shadows lengthen on autumnal evenings and a coolness stalks the stillness of this ancient and lichened churchyard... at that hour when bats and owls commence their vespertine callings, and fish rise heavily from dark pools for their last flies of the day... then, those that pass by with their prayer books who happen to look at the old yew closely, may, perhaps, in the dying light, decipher a form.

For I am here and always shall be.
Protector. Defender. Saviour.
I am the Green Man now.

# Frayed

WHAT *was* it about moths? bristled Bickersley.

The blasted things always managed to do their damage where it most hurt. One bite, or burn, or whatever it was… and always at the point of maximum impact. And – not that he much cared for fashion – *always* to an item of clothing he rather liked or, in some sentimental way, held dear.

He surveyed himself in the bedroom mirror, eyes on the ragged moth-hole in his midriff, the cotton of his shirt now semaphoring its presence beneath his punctured Guernsey sweater – a go-to garment he'd had for years.

He winced.

Never mind its smallness, to Bickersley the little white eyelet was like the lantern of a lighthouse, beaming on a navy-blue night.

Why couldn't the damned things strike somewhere *inoffensive*, for God's sake? Under the arm of a dressing gown… the tail of a shirt… the arse of his underpants?

That his clothes were old was neither here nor there. The point was, they were *good*… tailor-made, some of them:

shirts from Jermyn Street, suits that were near enough Savile Row.

And a frayed shirt held no shame. It actually possessed a certain *style*. Collars, if need be, could be bare to the bone. Visible maintenance to jackets was almost mandatory. Such things said that your money was 'old' (no matter if there was none left now).

But being… *mothed*. Well, it made one look… *seedy*, the sort who spent his days cigaretting with cheap Scotch in front of the racing from some small-time course on TV; even *trampish*… as if you'd been snagged by a hawthorn while sleeping it off under some hedge.

He threw on a tweed jacket over the Guernsey. In the hall downstairs, he added the Crombie coat that had been his grandfather's. He didn't bother with a handkerchief for its outer pocket. He couldn't be fussed with adornment. Not now. Not after this.

Moths! Why in Hell's name had God made them?

He set out on the lane to the village in a mood of disgust.

The place came into view: Llanwhereveritdamnedwellwas in Wales. He'd been there barely a week and already hated it. It had the cheek to call itself a town, but he – for one – wouldn't acknowledge it as that. It was a village – and full of idiots. And there it lay, in its hollow. No… such words were too kind by half. It *lurked*, in its gully… in its *pit*.

Dank, grey, charmless.

'Good place to get something finished,' Pandora, his agent, had said, offering him use of 'a friend's' cottage 'for a spell'. 'Off the beaten track.'

And the reasons for *that* were obvious, thought Bickersley. The sooner he got back to his small square inch of south-west London the better. Paradise his flat certainly wasn't, but any place was better than this!

He followed the lane down through the banks of wet bracken.

Out of the sun now, he felt the air turn chill.

At the porch to the library, Bickersley thought how hideous the building was: a Victorian eyesore whose once-red bricks were now charred and black. Weather – how bloody it had been since his arrival – and the years, he presumed, had rendered various stone gargoyles above the entrance considerably more monstrous than their masons could ever have meant. The carvings were blunt and indistinct: the bodiless heads like those of poor souls struggling haplessly in a mire.

Offensive also to Bickersley's aesthetics, were the low-hanging tube lights of the gloomy interior. These were strung from chains hung from high, Gothicky ceilings dismally washed with a lime-green paint. The tubes lit the rooms with a glow that somehow seemed deliberately weak. To Bickersley's eye, the whole effect was like being trapped in a toilet bowl… under an unending stream of pee. Old man's pee, he thought to himself, sensing a likeness with the hue that his own had started to acquire.

The shabbiness caused Bickersley to recall the several awful boarding schools he'd been forced to attend as a boy. The place had their odour… their taste: an unpleasant collision of cheap disinfectant, boiled cabbage and cruel and oafish masters, like moulting old crows, in ragged and musty gowns.

But at least it was warm. *Too* warm, in fact: the radiators discharging a near furnace heat from huge metal coils that lounged plump and lethargic in corners and halls – like snakes, he thought to himself: sunning themselves indulgently, having dined.

A rivulet of sweat ran down Bickersley's back. He wondered now why he'd even bothered with the Guernsey. His tweed jacket and the Crombie would surely have sufficed.

As he wandered the bookshelves, he unbuttoned his coat and let it hang loose.

He placed his intended withdrawals on the counter: a couple of Simeon Barrymores – not that they'd be any good: as well as being the most dreadful shit of a man, Barrymore was a truly woeful writer; a couple more Davinia Duvalls – not that her hackwork would be much better. Still, he thought to himself, in the circumstances, he might as—

'Who's been nibbling at you?'

'I'm… sorry?' said Bickersley, wrong-footed by a communication that seemed to be aimed at him. (Up till then, no one in the village had volunteered anything in his direction. Not that he had cared.) He was thrown also by the speaker's accent. Cosmopolitan as London nowadays was, he'd never heard quite such a… lilt.

'They've had a good lump-and-a-half. Out of your jumper,' the voice now added, as if by way of explanation.

Bickersley felt his way through what seemed his own private fog, his mind trying to make sense of the term 'yewah jumpah'.

Suddenly, he connected the words with the woman on the desk… who only a moment before seemed not to have been there.

'Moths, is it?' she went on. 'You'll want to be taking care of them. Spot of darning. That's what you need.'

Now that he knew her meaning, Bickersley's earlier ill temper returned. Of all the impertinence! What on earth was she trying to do? Humiliate him in front of the entire library?

He thought about storming out, struggled for something by way of a riposte. But then… then she flashed him a smile. And, in spite of himself, he found that he was being… disarmed (at least, to a degree).

The woman was red-haired and to use a word that he knew was no longer used very much… buxom. Some cleavage showed itself above the neckline of a black sweater that seemed to Bickersley to plunge rather low for a lady in a library.

'Yes, I um. Nuisance, aren't they?' he responded. 'I'm sorry – I didn't see you there. I was looking for the young man who served me yesterday.'

'Dylan?' the woman replied. 'Oh, he's finished. You know how it is with Dylans. Fireflies every one. They burn out so young. Can *I* help?' she continued.

'I'd like to borrow these,' said Bickersley, producing the card the youth had given him.

The woman studied it. 'Would that be *the* Gerald Bickersley?' she said after a moment.

'Well, yes it would, actually,' he replied.

Bickersley glanced either side of him for any signs of recognition among the other attendants and borrowers in the room.

Not a flicker.

He returned his attention to the woman.

While it was true that the library's shelves contained not one of his nineteen novels, her excitement – her eyes visibly lighting up – caused a quiet thrill to pass through him, not unlike, he felt, the pleasing warmth of a fine liqueur.

'We follow you in my circle,' she said. 'Never miss a Bickersley. Times may be changing, but your "sword-and-sandals" are safe with us.'

'Period literary fiction,' Bickersley – having doubts about his thoughts of just a moment before and feeling the need to defend his dignity – corrected her quickly, while forcing a smile.

The woman looked at the books he'd set down.

A photograph of Simeon Barrymore stared up from a back cover, as if with a sneer. The pompous creep's picture was twenty years old at least, thought Bickersley.

'Keeping an eye on the opposition, are we?' the woman asked.

'Not exactly,' he responded.

She stamped the books – one scarlet-nailed hand holding open each volume, the other plunging his return date firmly inside.

'You've got three weeks,' she said, looking up.

He took hold of the books in a manner he felt sure was sheepish. It was as if a vicar, or a neighbour with whom he was on speaking terms, had caught him in a shop where the newsagent was asking if he'd like a bag for his magazine.

'Well,' said the woman, 'and to think we've a famous author, right here, under our noses.'

'Yes, not stopping though. Passing through, really. You might call it a retreat. I'm here to finish something. The last chapters,' said Bickersley, who was enjoying her interest never mind the clumsiness of some of her remarks.

'Putting it all to bed. Isn't that what you writers call it?' she continued, flashing him (or so he thought) 'a look'. 'Well,' she went on, 'it will be nice to know that our little town has played its part. My name's Bronwen,' she said.

'And my name's…' Bickersley began. 'Well, you already know that.'

'Oh yes,' she responded, 'we've got all your particulars.'

'How very… efficient,' Bickersley replied.

She let out what seemed a sigh.

Women, it was fair to say, had only ever been a marginal force in Bickersley's life. There was Vicky, the barmaid at the Duke's… Pandora, his agent… Pandora's secretary, Leanan (or whatever her name was), who would seldom so much as look at him unless it was with utter disdain. Bickersley disliked the way this Bronwen had drawn attention to his sweater – her breezy self-confidence, her devil-may-care. And yet, he had to confess, she had… *something*. He found himself wishing that he had indeed bothered with the flourish of a handkerchief for his coat pocket

Uncertain quite what to say or do next, he took his books and made for the library's revolving door.

Pushing on its cold, brass rod, he sensed something strange: that the eyes of the lady librarian, and all of her attendants, were upon him: *boring* in the way that, earlier, he had been punctured… bitten… *denuded*, to his front.

In the afternoon, he worked on his manuscript at the cottage. From time to time, he opened the books he'd brought back from the library, comparing their passages with his own.

Simeon Barrymore's star turn was Sir Lucas Sheerbrooke, a still-young veteran of the Crusades. It seemed to Bickersley, turning the pages, that the creator of this dull 'shining knight' had a fetish for his hero's hands, which were always at work somewhere: pulling, entering, loosening... An episode rarely began without reference to his ring finger.

Meanwhile, Davinia Duvall's heroine, Lady Susan Shycroft, somehow contrived – as Bickersley already knew (from faint familiarity with her catalogue and reviews) – to be a lady-in-waiting not only to every one of Henry VIII's six queens, but Elizabeth after him, Jane Grey *and* Mary Tudor, while apparently never aging and displaying a 'unique' (Duvall's word) fealty to each.

Utterly ludicrous characters the pair of them, Bickersley said to himself. And it could only be a matter of time until TV or even a film studio brought them together: some epic piece of trash that would make Barrymore and Duvall – they sounded like an awful American police 'duo' – oodles of money... millions, quite probably.

Bickersley sighed and returned his thought to his own draft – the latest *Wulstan of Wyckmere*: untitled at present, but the newest in the long and – let it be said, Bickersley nodded – successful *The Catches of Wulstan of Wyckmere* series.

Yes, his fisherman-friar had been 'around' a while and there was, in truth, scarcely a river in England on which – while bending his rod – he hadn't solved a serious crime or righted some grievous wrong. In his time, his 'tonsured detective of tight lines and foul felonies', had caught everything from lampreys to sturgeon, master forgers to fire-starters, robbers of relics and even plotters of treason. After nineteen novels, his man had lost some of his mystique, Bickersley knew. But he surely still had *something* to offer – hadn't he? – in this ghastly age of portable telephones, baby-faced police officers, bearded academics (male *and* female) with all of their claptrap, and – worst of all, of course – the ubiquitous 'rights'.

Bickersley looked out at the moor of bracken beyond the window at which he worked.

Ugly, thorny trees stood hunched on its bleak plain, like beggars who'd become rooted to the spot. The sun was sinking, doing so in a seemingly slow and bitter way that made him think of a blood orange.

For some moments, he dwelt upon what Pandora, his agent, had said to him at her office. She'd been preoccupied, buzzing Leanan on her intercom with instructions to book a table at Avernus (or whatever the restaurant was called): for dinner with a client clearly much more important than him (never mind her not insignificant take from his titles over the years).

Perhaps Pandora had forgotten her words?

Bickersley hadn't.

*Good runs... dry wells... ends.*

But surely Wulstan wasn't dead yet? There was room for one more book... one more adventure... to round things off, at twenty.

And then, who knew what? What if it proved a hit? There were still some rivers to be fished, some waters that remained uncharted.

Besides, what of Wulstan? *His* life? Who had the right to take it? To lynch *him*... when he might yet reach new heights?

Bickersley thought of the words on Shakespeare's monument, written by Ben Jonson, he'd once read on a visit to Stratford: '... *still alive, while thy Book doth live.*'

Bickersley returned to his page and penned on:

*Wulstan had not long cast his line in search of* (add later) *on the waters of* (river / lake? – add later) *when, suddenly, he heard voices raised – as if in argument – coming from...*

That evening, by the light of an oil lamp, his parlour's coal fire smouldering miserably, Bickersley sat thinking... rehearsing lines for Wulstan, his companion of two decades and more. He did this as if his hero were there, sitting opposite him, at the hearth – a surreal act of ventriloquism in which he put words into Wulstan's mouth and listened to the robed and sandalled figure he imagined to be at the fireside.

Suddenly, Bickersley became aware of a tapping or bumping sound that, although never more than soft, gradually grew louder.

Rising from his armchair, he walked to the window and was confronted by the strangest sight: a great wall of moths at the uncurtained glass, so dense and numerous in their seething, fluttering mass that their cream and tawny comb fair filled the large frame.

The next day, Bickersley kept away from the library and the town. He continued to write, doing so perhaps more determinedly than ever, sensing that Wulstan's fate hung in the balance – and not merely in the way of those fictional battles of the past in which his hero had till then always triumphed, but in a way that was real and present.

Bickersley's manuscript grew. He scarce strayed from his desk. One big push and he would be through, he told himself. And the writing was as good as it had ever been, perhaps even exceeding that of his masterpiece *Angle of Attack – Wulstan & the Millpond Poisoner.*

He penned on, keenly:

*Abandoning all hope of further perch for the day, Wulstan turned his thoughts to the matter of…*

Later – as the sun dipped – shadows began to reach into the cottage from the moor and its mean trees, creeping over the bent figure of Bickersley, like black ink over blotting paper.

Such was his immersion in the world of Wulstan, however, that he was wholly unconscious of the darkness deepening around him.

*Up yours, Periodde Bookes!* he – with a reference to his publisher – smiled to himself as, relishing his penmanship, he toiled on.

For a delicious moment, he lifted his head and pictured himself flinging the finished manuscript at Periodde's managing editor: Olisha Stoke-Bliss, Pandora's bosom pal.

'You're going to need a bigger advance… *dear!*' he saw

himself declaring, as her eyes (in his, at least) fell rapaciously on his title page… *Wulstan the Outcast.*

'Period!' he imagined himself adding, magnificently.

Exhausted by his labour and the thrill of this vision, he slumped back in his chair, and slept.

Initially, his slumbers were peaceful. From the cottage's garden, the evensong of a blackbird lullabied him into deep and comforting rest.

Bickersley saw Wulstan, casting in bright sunlight from a reeded shore… his rod flicking and the line flying out over lovely, sparkling water.

In a fusion of the kind he had felt several times previously, and one that was perhaps not to be unexpected after quite so many novels about his hero, Bickersley and Wulstan then became one, so that, when Wulstan turned from the water to the shore, Bickersley saw that the face of the priest was… his.

The scene that had diverted the fisherman-friar from his angling was an ugly one on the bank: a hairy brute striking terror into a cloaked young maiden.

'Unhand her, you devil!' Bickersley heard himself / Wulstan say. 'Or – never mind my priestly garb and this cross I wear – I swear that I shall…'

The fiend fled.

The maiden, meanwhile, turned to face him, and lowered her hood.

But before he could see her countenance, Bickersley was distracted from his dream by the sound of something in – or was it outside? – the gloomy cottage; something bumping… something tapping.

His mind connected it with the moths that had swarmed at his window the previous night, and he now raised his head from the desk at which he had been sleeping.

To his surprise, the window's glass was clear: all that faced him was the blackness of the Welsh night beyond.

The tapping, however, re-started and, as Bickersley felt

the last strands of sleep fall from him, he came to realise that the sound was of someone knocking at the cottage's front door.

He stumbled in the dim light over the parlour's flagstones. He lifted the door's latch, drew it open and peered out, into the dark.

There, on the step, lowering her hood in the moonlight, stood the woman from the library who had announced herself as Bronwen.

'And what a night it is and no mistake,' she said, giving her hood a shake and letting it fall to her shoulders. 'Soggy as a sermon by a vicar named Squibb.'

Bickersley felt the droplets from her hood spray softly on his face, as if from a fountain. Still drowsy, he responded to her with an uncertain 'Yes'.

'Your house is in darkness. I couldn't tell if anyone was home,' she continued.

'There's no electricity here. I must have…'

His words petered as, once again, in the way that had happened in the library, he found himself at a strange loss.

He continued, haltingly, 'Do you want to…'

'Come in?' she said. 'Yes, well, seeing I'm here and you are here too. It won't take a moment.'

She was already in the parlour.

Feelings of unease and something else… something of a kind he had almost entirely forgotten – *excitement*, at the presence of a woman (an attractive woman, it had to be said) alone, with him, in private – jostled inside him.

He smelt her scent in the parlour's stale air.

Although inexpert in such matters, Bickersley quickly decided the fragrance could be nothing shop-bought. There was a wildness to it. And, more than that, it… she… this flame-haired *Bronwen*… had the intoxicating aroma of… *danger*.

'Dark in here, isn't it?' she said, in her sing-song way.

'Yes, um, I'll just…' Bickersley (preoccupied with his visitor's *un*librariness) mumbled.

35

He found some matches and began lighting candles and the wick of his oil lamp.

'There… that's a bit better,' she said, now illuminated in the half-light in a faintly ethereal way that Bickersley found rather lovely. Its softness, together with the compactness of the parlour, sent his mind scurrying for a moment to a trattoria of an intimate kind he had once visited in Palermo.

'Mind if I take this off?' she added, unbuttoning her cape-cum-coat.

'By all means,' said Bickersley, who hadn't forgotten his first sight of her Junoesque figure in the library.

'Well, it's about your sweater,' she continued (somewhat to his disappointment). 'We can't have you leaving us all holey like that. What sort of moth-eaten town will they take us for? Pop and fetch it, and I'll darn it for you. It won't take me two minutes.'

'Well, uh, that's…' Bickersley bumbled.

'Chop chop!' she said. 'You go and get it and I'll get this fire going. Goodness! There must be more warmth in a snowman's fridge!'

She bent to the hearth and picked up the poker.

Upstairs, in his bedroom, Bickersley located the Guernsey.

With a flickering taper, he scrutinised himself in the mirror.

Was that really him? he wondered with dismay. He looked like a corpse. Perhaps it was the gloom?

He thought about tarting himself up: putting on a jacket, perhaps a cravat. But then he dismissed the idea as daft: something that would have made him seem over-keen.

Even so, he tried to smarten himself, parting his hair with one hand. As he did so, his fingers touched something cold… something *bare*: a bald patch, which, till then, he never knew he had. It felt like an egg – a *big* egg, it had to be said – in a bird's nest.

Her voice came up the stairs from the hall. 'Mr Bickersley? Gerald? Are you there?'

He tapped his skull with his fingers. The hairless space was smooth, circular, like a clearing in a forest.

*Thank you, God!* he thought, with weary anger.

Still... given the gloom, she might not see it – with some luck.

'I'm coming,' he said, at last.

In the parlour, the fire was ablaze: its coals molten in a way that surprised him, given that he couldn't remember even having lit them prior to his visitor's ministrations.

Bronwen stepped back from the grate and put down the poker.

'That's better!' she declared.

A faint, pink light played over the walls.

Bickersley saw that, in addition to her coat, she had removed her smock, or whatever the garment had been, leaving her in a kind of dark T-shirt or singlet (if that was the term), in which her arms were bare.

She seated herself by the hearth.

'Give it here then,' she said, taking the Guernsey.

Bickersley found the fire's heat over-powering and retreated to a sofa set back in the room.

'Well, isn't this cosy?' said Bronwen, rising for a moment then returning to her armchair. She had in her hands what seemed to Bickersley a ball of wool, a reel of cotton and a little rectangular tin.

After a moment or two's perusal of the tin's contents, she drew out a needle and held it up to the light (in a way that reminded Bickersley of Wulstan and his fish hooks).

In the glow of the coals and the candles on the mantel, the needle's fine shaft and point now seemed to elongate and widen strangely, so that, as she held it aloft, her face was framed in its eye.

Bickersley felt his skin prickle and wondered how she tolerated sitting so close to the fire (where she seemed so at home, glowing like the coals).

Her arms, alternately silver and golden in the room's

quivering light, climbed and descended. They did so in a way that caused Bickersley to bring to mind salmon, bream, trout and other fish – their bellies rising, twisting, diving and returning – in a pool on an easeful reach of river where the dying sun danced in a fly-flitting dusk.

When his visitor first pierced the fabric of the Guernsey, Bickersley experienced a peculiar and painful thing: a sharp and determined stab to his own midriff that shocked him and made him shift on the sofa and look down at his chest, as if for a wound (though nothing showed itself there).

Although largely in shadow where he sat, he noticed that his seamstress seemed to register his discomfort (while pretending she had not).

Next, she drew the needle into and out from the sweater, and upwards… almost theatrically high. And, as she did so, Bickersley had the certain physical sense that he was *on* that taut thread, that tight line, on account of the tangible and fierce tug on his own concertinaed rib cage.

He felt, in short, as if he had been… *harpooned.*

'Won't be long now,' Bronwen said cheerfully – not looking at him – as her great needle descended and speared once again.

Seized by another awful spasm to his chest, Bickersley suddenly – and unpleasantly – remembered childhood visits to a dentist – a man with eyes like mineshafts, black briars of nasal hair and a mouth of rancid warm breath, who had uttered precisely the same words before leaving his juvenile jaws dripping with blood, monstrously swollen and horribly in pain.

Bickersley now felt a fresh puncture to his front, and – this time – a distinct drawing of himself towards her. He was no longer leaning back in the sofa, but sensed his buttocks slipping from its edge, one wrist on the armrest, his fingers digging – in agony – into its fabric.

Above all, he had the dreadful sense that he was being dragged… *reeled…* like a fish that had been hooked by

Wulstan. Not, though, to some bulrush shore and cleric's keepnet, but to the hole in his sweater, which was no longer a mere 'hole', but a portal... the mouth of something... a black hole... a place that would prove Hellish indeed.

A maelstrom of thoughts overtook him. He wondered if he was still alive: the cottage... the drab, deathly-dull, so-called 'town': if ever there were such a place as purgatory then that was surely it.

Maybe he was really on some mortician's slab? Being 'stitched back up' after the extraction and inspection of a vital organ to ascertain his cause of death: his heart, his liver, his kidneys (these even now being devilled in a pan by a scoundrel 'caterer').

Slowly, through this mental murk, he became aware that Bronwen was speaking, and that she and he really did seem to be *there*, in the parlour, in the cottage.

Sweat streamed his forehead. He dabbed at it with a handkerchief, wiped a dewdrop from the end of his nose.

'Oh yes, we must have you looking your best for your send-off,' she was saying. 'Standards must be maintained: a well-known writer like you. So... how's it all going?'

'I'm sorry?' said Bickersley, putting away his handkerchief and still trying to unmuddy his mind.

'Your project,' she continued. 'Whatever it is you are on now. You know – borrowing all those books: Simeon Barrymore... Davinia Duvall. *Not* that I'll tell. Your secret shall be safe with me. "Last chapters", I seem to remember you saying.'

'Barrymore and Duvall, did you say?' Bickersley responded, sensing the need to sound dismissive. 'Them? Oh, that's just some marginal stuff. I'm actually finishing a new book.'

He felt more comfortable now. The strange pains that had assailed him had passed. Indeed, as he watched Bronwen's motions, he found himself relaxing and growing reassured. There was something in her poise and rhythm that he found calming... even serene. He remembered a line that he had written once about Wulstan: watching a woman in a summer meadow, with a scythe. Bickersley cared not that the small hole in his Guernsey seemed to be requiring a great deal of darning, and he thought, again, how really rather pretty this Bronwen was (and how he ought to have put on that cravat).

'And would that happen to be a *Wulstan of Wyckmere?*' she asked.

'Yes. Number twenty,' said Bickersley, proudly. 'Quite a landmark.'

'Twenty!? Has it really been *that* many? Goodness, you must be running out of plots!'

'Oh no – I've a few more yet,' he replied. 'In my keepnet, so to speak,' he added, in the hope of sounding, if not Wildean, then witty, or literary, at least.

'Ever thought about writing something else?'

'How do you mean?'

'Another character. Another genre. Letting Wulstan... go.' Concentrating on her needlework, she added, distractedly: 'Killing him off.'

'*Killing him off?*' said Bickersley, with incredulity. Not only incredulity, but annoyance... annoyance that such a remark – such a *terrible* remark – had been uttered so casually.

'Heavens no! Why ever would I want to do that?'

'Well, he's been around a bit, hasn't he? And he did have that "brush"... caught on the wheel in the stream... in *The Millpond Poisoner*, wasn't it?'

'Yes,' said Bickersley. 'But that was number thirteen. I thought it needed some sort of cliff-hanger. You know, "Unlucky for Wulstan" and all that. Made a decent blurb for the back cover.'

'So you don't think he's getting a little... *tired* then?'

'Tired?' queried Bickersley.

'Frayed.'

'Good grief, no! He still has plenty to offer. Don't you worry about that. Besides, there are his fans. They'd never forgive me. If I so much as *dreamt* of doing a Sherlock Holmes death plunge – à la Conan Doyle – with Wulstan, they'd...

well, I don't know what they'd do. Burn me at the stake, I expect.'

In a quieter and less certain voice, Bickersley, having thought for a few moments, then added: '*Frayed*? What makes you say that.'

Bronwen now stopped darning, as if to gather her thoughts.

'Well, the world has moved on, hasn't it? Not for Wulstan though. He's stuck in the Middle Ages, obviously...'

Bickersley winced at her choice of words: he would have much preferred 'situated' or 'a character of'.

'He's in such a time warp, isn't he?' she continued.

'That's precisely the point!' said Bickersley. 'He is a character of—'

'Yesterday's man... *monk*,' said Bronwen.

'He is a friar, a wandering Franciscan friar,' corrected Bickersley, not caring for the turn the conversation was taking.

'"Wandering" certainly,' she continued. 'There can't be a river in England that he hasn't crossed. Adrift in other ways too,' she added (rather more quietly and as if to herself), '... made a right mess of his last case – lines of enquiry all rather tangled – I seem to remember.'

Her reference to 'Number Nineteen' – the ill-fated *Wulstan and the Scales of Justice* – made Bickersley shudder. He remembered – once again – Garfield Grist's 'review' in the *Examiner* (all three lines of it: 'a career low') under the awful pun heading 'Bleke House'. A piece by the normally charitable Dominic Gill in the small but influential *Dorsal* had been equally grim: 'One that ought to have got away.' And as for the little so-and-so at that 'listings magazine', or whatever it was... full of adverts from weirdos wanting to 'hook up'... why, she'd been out to spear him from the start. 'Jail Bait!' her poisonous piece had concluded. Twelve months on and the memory of it still riled Bickersley.

'I mean, where's the social relevance?' Bronwen, to his mounting exasperation, went on. 'Engagement with the issues of today?'

'Issues?!' Bickersley responded. 'The man's there to catch fish! And criminals! And to give the odd benediction or catechism! He's a member of a mendicant order! He isn't there for… *global warming*,' Bickersley spluttered, '… alternatives to… fossil fuel!'

She continued, seeming to him not to have heard a word he had said. 'I mean… he's a priest and he isn't even gay!'

'Well, I hardly think that—'

'And where are the women?'

'Women?'

'Yes! Where are they?'

'I think you'll find – if you remember – that Sister Anne plays a fairly prominent part,' said Bickersley.

'Yes, but she's always nursing, or praying, or grinding herbs in a bowl. Why can't she be catching salmon and capturing villains? And her relationship with Wulstan – it's all so… pure.'

'Well, he *is* a priest. And she *is* a nun.'

'But where's the sauce? Now, take Simeon Barrymore…'

'I'd rather not.'

'In *his* books, you can't turn a page without a healthy splash of spice. Bodice rippers. Sapphic encounters. *That's* where it's at. Advance requests for *The Shield and The Steed* nearly took down our computer. Book hadn't even been printed. Think of the public lending rights cash he's had back from that!'

She continued: 'And look at Davinia Duvall…'

'Davinia Duvall?!' Bickersley now broke in, angrily. 'Oh please! Spare me! What can an American *possibly* know about Tudor England? The very idea is preposterous! As are her books! Besides, she probably doesn't even exist. Nothing more than the made-up name of some idiotic lecturer called Marvin – or… *Dwight* – at some ghastly third-rate university where the students all wear dental braces and spend their days saying "like" and "neat". Every one of them on drugs or masticating on gum.'

'That didn't stop you borrowing a pile the other day.'

'I was—'

He chose not to continue. He sensed that he was losing his cool while she, never mind her nearness to the fire, was very much in control of hers. Whether it had been her intention or not, he knew – they *both* knew – that she had... needled him.

'And really, much as we've enjoyed him, all *nineteen* books...' she continued.

What on earth was wrong with the woman? Bickersley wondered. Couldn't she leave Wulstan be?

'... we've seen it all before: *Father* this, *Brother* that, *In The Name of* the other.'

Sensing his chance, Bickersley – like an old, bottom-dwelling pike... scarred but with an instinct for survival – now sprang.

'And not so much as a sprat between them, unless I'm very much mistaken!' he responded (a coup de grâce reference, so he felt, to the abysmal angling records of the clerics he believed she had invoked).

Checkmate, he told himself: he had withstood her slings and arrows to win both the hour and the day. The argument was over. Like a large chub, breathless after a game fight, it lay beaten and exhausted – and on Wulstan's bank.

His adversary merely adjusted the sweater in her lap.

'Are you done with the darning?' he asked, after what he felt was sufficient pause for his putdown to finish its victory lap.

'Almost,' she said. 'Just a few more lengths.'

A calm now came over them in which they no longer talked. Soon Bickersley had the strange sense that he was somehow drifting in the manner of a stick he might once have thrown into a stream as a boy, so that he was now able to look down on the scene in the parlour and see the figures who were seated there.

He watched her arms and hands moving in the lovely, hypnotic way that she had with them – quietly. rhythmically – in the pink and quivering light.

In time, he came to lean back his head so that it rested at an angle against the top of the sofa. And, as he lay there, he had the sense that she was behind and above him with her needle.

In his strange slumber, it seemed to Bickersley that Bronwen was darning his eyes – drawing her small spear with its length of wool through his brows and his lids and into his tingling cheeks.

A woozy memory came to him of an Oriental lady in London who'd once punctured his buttocks with pins, in response to his complaint of a glue ear.

He let out no sound now or single drop of blood, and permitted his visitor to go on darning… until his eyes seemed tight shut.

When Bickersley awoke, it was to the coldness of the dawn. Around him, the parlour was empty and silent, the fire a ruin of cinders. He took his Guernsey sweater from the armchair beside it and held it up. In the room's grey light, he saw that it was riddled… ragged. More plentiful with holes than a promise from a medieval pardoner.

In the days that followed, Bickersley shunned the town and the library. He also did his best to put from his mind the episode of the sweater. He worked on his manuscript in the mornings, and in the afternoons he took to the moorland that surrounded the cottage. As he walked the lonely ways through the wet banks of bracken, he rehearsed lines for Wulstan and the novel, speaking them aloud. 'Unhand me, sir! It matters not whether you are the bailiff for the King of England, or even of my liege the Pope. No one shall expel me from this water! Unseize my rod, I tell you, and do so at once!'

The bleak nature of the moor was itself strange inspiration. He felt himself more at one with Wulstan than he had been in their whole lives together. His progress pleased him, and his conviction grew that *The Outcast* would surpass the heights of even *The Millpond Poisoner* (for which – though many seemed to have forgotten – he had once been nominated for an award... given, in the cruel corruption endemic in the book world, to that great hand-fetishist and licker of arse, Simeon Barrymore).

The prospect of Pandora and all of the others – Garfield Grist, Dominic Gill, even Bronwen, whom he did his best not to think of – eating their words about Wulstan drove Bickersley on.

Such was the intensity of his immersion in his manuscript, that he grew increasingly unconscious of the world around him. At times, he became utterly lost in the tunnel-like wynds of the moor... its dun-brown lake seemingly closing over him as he wandered: the fronds of its bracken interweaving, like some great net, over the bobbing bald crown of his head.

In the cottage, he took less and less interest in cooking, or lighting the fire, often writing, after his return from the moor, until exhaustion forced him to stop.

One morning, in the sunlight at the window where he wrote, Bickersley noticed the strangest thing: a hole in his right hand: a narrow shaft, boring deep... midway between his knuckles and his wrist.

He held it up to the light and looked at the beam that passed through it and issued from his palm.

For several moments, he was shaken, confused, even awed.

He sought to rationalise the cavity... the well.

Yes, it was a hole, but the rest of him was... whole. Furthermore, there was no pain; it was his pen hand, but he could still write.

And that, he told himself, was what he would do. Finish his manuscript. And return in triumph to London... and a physician there, perhaps. But not here. *Definitely* not here, where at best there might be some provincial sawbones with scarce a word of English in his head. Finish... *finish* – that was it. *End* his story. End it he would. End it he must.

When, in the following days, other holes appeared – one through his left earlobe, another (a small crater) in the tip of his nose, and a third, conspicuously, through the forefinger of his right hand – Bickersley ignored all of them, as he had the very first.

Even when the holes became wider and deeper – one entering his head between his eyes and exiting the back of it in an oval he could feel with his fingers – he refused to be deflected.

He rarely left the cottage now, disregarding mealtimes and the hours of the clock, engrossing himself entirely in the fate of his friar.

Wulstan had been grievously framed by jealous enemies: convicted of not only plundering a cardinal's stew pond but celebrating a black mass. The latter – which had witnessed all kinds of foulness – perplexed Bickerlsey greatly. He wondered how he had written such scenes of debauchery, eventually settling on the explanation that his hand had moved in some sort of semi-conscious attempt to satisfy the 'sauce' that had been called for by Bronwen. Bickersley vowed to clear his priest's name at all costs (albeit that the mystery of the prelate's poached carp was the major and pressing concern). Putting pen to paper, Bickersley swore he would rest at nothing till he had righted these monstrous wrongs.

Returning one day from a rare outing to the moor, he caught sight in a window of a strange figure whose movements seemed to mirror his own.

A cheekless, chinless, partial man.

Bickersley's last lines came on a cold, clear morning in which frost rimed the windows of his cottage with queer patterns of a kind he remembered scissoring into sheets of paper as a child.

He had worked through the night by the glow of a candle that had burnt itself out. Any fire that there might have been had long died in the hearth.

With intense effort – his whole body seeming numb and bloodless – he now wrote:

'Worry not, child,' the goose girl's mother told her daughter as she braided her hair by the firelight. 'I doubt very much that that is the end of Wulstan of Wyckmere.'

He then added:

### THE END

Satisfied that he had restored the good name of his fisherman-friar, he put down his pen at last.

He glanced at his wristwatch. The date told him it was just over three weeks since his arrival in the village.

Looking now to where his pen-hand – his right – ought to have been, he realised that it was barely present… so eaten away had it become.

He reached with this ruined claw at the window in front of him, to scrape away its rime. In doing so, he dislodged several of the library books that he had stacked on his desk. They fell to the floor, the covers of one coming open.

Bickersley retrieved it and saw that they were due for return that same day. He considered the matter for a moment, then decided: no, he would not. Why should such rubbish be on the shelves of a public library, especially one that didn't deign to stock anything of his? He would not set foot in that damned village. He would pass (no… *hasten*) through it when he left, and that would be it.

And so, donning his overcoat and a silk muffler (which, through its decimation with moth-holes, almost disintegrated as he tied it), he walked out with the volumes, onto the moor.

Ice crystals coated the moor's bracken and brambles. In the sunrise, they radiated shimmering, iridescent light. In an opening, where the bracken had been beaten back, Bickersley stopped and – his breath rising in white plumes above him –

thought how magical the setting was. A hare entered the enclosure. Bickersley held himself completely still as the animal eyed him for a moment before lolloping on.

Bickersley now continued in the direction of a ravine he had come across on his previous excursions. Standing at its edge, with the bloodshot sky at his back, he tossed the books down into the gorsed and rocky gully.

They fell, one by one, like ungainly, flightless birds.

Turkeys the lot of them, Bickersley thought.

He turned and went back to the cottage.

In the parlour, he cleared away his papers, leaving only his manuscript on the desk by the window. He began to tidy his bedroom similarly and to pack his clothes and things.

In time, fatigue forced him to lie down, on the cover of his bed.

The combination of the intensity of his work on his manuscript, his self-neglect and the hypothermic shock to his body of his walk onto the frozen moor now rendered Bickersley feverous.

A strange vision beset him, in which a flock of moths hovered above his supine form.

In the manner of small fish in a sunlit sea, the moths shoaled downwards and entered him through a cavity in his chest, after which he seemed to hear their wings – beating – in the cage of his ribs.

Some while later, in darkness, when all sense of time had deserted him and his weakness was such that he felt hollow and almost without weight, he found himself distracted by a disturbance at his window.

He rose from his bed and in the moonlight saw a great mass of moths, bumping… beckoning, so it seemed… in a bronze and silver tapestry of wings and bodies at the pane.

He unfastened the window and admitted their armada, and felt their warm, soft forms swarm upon his.

Soon – with the exception of his eyes – they covered every inch of his being.

Next, he felt them lifting him and taking him bodily through the open window so that he was with them now, flying beneath the stars and above the frosted moor, whose creatures seemed to stare up as he and the moths passed over them in their strange and wonderful flight.

A moth which seemed the queen led him by his nose… her attendant creatures supporting his ragged hands and depleted feet.

With all of this, Bickersley felt a peculiar entrancement, an elevation of his spirit that he had never before experienced.

He wondered where the journey would end. Another galaxy? The Moon?

Suddenly, though, he sensed himself descending… leaving the stars behind.

Falling.

Plummeting.

Like Icarus.


A horrible bolt of pain through his shoulders brought him to his senses. Bickersley saw that he was now in the lending room of the library, where – to his bewilderment – he was being hoisted by his arms, above its many shelves and bookcases. This elevation was being achieved by way of two of the chains whose day-job was the suspension of a tube light, but whose purpose now was as instruments that Torquemada might have envied. This operation was being supervised by Bronwen, whose attendants busied themselves with various tasks. As Bickersley was hoisted ever higher, one of them climbed a stepladder and, with a firm push on a 'Return By' stamper, plunged the day's date on his forehead.

'This is madness!' said Bickersley, as he continued to be winched. 'All for some overdue library books? Shouldn't I be having a letter? Some sort of fine? *This*… this is like the Inquisition, for heaven's sake! What on earth has got into you?'

He stared down at the scene below him in the weak, yellow light.

He saw that Bronwen's eyes had become enormous and that her back had sprouted a pair of glistening wings. The other attendants of the library were in a similar state of metamorphosis, though she was by far the largest and most dominant.

'This can't be happening! I must be imagining it!' Bickersley shouted.

'I'm afraid not. It's all very real,' Bronwen answered him, her wings spreading behind her. 'Besides, after nineteen Wulstan mysteries the limitations of your imagination are known only too well.'

'What do you mean?' demanded Bickersley.

'The fact is, you've been booked-in here for years, Gerald,' the mutating moth-woman that was Bronwen shouted back. 'But, as with everything else in this world, there's a waiting list. Only so many we can get through in a week.'

'What in Hell's name are you on about?' he responded, as plumage in sundry shades of brown spread itself over her front.

A proboscis-like tongue now flicked from her mouth as she spoke.

'Leonora Learmount... Randolph Hillyard... V.K. Schmidt... Kwezi Abebe-Nkrumah...'

In his suspended state, Bickersley put faces to the names quoted by the now fully-fledged queen moth who'd been Bronwen.

Authors, every one of them.

Learmount, the prolific romantic novelist and winner of twenty Swooning Hearts, Bickersley, of course, knew instantly. Hillyard, the so-called 'unstoppable' Australian – the octogenarian warhorse of eighty action adventures – was just as familiar. Schmidt, he remembered as the painfully morose German whose awful books always ended with the end of the world (until it somehow managed to come back for his next one). And Abebe-Nkrumah – who could forget him? (no matter how deep the desire) – the faithful chronicler of humdrum goings-on in his small African village for a heavily wearying seventy-seven years.

Bickersley recalled their reported – and publicly accepted – fates: Learmount's in a 'choking tragedy', in which the guilty party had been a soft-centre dark chocolate (the Press headline 'Fondant Cream Killer' and the words 'raspberry roulette' flashed before his eyes); in Hillyard's case, a 'freak tragedy', the circumstances of which were never fully disclosed, but somehow involving a koala bear; as for Schmidt, a 'drugs tragedy' among a 'lost' tribe associated with a ritual that required the licking of the anus of a highly toxic toad; and, finally, Abebe-Nkrumah, a 'tragic' goring to death by some rare horned beast the world had thought extinct – which, for its pains, had subsequently been shot dead (its blood-spattered horn later fetching millions on the Far Eastern black market in erectile aphrodisiacs).

*All* of them tragic 'tragedies' in which – bizarrely – every last remnant of the writer in question had disappeared… with not so much as a notelet, earring, wristwatch or shoelace ever being found.

'… Philomena Mee…' continued Bronwen.

Her reference to the shamelessly self-promoting poet and academic – a particular bête noir – left Bickersley in little doubt: Professor Mee's cause of death, as given by the newspapers – a rockfall in the Netherlands – had always seemed to him suspicious.

'There's no prejudice here, of course,' Bronwen continued. 'We're an "equal opportunities" facility. We did one of our own last week – Gwynfryn Gwynne-Owen. Ever heard of him?'

'"Did"?' queried Bickersley, to whom the name meant nothing.

'A petition in his case, with a *large* number of signatories. A day-and-night job for us, it was. The whole committee of the Llanymaen Literary Festival had to go with him.'

'"Go"?'

'Well, after winning their prize nine years on the

bounce… and then the tenth under the less than clever pen name of Gwendoline Gwynne-Owen… it all got a little fraught. Small countries… second cousins. You know.'

'I still don't under—'

'Pandora, your agent, and Olisha at Periodde Bookes… they've had you down for years. And *don't* say we didn't try to stop you. I mean, look at the state of your head and your hands. More holes than a plot by Barnaby Bellamy. He's up next, I believe. Butty of yours, isn't he?'

'"Butty"?'

'On and on you went, Gerald. I've never seen a writer so… *possessed*.'

Her reference to Bellamy – a rather duff author of the old school and sometime dining companion at the Quimbury Club – sent a wave of nausea through Bickersley: confirmation that what was happening to him was indeed all too real.

He saw that at his feet Bronwen's attendants were now assembling a mound of his books. The cover of *Wulstan and the Rod of Ages* stared up from the pinnacle of the pile, the golden instrument of the title glowing at its creator… or so it seemed.

'And what if I elect *not* to "go" gently,' he responded, inspired by the sight of the shining staff, 'but to rage and even to sing in my chains – as your noted countryman put it – "like the sea"?'

'Well, you must do as you please. Dylans, as I told you, burn quickly. Moths to the flame, so to speak. But we… *we* have eternity. Sing, though, if you want to; this is Wales, after all. Anyway, time to crack on.'

As if about to peg a pair of capacious bloomers on a line of laundry, she now held aloft what Bickersley recognised as his manuscript, never mind – after a mass attack by moths – its resemblance to a giant slice of Swiss cheese.

'No!!' screamed Bickersley, as one of her flunkeys put a match to his punctured papers.

'I'm sorry, Gerald – but it has to be,' said Bronwen, flinging the flaming manuscript to the pyre beneath him.

'It *isn't* Gerald – it's Wulstan!' he shouted down, truly and unashamedly now at one with his hero, as the flames rose around him: a union for which a part of him had somehow always longed.

As his books burned in the bonfire and the flames began to consume his hanging form, Wulstan Bickersley now declaimed the 23rd psalm (according to the Christian Bible of King James): 'Yea, though I walk through the valley of the shadow of death, I will fear no evil: for thou art with me; thy *rod* and thy staff they comfort me.'

And, after that, his voice rising and jubilant as the flames licked and flayed, he called out, his eyes shining brightly: '… the kingdom of heaven is like unto a net, that was cast into the sea, and gathered of every kind… Matthew, Chapter Thirteen, Verse Forty-Seven.'

Then, finally, to the delight of those around him, their wings aflutter, he began to sing lustily – not knowing from whence his words came – the verses of the Welsh hymn *Cwm Rhondda*.

> Open thou the crystal fountain
> Whence the healing stream shall flow;
> Let the fiery, cloudy pillar
> Lead me all my journey through

And, faltering now, as the flames leapt and the fire showed no mercy in that Hades of a lending room:

> When I tread the verge of Jordan,
> Bid my anxious fears subside;
> Death of death, and hell's destruction,
> Land me safe on Canaan's side

And, as his words withered to nothing in the fire's almighty roar, the queen moth and her attendants lifted up their wings and voices, and chorused:

Bread of heaven, bread of heaven
*Feed* me till I want no more.
Feed me t-i-l-l I-I want no more.

Amid the grotesques and the gargoyles above the entrance to the library, a new face now made itself felt; the countenance in question pressing its pained features to the surface of the sand-coloured stone, in the manner of a death mask.

As it did so, the flames that had cremated both Gerald Bickersley and Wulstan of Wyckmere climbed in towering tongues through the raised sash windows of that awful charnel house; the effect of this being that their bright beacon could be seen for a great many miles.

Hundreds and then thousands of moths flew towards it in vast golden and silver clouds, as if the winged creatures bore on their backs personal invitations to some millennial bug ball.

And, for all of that long night, they shoaled and danced in delirious circles in the smoke and spark-filled sky above the otherwise dark little town of Llanwherevertheplacedamnedwellwas… in its hollow – or, if you prefer, its 'pit' – somewhere in the land of Wales.

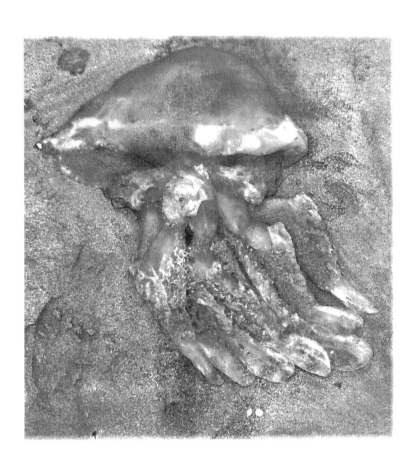

# Under-Wall

SCALING the dune's soft, down-sliding sand was like struggling upstream against a river – an attempted advance against Nature, her grain and all that was ordained. Robbie had made it though, never mind his slipping, splaying limbs. And now he stood amid the tufted peaks in the strange, quiet upland of the sandhills, away from the sounds of the beach and the sea.

Not that at his age he knew, but to many of the townspeople the dunes were a blight: blocking their view of the sea and having a quality that was sordid, like certain ragged woods and unkempt banks of canal that skirt and cross other, inland towns of England.

This stemmed in part from their shabbiness: the way their sharp grasses and the barbs of their brambles spiked and hooked litter. Bits of tarred rope, netting and fishing-boat floats straggled there also, brought in on the high tides that at times toyed with the town.

Behind them, on the road along the seafront, the town's cheaper hotels paraded. Not infrequently, their signs lacked letters in a way that made them look more rundown than they really were. One boarding house whose front garden was covered with cracked paving slabs announced itself as the 'Seashore H..el'. In their traffic-grimed windows, tube-lights pulsed ROOMS, in scarlet and blue.

Finally, there was the matter of what many entered the dunes for, especially at night, evidenced by discarded condoms and the paraphernalia of drugs.

The man who now greeted Robbie seemed to have been sleeping. He was tall and angular – in an irregular, misshaped way that made Robbie think, at first, of an old, leafless tree.

He rose from the foot of the seawall where its stones met the sand, emerging in a manner that suggested he had been under the wall, as if in a cellar.

Robbie *presumed* him to be a man, for, in truth, sand covered him... coated him, from his head to his feet. Although he moved, he was like some scarecrow that had been planted there, pinned to a cross, against which the sand of the beach and the dunes had blown and caked.

Standing now, in front of Robbie, some of the grains slipped from him, in fine, vertical showers.

For several moments, Robbie and the man stared at one another.

Robbie seemed to hear only the hard beating of his own heart, which felt big inside him after his scrabble up the dune.

Suddenly, the voice of his mother, who he'd left elsewhere on the beach – sitting on a towel – broke through the loud sound of his heart.

'Robbie! Robbie!! Where *are* you?'

In her words was the scold that was familiar to him.

'Come *out* of there!'

He turned from the man towards what seemed the source of her call, conscious that she might even now be struggling up the same slope: skirt blowing, shoes slipping, mouth swearing.

'Robbie! ROBBIE!! I won't call you again!'

He pivoted to the man... or where the man had last been,

because the man was closer now, much closer, his skin oozing its silky showers of sand.

'Robbie! I'm telling you!' his mother's voice called again. 'Last chance! I'll leave you! See if I don't!'

And Robbie ran then, without stopping, away from the man, away from the hollow, up and over the tufted peak and down the slope of slipping sand on the other side of the dune – the side that the town saw and that the sea sometimes washed against, when it came close to the town... when it wanted to.

The house where they lived – Robbie, his mother and, at times, his grandmother – was a lean four-storey at the end of the esplanade furthest from the dunes: part of a terrace that had at one time been sought-after. Several slips of the headland which, by diminishing degrees, extended beyond them, had made the houses unsaleable. The spur sank into the sea – sometimes by night, sometimes by day – as if in some game of hide-and-seek. One of the houses had become a squat. The endmost, closest to the rocks – and riven with cracks – was occupied by an old woman – Mrs Kidd – and her abundance of cats. Robbie's mother admitted no one save his grandmother to their own house. If anyone knocked, she would open the door an inch and snatch whatever it was they were delivering, as if fearful something unwelcome might enter... or escape.

The house had a musty smell and had grown gloomy and bare. This physical emptiness was on account of the things Robbie's mother had sold: a piano, pictures, some porcelain... small pieces of silver and brass. Sometimes a television was there in the lounge and sometimes it was not. His toys were not immune. A tinplate train, wooden fort and space rocket vanished in one night. Poorer, cheaper toys took their place: lorries with loose wheels, plastic dinosaurs lacking eyes and teeth, soldiers with broken arms and legs whose rifles had been snapped.

In those times of the TV's absence, his mother played

(though didn't seem to listen to) a portable radio. Voices from the wireless climbed the stairs of the house, from the kitchen to his bedroom. This, save for an attic room that would once have been the maid's, was at the top of the house. Now and again, there'd be a man's voice on its own on the radio, perhaps reading the news or commentating on something in a sparse way, such as a cricket match. This made it seem as if the man was in the house. And Robbie noticed that at such times his mother tended to turn the radio off.

His mother and grandmother, whenever she stayed at the house, communicated in words and glances that Robbie did not understand completely, but which he knew referred to a man who had once lived in the house.

Frequently, his mother would interrupt these conversations to tell Robbie to go to his room.

From the landing, he'd hear the voices of the women – his mother's becoming raised – and he'd catch sight of her crossing the hall to the kitchen to search for her cigarettes. His grandmother would enter the kitchen after her, his mother more often than not now crying as she pulled open cupboards and drawers. Afterwards, she would re-cross the hall and shout up at where he stood by the banister.

'I told you to go to your room!'

From his window, he could see right along the beach: the seawall tapering into what seemed like infinity and, to one side of it, the forbidden land of the dunes.

Eventually, his mother's voice would be smothered by the hushes and shushes of his grandmother, who would say things like, 'Carol... please. Robbie will hear.'

Sometimes, at night, he'd hear his mother crying. Not tears of pain or hurt, but tears that were hot and angry.

He had cried these himself and knew the difference.

Normally, they would never walk that far. Normally, they walked the *other* way: on the green swards of the headland and cliffs. Excursions to the beach would invariably end halfway, where there were steps up the seawall to the esplanade.

That day though, the day of his discovery of the man, Robbie and his mother had for some reason drifted further.

On their way home, he told his mother about the stranger he'd met in the dunes, the sand that had slipped from him, as if it were gold.

She rebuked him.

She said that if he didn't stop his 'silly stories' she would end their walks on the beach entirely and, in future, they would go only to the park. The latter he disliked (being nervous of the other children there). He knew that his mother knew this.

'Keep on and I'll send you away somewhere,' she added.

'Where?' he asked.

'A school – with horrible teachers and boys.'

His mother walked on quickly, angrily, jerking him by his hand to keep up with her.

And so he said nothing more about the man and the sand and the wall from under which the man seemed to have come.

At tea there was a sudden great rumble of noise. It rattled the cups and saucers and caused the sash windows to vibrate. Robbie ran from his seat at the kitchen table to the bay window in the lounge. A fresh piece of the headland was being sucked into the sea. He saw scree falling into its foaming, smoking water. A sward of grass and gorse clung oddly, in suspended collapse, to an otherwise new – and sheer – cliff.

In his eyes, the horn of rock, in its various altered states, had, over time, passed through a series of incarnations as animal and mythical beast. At one stage it had been a dragon. At another a dozing dog. At still other stages it had seemed to him a snake and even an eagle (or at least its fierce-beaked head).

But with this latest fall its metamorphosis seemed to have stalled.

It was as if the headland had not merely been shorn of its snout, but – like some fallen statue – had been severed of its entire skull and neck.

That night, Robbie dreamt of further, deeper advances by the sea. The old woman – Mrs Kidd – and her cats had been swept from their house and were struggling in dark waves amid a wail of horrible mewing. His grandmother meanwhile was clinging to her bed – afloat in the town's park, where children had gathered in a crowd on the slowly-spinning roundabout. The roundabout was surrounded by water, its structure like the capsized hull of a boat. It was as if the children and their vessel had been abandoned by all adults.

Robbie had the sense that the sea was slapping the stairs of the house, where he and his mother lay immovably: its dark water unhooking pictures and carrying them off, in a flotsam of shoes and books and hats.

A creak, as if from someone on the staircase, caused him to wake.

He pushed back the covers of his bed and went to his room's bay window.

Through the right-most pane, he saw the dark, cragged shape of the headland. Through the centre pane, he saw the moon, low over the sea (which was smooth and still and lying as it ought to have been). And then, through the left-most, he saw the beach.

On the shore, something… some*one* was moving… walking. A small, beetle-like figure in the silver light.

For a moment, the figure seemed to stop and look back – at the house… at his window – and then walk on, in the direction of the dunes.

Robbie checked the sill of the window to satisfy himself that those things that he had recently collected from the beach were still there: a white clay pipe, the red plastic case of a shotgun cartridge and a dry and sun-bleached starfish, whose setting on the sill he now adjusted slightly.

After this, he stood on his bed and pushed a mobile of an aeroplane that hung from the ceiling.

He climbed back into bed and watched the plane spinning, as the sea kept up its rhythmic fall on the shore.

One morning some days later, his mother told him she had something to do in the town. She said that there was milk and bread – cut in the kitchen – with some jam, and that he was to stay in the house until she came back.

From his window, he watched the butterfly-bright daub of her pink mac disappear on the drab esplanade. On the landing below his, the odour of perfume lingered outside the locked door to her room.

He went downstairs and ate and drank what she had left for him.

He then let himself out through the back door of the house by way of the key – the one that he wasn't supposed to know about – that his mother kept in the cutlery drawer.

Robbie locked the door after him and walked through the overgrown garden to the gate to the back lane. Then he wandered to the beach.

The tide was out and Robbie combed what it had left, kicking at weed, driftwood and shells.

He picked up and tossed back the rough white bone of a cuttlefish but retained some small lozenges of brown and green glass that the sea had made smooth and gem-like.

In time, although he had not been consciously heading for them, the trail took him to the dunes.

He began to climb the same sandhill as previously.

Some way below the peak, he glanced back to the esplanade, wondering if he might see his mother in her mac. There was no sign of her, and so he carried on towards the crest. The sand – thanks to the dune grass that scruffily bearded it – hardened here and should have been easier to scale. Yet he found himself slipping and sliding, even so.

Suddenly, an arm reached over the ridge, and pulled him up.

In the bowl inside the dunes, things were quiet and still. The sea – distant on the flats – mustered barely a whisper. The town, although close, seemed equally remote... almost imaginary. No birds shrilled above them and no breeze touched Robbie or the man, who, having hitched him over the ridge, now let go of Robbie's hand.

They stared at one another in the shabby hollow. As with their first encounter, sand covered the man. If anything, the coating was thicker now. It was as if he'd been blasted with it… his scarecrow form stepping down from the dunes to wander the shore, both in storms and the winds that swept it at night, when no one else ventured onto the beach

Robbie watched as the man's face shed flakes… as his crusted hair streamed golden showers to his shoulders and his chest.

The man reached into a side pocket, then drew out his hand.

Saying nothing, he moved a clenched, grain-covered fist towards Robbie. Then he turned his wrist and opened his palm.

On it, Robbie saw a toy soldier that had been his. A guardsman in a black bearskin and scarlet tunic. One of the many that had gone missing from his room.

Robbie's eyes grew wide. His mouth opened to speak.

The man, however, raised a sand-streaming finger to his lips. These were pale as sticks of driftwood that the sun had bleached; on them, tiny grains that had a gold-dust glitter.

And Robbie knew to say nothing.

He took the figure from the man and wiped some grains from its face. He tucked it in a trouser pocket.

Suddenly, his attention was seized by a plastic bag snagged on brambles to one side of the man. The bag rippled and rattled in a way that Robbie found oddly loud, as a gust blew through the hollow and pulled at the bag on its bramble barbs.

The breeze died and the bag became limp. When Robbie looked back, the man had gone.

Robbie scampered up a dune.

Beyond it, through a gap, he saw the shape of the man, retreating to the stones of the seawall.

And then he felt himself sliding – as if sucked – down a

steep slope, till he came to a hard bump and a stop, on his backside, on the beach.

He began to walk home, puzzled, fingering the toy guardsman in his pocket.

Forgetting that he was supposed to be indoors, he climbed some steps to the esplanade and wandered the seafront.

Down a side-street that he knew from the barber's pole that leant into it, he thought he saw his mother's mac, moving amid people on the pavement and then up some steps that had railings, as if she were behind bars.

He lowered his head and hurried home.

It was dark when he heard her unlock the front door, close it and climb the stairs. When she sat on his bed and kissed his cheek, her breath was warm and sweet, in a way he didn't like.

In the following days, she often left him on his own in the house. To begin with, she left food on the kitchen table. Then money took its place. Coins – one and two-pound pieces – and sometimes five-pound notes. She no longer said anything about him not going out.

He bought candyfloss, chips and ice-cream from the shops and stalls along the front.

Nobody asked why he wasn't in school. Nobody said anything much, apart from one man whose car window had been down on the road along the seafront, who wanted to know the way to the headland.

Bags of sweets glistened on his dashboard.

'I need you to help me,' said the man.

A van came up behind his car and honked.

With an irritated look at Robbie, the man moved on.

On such days, he found himself walking to the dunes. Not through design, but because the tide's strandline of weed and shells seemed to take him there.

In the inner world of the dunes, the man would be waiting with one, and then another, of Robbie's missing toys:

his clockwork frog, his racing car, the monkey with its drum – small but important things whose disappearance Robbie had noted… toys his mother had said he was 'too big for' – all now returning to Robbie, on the palm of the man's hand.

One day, the man produced an American Indian – a brave in a headdress – that had been one of Robbie's favourites.

Bending towards Robbie, the man raised it to his mouth on the flat of his palm and blew grains from the figure's face.

For a moment, the white and black-tipped feathers of the headdress seemed to come to life, lifting and blowing backwards in the draught of the man's breath. Then they settled and were still again, like birds that had been disturbed in a tree.

After these visits, the seawall – hemming the shore, so it seemed to Robbie, like a train with extra-long carriages – transported him back to the house.

Sometimes he dawdled.

Once, he saw his mother in the window of a café. She was sitting at a table with a man he didn't know. She saw Robbie, and looked away.

Sometime after that, she entered his room and held him and sobbed.

She said that she was sorry for the way that she had been 'busy'. She kissed him and told him that in the morning they would go out together.

He had to wake her. He'd hoped they might catch a bus and visit a castle. Instead, they went to the beach. His mother smoked, fiddled with her phone and answered him in a way that he knew meant that she wasn't listening.

The sour stream that was the town's 'river' slithered to the beach via a grey, concrete pipe that looked like the half-submerged cylinder of a giant toilet roll.

It tunnelled under the promenade and seawall, its mouth (and the slimed and rusted grille that covered it) emerging on the sand… short of the water, except at high tide.

Congealed with junk, its flow seldom exceeded a trickle.

But that day, as Robbie poked in the shallow and cloudy pool at its mouth, it acquired a much more forceful flow.

It was as if some obstacle upstream – a shopping trolley, traffic cone, or an old tyre heavy with silt – had been dislodged after years of holding back a great accumulation of filth.

A dam-burst of detritus now slurried downstream and spewed from the pipe.

It swept Robbie from his feet, bowling him backwards, bringing his head down hard on the damp sand.

He got up for a moment before – in almost the next second – the black torrent bowled him over again.

And now he was being forced, *jetted*… from the shore to the sea, as if he were a piece of jetsam, something that the town had always secretly hated and, having sensed its opportunity, was determined to dump.

The river's scum was in his mouth and in his eyes. It was on and under his tongue, in his hair, his trousers, his underpants, his ears.

Gritty. Stinging. Choking.

A grotesque and rancid tide stormed from the pipe: soiled condoms, used syringes, rusted needles, torn betting slips, soaked bingo cards, crumpled beer cans and empty vodka bottles. Bobbing on it, were flotillas of white plastic cups and – horrifically bright – the slung, polystyrene cartons of part-mauled and rejected takeaway meals, like some ghastly mockery of fishing boat floats.

The ceaseless, stinking trash-slide sent Robbie further and further towards the sea.

He was on his back now… skidding, spinning… in the sludge and the slime.

As he was thrown and hosed and swept and tossed, he sensed that the force doing this had to be more than the mere river that in ordinary times crawled greasily through the town.

For an instant, he remembered his grandmother lancing a boil on his leg with a hot needle of the kind with which she sewed… the lava flow of pus that oozed onto his skin… her fingers squeezing his limb's little volcano.

And he knew… he knew that the roaring sewer-river was in fact some great tsunami of the town's own making – its own gangrenous poison.

In the midst of the deluge, he seemed to grasp so many of its secrets now. He saw and understood clearly the bribes taken by policemen and councillors in laybys on the clifftops; the beatings given to women and children behind closed doors; the cash-in-hand that was the currency of the town's tradesmen, barmaids, waitresses and sundry sellers of tat; the *real* intent of the man in the car who claimed he needed to know the way to the headland.

He also saw the other men and what they did with his mother – in hotel rooms that were warm and airless and had nothing but a bed, kettle and cups with sachets of coffee, sugar and powdered milk with which to whiten it, if they so wanted (amid their other desires).

Robbie understood now how and why the town was rotting, how it was the *town* that was falling into the sea rather than the sea claiming the town.

The sea, surely, would have been revolted by it. The headland was no living creature. It was something decaying, dead, like the rabbit he'd once found on the cliffs, flies over the drying jelly of its staring eyes… swarming.

And now the sea began to carry him – away from the beach, away from the town.

A black bloom opened in the water.

After some while, the swell seemed to lift him, so that he saw the headland, its line of stacks and stumps, stark in the sunlight, the flecks of the seabirds that circled them.

He could hear them.

Shrilling.

In the coldness, Robbie sensed something take hold of him, *curl* itself around him.

He saw the seawall: its high, dark stones and grey mortar,

peeling from the town and the seafront, reaching out into the water... taking him... back.

On the shore, the man stood dripping. Crags of wet sand fell from him, as he held Robbie.

'Give him to me!' Robbie's mother screamed.

In her arms now, Robbie stared at the man, whose cloak of grains wasn't merely slipping from him, but separating – in lumps and screes, like the collapse of the headland.

Robbie realised then that he knew the man and had always known him.

His mother, sobbing, carried him across the weed and the wood and the cuttlefish bones of the strandline, away from the sand, away from the beach.

Later, much later, when theirs had become the end house of the terrace and his mother had left for an inland town, Robbie continued to do those things he long had done: watching the headland, combing the beach, clearing rubbish that had become jammed in the bars of the outfall pipe where it snaked onto the sand.

In time, as with the man before him, the house became a place where he no longer lived.

The dunes and the under-wall and the boys and the girls who came to him – secretly, in search of those things that had been stolen from them – were now, instead, all his.

# An Exhibition

VILE! That's what he was. In her eyes. The mere thought of his... *creations*. It made her shudder; it *polluted* her, his... *effluent*, so that her tea, yes even her tea, the very tea in her very cup, tasted bitter.

Julius Blunt, the little... *darling* of the London art world, the *enfant terrible* of English culture, who claimed he was 'still a simple Nantborough lad at heart'. Never mind his mansion in Bermuda. Let alone the complete accident of his local 'connection': delivered at Nantborough General, silver-spoon son to a father who'd been some sort of top diplomat and a mother who, according to all the magazines, had been both a beauty queen and a ballerina, in whichever country it was that Blunt Senior had been doing his diplomatic act... Denmark, or was it Sweden?... the infant genius Julius entering the world in the General's maternity ward on the night of a storm that saw flash floods submerge all roads and railway lines south to London.

Never mind also, the young Blunt's education at a top public school, followed by a highly fashionable art college and, with it, possession of an accent posher than H.M. the Queen. No, the way *he* and his PR people spun it, he was just 'an ordinary northern, Nantborough lad'. And so the town gallery, suckered like so many others, actually took in his… *trash*, rather than dumping it in the gutter where it belonged; the council – yes, the 'cash-strapped' council, as it liked to proclaim itself – even bidding for the (lower-priced) stuff at auction. And how Blunt was hunted… nothing of his ever fetching less than five figures; the average for a 'statement piece' being well into six. And now, according to the paper, another atrocity was on its way, though they didn't call it *that*, of course: something that was still 'under wraps', but 'daring', according to a report – labelled 'Exclusive' – by the *Gazette's* TV, Gaming and Arts Correspondent Gary Trott.

Her heart sank. She put down the paper and took another sip of her tea. She'd earned this cup. And she'd get through it, bitter or not. Hadn't Blunt made her suffer enough? As for that fortnight covering his room when young Sheena Sidebottom had been off on holiday with her boyfriend – Ibiza or wherever it was the dizzy pair went… Worst two weeks of her life! Thank God for the mercies of H.F. Moss. How glad she'd been to get back to his pastoral scenes next door, never mind that she'd been staring at them for thirty-five years.

*Thirty-five years…*

Yes, it really had been that long. She could tell a cow's arse by Hubert Moss from five hundred paces, they were that familiar.

But Julius Blunt…

She didn't know which of his *things* she loathed most. The horse's head was up there, to be sure. And not a fake head, of course. Not something done in gouache, or stencilled, or sculpted. Oh no, not with Blunt. For him, everything had to be a stunt. And so it was a real, actual head. Dead and decomposing. With lightbulbs that glowed through the holes left by its dropped-out eyes, skinless nostrils and part-open jaws. Press a button and the 60 watts – or whatever it was –

shone through. *Neigh Lad: Strong and Stable.* A 'statement piece… an installation' – those were the words the gallery used. She had her own for it, of course. Then there was *Wired For Sound.* She winced at the very thought of it: a roll of old barbed wire coiled around a giant plasterwork ear that had been salvaged from some medical school. And as for those sordid little booths of his with their pervy films of women in white macs walking dogs in parks… and that *disgusting* box of sand where you were supposed to bury your hands while listening on headphones to sea shanties sung by fishermen in Devon, or Dorset, or wherever it was. Folk wouldn't have been half as keen if they knew it'd been dug from Dredgley Beach (famous for its nuclear plant and sewage pipe), courtesy of a bunch of upper class interns sent North by 'Our Julius' to sample 'life's grittier side'.

Oh, the Julius Blunt Room was full of it, all right.

And to think… to think of all of the wonderful things that had been ousted to make way for his horrors – lovely porcelain, beautiful miniatures, oils of nineteenth century scenes. *Proper* art. All of it now archived, mothballed… moved away. Sometimes, after-hours, she'd go down to the vaults and open drawers, remove shrouds… look at – *touch* – those things that had been 'lost' because of that… Blunt.

And now her very last day was near… after thirty-five years… thirty-five years of stalwart near-invisibility, passed in the same attendant's chair (you could see the curves her behind had left in it). All in the service of Nantborough and its most famous son, H.F. Moss (before Julius Blunt – the little Caesar – had swept onto the scene). And who would speak up for Hubert now, she wondered (his spires, his meadows, his cottages, his cows), after she had gone? Certainly not Nigel (the curator), who scarce made a secret of the fact that to him Nantborough was a mere pit stop on the way to somewhere swankier, in London or abroad. Nor, for that matter, any of the trustees – dull worthies who downed an expensive dinner once a year, none of them knowing their Arts from their elbows. They'd all as soon use H.F.'s room as an overspill for Blunt's junk. No longer the Julius Blunt Room... but the Julius Blunt Wing. Didn't he always have some fresh piece of foolishness on the go – a new stunt, even sillier than the last – to be lapped-up by London's luvvie crowd?

As her departure date drew near, her worries about Moss having to make way grew. She pictured his frames in the rough hands of removal men, not even bothering to wear gloves – their new 'home' a warehouse on a derelict industrial estate where no one ever went... his canvasses crawled over by spiders, gnawed at and peed on by rats.

An awful vision of one ghastly rodent – all horrible teeth and long, scaly tail... scurrying over the golden clockface of Moss's *Nantborough Priory* (1860) and down its sturdy stone tower – haunted her dreams at night.

She woke feverously, reciting the words of the nursery rhyme *Hickory Dickory Dock*.

'The mouse ran down...' she repeated in the blackness of her bedroom, seeming not only to see but to *feel* its hideous, scampering claws.

The clock was ticking. The bell was tolling, both for her and for Hubert. Time was running out.

In the day, at the gallery, ideas began to enter her head – their thrust being her need to 'neutralise' Blunt. Not by any assault on his person – he hardly came to Nantborough anyway – but in an attack on his room, his chamber of horrors, his so-called art. And 'attack' wasn't the word. *Sabotage*. Yes, it would be that, and *resistance... defiance... liberation* – those words too.

For the sake of art, Julius Blunt *had* to be stopped. What *would* the young show-off do next?

She began to consider ways. A slashing of one of his 'paintings'? Little chance of her being caught if done at the end of the day – the gallery was always nearly empty by then. After-hours would be best... to be certain she wouldn't be seen. She'd need a hoodie. And a mask, of course. After all, she needed to look out for her pension. *Pension...* What had she done with her life, she wondered, other than look after H.F. Moss? Well, *now* was the time for action. Anyway, there was no need to hurry home. Not since her mother had died. Conversation and companionship? That all rather began and ended with Hubert (and him a confirmed bachelor, by all accounts).

Yes, she thought to herself – as her sense of the need for a deed deepened – the rip of a blade through *Pool of Vomit* (2019) would indeed be satisfying. And yet... Might not a gesture like that prove counterproductive, provoking support for The Great Pretender? She could see Blunt playing the victim... whining about assaults on art, culture... reaching for the martyr's crown. But what about *Neigh Lad*? Surely *that* piece of idiocy deserved to go up in smoke? She wondered about swapping its bulbs for some of an inappropriate wattage. With luck, they'd explode in the poor creature's head. The crummy nature of the work might then dawn on the public. She pictured it: eye-sockets aflame, smoke streaming from its nostrils, grey teeth aglow – like some hideous, fiery nag that the *real* Devil – not just Blunt – might ride.

On the plus side, the room's sprinkler system would almost certainly come on, soaking the rest of Blunt's ridiculous wares. And yet, again, there was the question of the sympathy this might elicit. On top of which, there was the lack of satisfaction in something done surreptitiously. It didn't have that same delicious smack of humiliation that a put-down in public possessed: a custard pie in the face, an egg to the head, a debagging of trousers, a V-sign and pithy remark – loud and proud – amid the flashbulbs of the Press. In *these* lay the true thrill of triumph.

Even so, temptation tingled inside her. Oh, if Julius Blunt only knew how he was being hunted now!

Halfway through her last week, she had a message from Nigel, the curator: a note in her pigeonhole that concerned no less a person than 'JB' (as Nigel, an undisguised fan, liked to call him).

Nantborough's favourite son had heard of her impending retirement from her 'splendid career of service' and would like to meet her, if that would be all right, 'as part of her send-off'.

A frisson seized her. It was as if she'd been caught dragging a kitchen knife through one of Blunt's 'paintings' – by no less a figure than the silly young fraud himself.

She spent the next day discreetly perusing photographs of Blunt on her phone in the Moss Room, reading interviews he'd given to trendy websites and magazines. In one, he was pictured wearing a flat cap, declaring his love of 'all things Northern', including hotpots, Eccles cakes and whippets.

*As if!* she thought.

Meanwhile, she had the mounting sense that Moss and the subjects of his paintings were aware of her looming departure.

Although her thirty-five years in his room had been passed in near silence, she now seemed to hear the shifting hooves and soft whinnies of horses, the distant lowing of cows, the occasional bleat of sheep.

At times, her nostrils seemed to catch whiffs of tobacco smoke. Hubert had been 'a pipeman', she knew (from sundry portraits and old photographs).

It was as if he'd been there when she'd been fiddling with her phone: puffing quietly, in a corner, in some moment of contemplation, perhaps even thinking of painting her, assessing how she might best be captured (in oils, pencil or watercolours).

And now – upset by divination of some kind – he'd packed up his palette and gone.

Looking around the room at his canvasses, she had the momentary but distinct conviction that his animals had all either turned, or lifted their heads, and were now staring at her, intently, in the manner of creatures whose grazing had been disturbed.

A breeze seemed to ripple the swards of his water meadows and sway the stalks of his wheat fields.

The petals of sweet peas and wildflowers tumbled, or so it appeared to her, from Moss's heavy, gilded frames.

On her last afternoon, she left the premises punctually. At home, she tried on a series of frocks, finally settling on a little red number she'd not worn for years. She found herself attempting to remember who'd been Top of the Pops the last time she'd worn it, as she wiggled and fiddled.

A squeeze, but... a fit, just. She was in!

After that, she fixed her lipstick, eyeliner and mascara. God! How long had it been since she'd used any of them?

She paused for a moment and thought about Blunt.

While of course his art wasn't *everyone's* idea of the word, there was no denying that Julius – yes, it was Julius now – had done rather well, put the town on the map. And who could blame him for so rarely coming back? I mean, the place was boring, wasn't it? Known for its 1970s flyover and (to the half-dozen who'd heard of him) as the birthplace of H.F. Moss. That had been it... before Julius jumped on the scene. And his art – yes, it was *art* now – wasn't *all* bad, was it? Some of it was really quite clever. If nothing else, you had to admire his cheek. And the boy could draw when he wanted to. There was no doubting that. And the *other* thing about Julius – devil that he undoubtedly was – was that he was... well... just a teensy-weensy bit good looking: those Nordic high cheekbones, that thatch of fair hair. If anyone really thought about it, hair on a bloke was a rare thing in Nantborough. Most men shaved it off, or were naturally bald, like Nigel.

And she would soon be seeing Julius, this bad boy, in his private suite – for that was where they were meeting – in his hotel (the one that he owned) – for her special send-off.

She smiled in the mirror as she finished her make-up.

*Go get him girl*, she winked.

'Don't go making an exhibition of yourself!' her mother's ghost called from her chair by the gas fire in the living room, as she made for the front door.

'Not now, mother!' she answered. 'I've been waiting thirty-five bloody years for this!'

The receptionist at the hotel's front desk gave her directions to 'Mr Blunt's' suite. 'He's expecting you,' the young woman smiled.

She went up in the lift. It played music: Vivaldi… *Winter*, unless she was mistaken.

Between floors, she plucked a hair from her right nostril in one of the lift's mirrored walls. Her eyes watered a little.

Blunt greeted her effusively at the door of his suite. He wore a dark silk gown embroidered with fire-breathing dragons and, on his seemingly sockless feet, slippers that bore his initials.

There seemed no other guests.

A *little* forward Julius, she thought to herself.

*Still, that's what you get with a genuine bohemian.*

He took her mac from her shoulders, and she sensed – as she'd hoped – a slight tremble in his fingers: her coat being one she'd dug out deliberately on account of its resemblance to those worn by the women who walked dogs in wet parks in his odd little films.

Blunt was flattery itself, directing her to a trolley of 'nibbles' in the softly-lit suite. He plucked a bottle of vintage champagne from an ice bucket and uncorked it, with a pop.

'Honours are in order!' he gushed. 'Service like yours needs to be celebrated… commemorated. Thirty-five years in the attendant's chair. We can't let you go without something to mark dedication like that.'

The bubbles of the champagne seemed to go up her nose. She felt herself blush.

He guided her to a large and deep sofa where, for the next hour or more, they talked art. Diverting discussion from his own work to that of H.F. Moss, Blunt surprised her with his knowledge of Hubert and his scenes. 'Yes, but I think that particular cow was painted on Myrtlewick Meadow. If I'm not mistaken, Sissy-Belle was her name…'

And now, never mind her intentions of all the previous days and weeks, she found herself wanting to pay him – 'JB' – a compliment.

'You're a very productive artist. The *Gazette* reckons you've something big on the go. A workload like yours must be very tiring.'

'It is, but it has its compensations,' he answered, with (unless she was mistaken) something of a mischievous grin. 'Let me get you a refill.'

Another thing she noticed was that each time he rose to top up her champagne he seemed to return and seat himself a shade closer.

Eventually, their conversation was being conducted with his hand on her knee.

*Cheeky*, she thought.

But she decided not to remove it. After all, wasn't that the hand of England's greatest living artist? *His* palm on *her* patella, of all people?

What also dawned on her (albeit somewhat hazily), through the copious flutes of champagne and the fogginess they induced, was that her dreams and schemes of humiliating Blunt, of wrecking his art, seemed to have evaporated... gone 'pop', like the bubbles of the champagne.

In fact, rather than throttling him with the belt of that gown of his, making him beg for mercy and swear that he would never paint, sculpt or *install* anything ever again, she found herself rather hoping that he would undo that same silk sash and perhaps even install...

'You know, I'm really not supposed to say a thing like this, in this day and age, particularly not to a guest in my hotel room – and I understand that *fully*,' Blunt began. 'But the truth is – how can I put it? – an older woman, a *mature* woman, a woman of the world...'

'Can't be me,' she broke in with a hiccup and a giggle. 'I've never left Nantborough. Except for a week in Benidorm – if that counts. Can't say I cared for it. And the odd coach outing, to Dredgley Sands.'

'… that's the kind of woman that I've always wanted to capture.'

She sensed his blue eyes stare into hers. He leaned closer.

Her face lifted to his. She puckered her lips.

Blunt rose smartly from the sofa. He disappeared to a dimmer part of the suite. 'I'm just going to…' His words petered.

A moment or two later, he called out, rather more loudly: 'There's a hot tub on the balcony. Lovely view of the town. We can finish all this out there. You'll find a robe in the bathroom.'

Having wondered about the wisdom of it – certain parts of her had undeniably grown saggy with the passing of the years, as the mirrors in Blunt's bathroom had cruelly made plain – she was now out on the balcony.

Before and below her, grimy old Nantborough did its best to glitter.

The tub's cauldron steamed and bubbled at her toes.

She had never been in one before and wasn't quite sure what to expect.

Scandinavians like Julius did it all the time, though, didn't they? she thought to herself. For them, it was a cultural thing: stripping off for a sauna and then a soak. And Julius was certainly cultured. Did any man alive know half as much about the cows of H.F. Moss?

She thought the tub smelt a bit… funny, that its water looked a bit… gooey.

But she let her robe slip, even so.

And baring her body and her soul to Nantborough – its multi-storey car park, its pound shops, pawn shops, nail bars, chicken bars and launderettes, its betting shops, charity shops and its pavements full of druggies and dog mess, and with her mother's refrain ringing in her ears, 'Don't go making an exhibition of yourself!' and her own rouged lips issuing the rejoinder, 'No mother, I *will*. I *bloody well* will!' – she stepped forward, and in.

Of all the exhibits at Nantborough Town Gallery, the one that really draws the crowds – for its shock value, if nothing else – is that of a woman of near pensionable age in a piscine pose, suspended as if swimming through the clear 'water' of a rectangular tank: hair spread rather wild, bosom rather sagging, her mouth rouged in a rictus grin. The fake figure – for it is surely that and cannot be real – looks (with poignant longing, some think) towards the adjoining room of Nantborough's second most famous son, the landscape painter H. F. Moss, and the gentle scenes that – for the time being – still hang there: Victorian vistas of spires and water meadows, cottages and cows.

The title of this installation – spot-lit and raised reverentially – to which worshippers weary of Botticelli's *The Birth of Venus* and da Vinci's *Mona Lisa* journey in new pilgrimages of adoration, all in the name of art?

*Attendant Pleasures*, Julius Blunt (2020).

# Hide

RINCH'S tongue ran over his top lip. 'Oh, you beauty. You little, little beauty. You *cheeky* thing. Come on now. Come on. I can s-e-e y-o-u. Yes I c-a-a-n. You *are* a pretty one, aren't you? Hey? A pretty, pretty one. And do I get a twirl? I do! Very nice! Oh, that's *very* nice! And where do you think you're going? Not leaving me, I hope? You little minx! Very well then. Be off with you… I shall see *you* later. I'll be w-a-i-t-i-n-g.'

He lowered his binoculars and opened his journal. Under the day's date he wrote 'BTG' – his abbreviation for bar-tailed godwit – adding: Adult. Female? (Bit of a tease.) Western marsh. Reeds.

Rinch put down his pen, lifted the loop for his binoculars away from his head and rested them on the shelf below the viewing hatch. He took a Thermos from his knapsack and poured some soup ('Farmhouse Vegetable' the packet had claimed) into a grey plastic cup. Next he peeled back the lid of a Tupperware container and bit into a sandwich whose cheese he'd grated that morning having scraped mould from the small block of Cheddar in its foil in his fridge. (A natural enough growth, he'd told himself, re-wrapping the block.)

He was the only person in the hide and had been since his arrival at ten o'clock. He liked it like that. Weekdays were always the best. On Saturdays the place was like a zoo. Sundays were even worse: the world and his wife in there, squashed like sardines. He'd known six to a hatch, all peering and chattering. Where was the joy in that? Maybe he'd bring it up at a committee meeting. Maybe not. Maybe he'd just stick to his weekdays, keep things quiet.

A slice of tomato slipped from his sandwich to the floor. He picked it up. Fair enough, the hide was little more than four walls of larchlap and creosote, a glorified garden shed. But it needed to be kept respectable. Rinch glanced at the sign – the one he'd made and pinned above the door: 'Please Leave This Hide As YOU Found It.'

He looped his binoculars back over his head and returned to the hatch. He'd seen some 'fluff'. Now how about some gore? The previous week he'd watched a peregrine falcon seize a starling in mid-air, swoop to earth and disembowel it – all in a trice. TV… those games teenagers fooled with on their phones and computers… they had nothing on that. The marsh was life and death in the raw. There was no one… no*where*… to run to out there. Peaceful it might seem on the surface. But red was its real colour – red in tooth and claw.

Scanning the reserve, Rinch thrilled quietly at the power of his binoculars, which were Russian, military issue and night-capable (if you knew what to do with them). He congratulated himself on his purchase: the best he'd ever bought. As far as he was concerned, there was no point investing in anything less. With inferior gear, plumage was just a blur. And as for eyes and legs? Well, you could forget anything like that. He wondered why some of the others even bothered, given the equipment they brought. Nothing escaped *his* magnification though. He got every last feather, nailed every squirming grub. One night soon, he'd survey it in the dark, put his purchase to the test, see what was lurking… 'going on'… out there, on the reedbeds and the bogs, in the blackness 'after hours'. First though – for safety – he'd get a bolt put on the door. Never mind the reserve's remoteness. You couldn't be too careful. Not these d—

Suddenly, his lenses swept over something. Something… odd, something alien: a collision of colours: blues, blacks, creams… disproportionate and out-of-keeping.

He swung back, panning the northern edge of the reserve, along a ragged line of alders that entered the wetland like nervous bathers. He steadied the lenses, re-calibrated, zoomed in.

His finessing brought into focus a black jacket, blue jeans… lowered… of… a young man. And, behind him (what Rinch could see of her) a young woman… lying… on her back, against one of the dun-coloured rocks that rose on a slight incline (where the land was drier).

Rinch reared from the glasses.

Their strap tightened at the nape of his neck.

He let go of them and they fell – heavily – against his chest.

He blinked, shuddered, blinked again, widening his eyes as he did so, as if needing to expel some bug or speck of dirt.

He looked around the hut, his attention falling on a faded poster to the left of his viewing station: pale pictures of damselflies, butterflies, bats, birds and bees. *Wildlife You May See Here* was the heading, above notes about feeding and mating that Rinch knew by heart.

He stood still for a moment, then raised the binoculars and looked back through the hatch.

The youth was moving rhythmically into the girl. She was drawing him in: her thighs and knees around his hips: locking, unlocking, relocking.

'Stop it!' Rinch said, still looking. 'Stop it!'

He lowered the binoculars, marched to the door and stormed from the hut.

In the sodden ground of the marsh, Rinch's determined strides drew squelches and splashes, peaty water spraying his high, woollen socks. He brushed his way hotly through tall stalks of fescue and foxtail.

After about fifty yards he stopped and checked with his lenses. They were still… *at it.*

Rinch splashed onwards, binoculars swinging, banging his chest. A sheep browsing behind some ferns jumped out of his way, with a bleat.

Suddenly, his left leg sank in a small bog. He pulled it free, to the sound of a horrible suck.

Having extricated his limb, he stood panting… looking down at the mess he'd made of himself. His boot, sock and corduroy breeches were filthy, almost to the fly.

He cursed, brushed himself, his hands now also becoming soiled… his anger towards the young couple intensifying. His face flushed and he felt a prickling in his scalp. To Rinch, *this* was all the fault of the youth and the girl: their *grotesque* intrusion. It was as if they had pushed him into the bog and had stood there, at the edge of it, laughing.

He bent and wiped his hands on some grass.

As he did so, he found himself remembering something that he thought he had forgotten – something that the marsh and the mocking couple seemed to conjure and spread – sardonically – before him.

Straightening himself, he saw – for the first time in a very long time – the slum of shanty houses, its mazy streets no more than sewers, the flint-faced woman with whom he'd bargained; her cruel, black eyes.

The whole, ghostly scene unfolded, as if from the lingering bacillus of an old fever.

Rinch told himself to get a grip, to think of something else… *anything* else. He didn't want to go back. Not to those ugly lanes. Besides… that was ancient history. Wasn't it? There was nothing to be gained from returning there.

He forced his mind to his journals: the jenny wren – pretty as you like – he'd seen in a thicket some days previously, the kingfishers whose lightning darts he'd struggled to follow. There'd been so many spottings and jottings: the curlew, reed warbler, dipper, moorhen, little *and* great crested grebe. And what of the swallow, snipe, the harrier... gliding imperiously, feasting on glistening frogs? Not to mention the redshank and red kite.

There it was again, thought Rinch. There it was! Red: the colour... the *real* colour... of the marsh. And not just birds, but insects, too: lovely ladybirds, glossy as you like; cardinal and willow leaf beetles, humping their scarlet shells; butterflies: red admirals roaming the ragged-robin; not to mention the papery wings of cinnabar moths, beating day and night in the ragwort of the sandier reaches. And, finally, damselflies – he'd seen plenty of those, hovering then dashing with astonishing speed... amazing displays of rainbow rocketry, over the water lilies. Yes, in many ways, the marsh was the perfect haunt for damsels. They came in all colours: white-legged, southern emerald, blue-tailed, brown hawker, red damsel – *red*... there it was again – shiny as a satin dress... as a very bonnie bodice.

Yet – never mind his attempt to distance himself – there *she* still stood: the hag from the slum, her awful hand drawing back the same rancid curtain. And, behind the disgusting drape, the young girl, the very young girl... like a chick, in her nest.

But there were reasons, justifications, Rinch told himself. For one thing, he'd been serving and sometimes men in his position, his circumstances... Besides, he'd made sacrifices, hadn't he? Gone without? Suffered? What about his malaria? Anyway, it had all been so different, back then, so very long ago.

He steadied himself and walked on through the marsh.

He reached a rowan and propped himself against its scaly trunk. The tree clung there, like some ancient ruin, its bark blotched with blue lichen.

Rinch rested, got his breath, lifted his binoculars, watched.

The young man and girl were still there, though their position had altered: the girl bending forwards now, the youth behind her, his hands at her shoulders.

*Souls of dogs!*
Rinch heard his mother's voice, scolding as he peered.
*The spectacle!*
There were orchids there, he thought, indignantly. *Dactylorhiza*. Right at the very spot. Yellow irises not far away. Marsh marigolds, too. Doubtless half of them now crushed. Under their hooves. Their cloven, bloody hooves.

Rinch lowered his glasses. He noted that the sun – it was now past noon – was lowering also, which meant that he would have to be careful not to catch it in his lenses.

The alteration in the light was beginning to shadow and blacken certain parts of the marsh: hollows, channels, pieces of the marsh where the vegetation – collapsing under the burden of its decay – gave way abruptly to deep, black water. Rinch had long sensed something conspiratorial in the way these areas of the marsh retreated into darkness. He reminded himself that he would have to tread carefully.

A covey of shelducks broke from a reedbed with a clatter.

He walked on.

As Rinch crossed a stream, a shoal of minnows scattered in the water.

His anger boiled inside him. Anywhere else was *their* affair. But not *here*. Not on the reserve. Not on *his* watch.

Once over the stream, he began to hear their exchanges – the grunts of the youth… the shrieks of the girl – across the wetland's emptiness.

Soon he was close enough to see them quite clearly, without need of the glasses.

Suddenly, the girl seemed to look his way. Rinch dropped to one knee, dipped his head behind a wall of reed-sweet.

He held his breath, listened… heard.

They were *still* at it.

Kneeling now, he parted the stems of the reed-sweet with one hand, raised his binoculars with the other. Through the lenses he saw the buttocks of the male, pumping as before. Shameless… bloody shameless, thought Rinch.

The buttocks paused for a moment, their owner stopping to sweep a mop of hair from his eyes.

As the young man did this, Rinch saw that the face beneath the drab locks belonged not, as he imagined it would, to some hostile youth of the kind he'd encountered in shopping precincts and bus stations come evening, or indeed to any youth at all, but was in fact... his.

Rinch rocked backwards, dropping the glasses, which landed painfully against his sternum.

A bumblebee buzzed idly around his head.

He batted at it with a hand, flailing and rocking, moving absurdly on his arse, in the manner of a child in a nursery who couldn't walk. Cursing his idiocy, he eventually rolled back to his knees, and again raised the glasses.

In their lenses now, he saw not the eyes of the young woman of before, but those of the younger girl, the *much* younger girl, looking up at him, in the way that she had in the hot, airless dark of that stinking cubicle. In that hideous hovel. In that squalid street.

He let go of the binoculars, snatched his hand from the grass, let the reed-sweet shut out what he had seen.

A fly whined in his face, crawled on his cheek.

He slapped himself, inspected his palm, saw the crushed black dot, and blood... in a little, sloe-coloured smear.

All of a sudden, the sun became ferociously bright. An impenetrable white light imposed itself across the marsh, disorientating Rinch utterly.

His mind struggled to make sense of what was happening. He wondered whether, in spite of his caution, he had somehow caught the sun's slipping orb in his glasses — momentary blindness, the result.

He could hear the shrill cries of birds and, among them, the noise of something scudding the surface of one of the channels in the marsh. A dizzying confusion of brilliant flashes and macabre shadows passed before his eyes.

And now he had the awful sense that his mouth was filling with marsh-water: small twigs and leaves trapping themselves between his teeth and under his tongue. And though he tried to reason that it was not happening, that it could *not* be happening, he felt as if his body were sinking, submerging, in a dark narrow of water over which the reedbeds were now creeping and closing, their hanging roots taking hold of him in the foul, black depths, coiling horrifically around his legs and his arms.

Rinch struggled, scrambled, spat, flailed on the floor.

He ran his hands over his face, felt a film of sweat on his palms.

As he drew his fingers from his eyes, the blinding whiteness passed.

He looked up and saw that a great cumulonimbus cloud now masked the sun, neutering its dazzle.

The marsh re-appeared as before, albeit darker than previously. A breeze bent the vegetation that lay further out, near the open water.

Rinch rose and now began marching – openly – through the marsh, in the direction of the young couple.

And it *was* the young couple who he'd find there, he told himself. No one else. Anything beyond them that he might or might not have seen had been mere tricks of the light, deceits of his mind. That was all. Nothing need distract him, he said. He would do his duty.

He strode flagrantly now, no longer trying to hide his presence.

'Brown hawker… marsh harrier,' he incanted as he advanced. 'Nothing to hide. Nothing to hide.'

The girl saw him first. She was on her back, blue denim jacket against the dun rock. It seemed to Rinch that she was staring at him – deliberately, defiantly – as he closed in.

Finally, when Rinch was no more than a few yards away, she turned her head, looked at the youth and said something in the language that – in echoey shards – Rinch had heard during his approach.

The youth turned and looked at Rinch while drawing himself out of her.

The young man staggered, pulled up his jeans. He threw back his hair with one hand, swore (or so it seemed to Rinch) and began talking loudly to the girl.

She pulled on her own trousers and reached for some shoes – a pair of platforms with cork heels – in a clump of marsh horsetail that Rinch noted with dismay had been damaged.

'Yes?' said the girl. 'What do you want?'

She forced the end of a floral-patterned blouse into the front of her white trousers. Rinch looked away, looked back when he thought she might have finished.

'I want you to… STOP!' he shouted, the indignation that had mounted in him as he'd crossed the marsh now erupting.

'What?' she asked.

'This!' said Rinch, reddening with rage, her question stoking his fury. 'Here!' he added, flinging out an arm.

The girl reached casually into a pocket of her jacket, drew out a packet of cigarettes. She took one then threw the pack to the youth. He removed and lit one then tossed her his lighter.

'Stop it!' said Rinch. 'Stop it! This is a reserve!'

The youth said something to the girl that Rinch didn't understand. The youth spat on the ground, drew his sleeve across his mouth.

'Excuse me?' the girl said to Rinch.

'A *nature* reserve!' said Rinch. 'A special place! For plants! Birds! Wildlife! You can't just… make merry *here*. There are rules! Regulations! Laws!!'

The girl spoke to the youth. He said something back. A phone rang in one of his pockets. He answered it and began talking to the caller.

'Stop it!' Rinch said again. 'This isn't the time or the place for… *phone calls.*'

He stepped towards the youth. The youth waved him away, went on talking on his phone, finished the call.

The youth spoke to the girl. She addressed Rinch. 'He wants to know, *if* it is a special place, why it smells so bad?'

A sulphurous stench blew over the marsh in the gathering breeze.

The youth waved a hand up and down under his nose. He smiled mockingly and drew on his cigarette.

'That's because it's a wetland,' said Rinch. 'A wet *land*. Plants die here... there is animal matter here... *waste*... *bacteria*. Things rot. It all creates a... smell.'

The girl and the youth stood looking at Rinch.

Try as he did to resist her, the reek of the marsh now revived the woman... the crone. It was as if she were there... on the marsh, relishing the mire, stirring its stinking stew. And with the woman, of course, came the curtain... and the girl.

Oily rivulets of sweat ran down Rinch's back. They welled above his buttocks at the tight dam forged by the belt on his breeches. And, again, he sensed himself not *on* the marsh, but *of* it... as if he were part of its rotting fibre, its awful, ink-like liquids.

For a moment, he saw the crone quite clearly: brown hawker – her claw hand out for more money, never mind the notes he'd placed in it. She snapped words he didn't know, though her meaning was clear.

And this time it was no use him seeking sanctuary in his journals and his spottings. For when he turned his mind to their pages, she was there also: sketched and annotated in the margins of leaves, as if penned by some taunting interloper, some jealous rival from the hide.

Elsewhere, on other pages, the words RED DAMSEL... RED DAMSEL screamed, defacing his neat entries about warblers and widgeons, shovelers and dippers, buzzards and swans... the letters hideously scrawled in scarlet crayon.

The young couple conversed for a moment. The sound of their words – though unintelligible to Rinch – brought him to his senses.

He shut his mind to what he'd seen in his journals, re-found his focus.

'You *must* stop smoking!' he said loudly. 'I mean it,' he added. 'Now!'

The girl looked at him, drew heavily on her cigarette, then extinguished it on the stone. Rinch winced. The youth did the same. They put the unsmoked remnants back in her pack.

'Cigarettes... UK... expensive,' said the youth, grinning and looking at Rinch.

'Where are you from?' the girl asked.

Her question wrong-footed Rinch (who thought that this was something he should have been asking them).

'I'm sorry?' he said.

'Where have you come from?' she said.

He then realised her meaning, turned and pointed to the hide. The boards and roof of its low rectangle were faintly discernible, across the marsh.

'There,' he said.

The girl gave him a puzzled look.

He added: 'I watch birds.'

'Ah,' said the girl.

She again translated to the youth, who leaned forward and felt Rinch's binoculars, lifting them slightly, in a way that Rinch didn't like. The youth said something to the girl.

'Will you show us?' she asked.

'Show you?' said Rinch, wiping at the sweat on the back of his neck.

'Your place,' the girl said.

'It's for members only,' said Rinch.

'We would like to see it,' said the girl.

Something about the scale and weight of the marsh – so matted... fetid – seemed now to oppress him. He felt exposed, vulnerable in its openness.

Yes, the hide... the hide, he thought. It would be good to get back there: to its coolness, its shade.

'Well... all right,' he said, uncertainly. 'If you're interested. I don't suppose a quick look will do any harm.'

The girl said something to the youth, who nodded and smiled. Rinch turned and they began to follow him across the marsh.

The girl caught up with Rinch and kept in step with him.

Her shoes were open-toed and Rinch watched as her pink-varnished nails sank and rose in the sodden ground.

'Members only?' she asked as they walked.

'Yes. You have to belong. It's private. People can't just barge in. I'm on the committee,' Rinch told her. 'Practically in charge.'

A small, black-capped bird flitted in a tree that hunched itself ahead of them.

'Now there's a queer visitor,' said Rinch, stopping. 'Marsh tit. Shouldn't be here at all. Woodland bird, in spite of its name. Cheeky thing.'

They carried on towards the hut, the bird's squeak and chirrup diminishing behind them.

At the stream, Rinch took the girl's hand and helped her over. She was bigger than him, in her shoes at least. As she crossed, she brushed against him.

For a second, Rinch felt the plumpness of a breast beneath her jacket. The girl seemed to know this but said nothing. Rinch, however, felt the need to say something and described how, quite recently, he'd seen a spoonbill... wading... on the edge of the marsh. The bird was really very rare, he said.

From behind them, the youth said something to the girl, which she translated to Rinch.

'In our country there are people who go crazy to see a small bird. They will drive many kilometres. They just have to have that bird.'

'Oh, we have that too,' said Rinch. '"Twitchers" we call them. But I'm not a twitcher. I'm a watcher. There's a difference. Watching is more like a relationship. You become familiar... friendly, with the birds. Twitching? Well, that's more of a one-off. Hurrying somewhere to catch sight of a bird, usually with a flock of others: other twitchers, not birds, I mean. There's some satisfaction to be had in it, I grant. Thrill of the chase and then the spotting: a few minutes... maybe longer, if you're lucky. And then it's all over. But if it's real appreciation you're after... habits, calls, feeding, mating... then "watching" – that's the thing. I come here to the marsh, to the hide, to watch.'

'Hide?' said the girl. By now they were nearly there. 'Hide and seek – that is a game, yes?' She indicated Rinch's binoculars and continued: 'You seek with these?'

'Well, yes, that's the gist, I suppose,' said Rinch.

They were at the door of the hut now. Rinch showed them in.

The dry, timbery, tarry smells of the hide replaced the gaseous odours of the marsh. Relieved to have returned, Rinch thought how – after the menace of the marsh – the place was like a small fort. A *lonely* outpost, it was true – but rigid, secure: a haven.

He let out a sigh of satisfaction.

The young couple wandered around, glancing at the faded wallcharts, peering through the hatches, onto the wetland.

Rinch gave the girl his binoculars. He looped the strap over her so they hung at her neck.

She trained the glasses on the reserve and looked through them for a few moments, then gave them to the youth (who did the same). They spoke to one another, briefly.

The girl looked around the hut. She took in Rinch's knapsack, the Thermos flask beside it, his Tupperware, his collapsible canvas chair.

'It is cosy here,' she said.

'Yes, I suppose it is,' said Rinch. 'I like it.'

'You're alone?' she asked.

'Mostly, on weekdays – that's why I come.'

'It's nice to be alone, sometimes,' said the girl.

Rinch's earlier behaviour began to embarrass him – the manner of his interruption, his aggression, out on the marsh. 'May I offer you something?' he asked.

The girl looked at his knapsack; saw a bottle of water, protruding.

'Some water would be nice,' she said.

Rinch handed her the bottle. He undid the strap of a side pocket. 'I've a beaker... somewhere.'

The girl unscrewed the top of the bottle, drank from it and handed it to the youth, who swigged from it similarly.

The youth then went outside, closing the door.

Suddenly, Rinch was nervous. He was worried that someone might come, one of the members, and see the youth out there, pissing, smoking, whatever it was that he might be up to, and come in and find him – a committee man – with the girl.

'Where's he going?' Rinch asked her.

'Only outside. For some air. It is – what is the word? – *stuffy*... in here.'

'I suppose it is, a little,' said Rinch. 'He mustn't smoke though,' he added quickly.

'Don't worry,' she said. 'He won't be doing that.'

With a swiftness that surprised him, the girl began to unbutton Rinch's shirt. Next she undid the belt of his breeches and pulled them down.

'I think you've done this before? Yes?' she said.

Rinch sensed himself trembling. 'I don't—'

'In a place like this?' she continued. 'A hiding place?'

Before he knew it, he was on his back on the hide's wooden boards, his underpants near his knees – the girl on top of him, straddling his stomach in her white trousers, rocking, clamping him, pinning him to the dusty floor of the hide.

She reached and took his binoculars from where the youth had left them, on a shelf below one of the hatches, and looped the leather strap over her head.

Holding down Rinch's arms, she swung herself so that, inside her curtain of hair, the ends of the binoculars struck him again and again, beating his head and his face.

Through one of the open hatches, Rinch glimpsed the blurring shape of the youth, who was outside, looking in. He was laughing and holding up what might have been his phone, sunlight glancing from its screen.

'Seek and hide,' the youth cackled as the girl swung herself over Rinch.

Steadily, Rinch's features melted to a morass of bruises, mucus and tears.

'Stop it!' he begged. 'Please stop it. Someone could be coming.'

He sensed the eyes of the creatures on the posters on the walls – the fox by a purple foxglove, the peregrine falcon on its ledge, the otter emerging from a holt, the badger sniffing the air, the small water shrew, the bats… No longer drab photographs, but alive… all of them: vigilant, vivid and staring at *him*.

It seemed to Rinch as if everything in the hide and on the marsh had been reversed – as if all of its creatures knew *him*, had been keeping notes on *him*, his rituals, his feeding, his mating… that the marsh, for all of the years that he had been going there, had been watching *him*, closing in on *him*.

For a moment, the girl raised herself slightly and swept back her hair. As she did so, the binoculars at her neck swung free above Rinch. He seemed to see himself in their swaying lenses – except that, now, on his face, he wore a horrible mask… of awful bogs, oily narrows, rotting beds and hunchback trees.

*He* was the marsh. Its whole, stinking foulness.

It covered him… from crown to chin.

The two, separate, swaying glasses now melded in his vision to a single mirror.

Rinch seemed to see his grotesque self in the giant eye of a great bird.

He remembered the mighty marsh harrier and its feast of frogs – how he'd sat ringside those days earlier, delighting in the raptor's every rip and swallow.

'Someone…' Rinch began again. 'Someone…'

'No one is coming!' said the girl. 'No one is coming!'

'Brown hawker? Red damsel?' Rinch whimpered now, thinking he could see the crone and the young girl, walking steadily… advancing through the marsh, closing in on his little wooden fort.

With them crawled all of the marsh's worms and its

leeches and its snakes and – up above them – the great raptor, red in tooth and claw, its heavy wings beating… beating.

'Marsh… harrier?' Rinch added, with a gasp, to the hawker and the damsel.

'Oh, they are coming!' said the girl. 'They are coming!'

# Dog Years

IN the park he lies at her feet. Watery eyes watching.

A bench by the railings is their usual spot, though sometimes – when it's hot – she stands in the shade of a copper beech.

Under it they have the faint look of mistress and hound as sometimes found on a tomb in a church.

She does the crossword: her newspaper (halved or quartered) in one hand, a Biro in the other.

He is white-muzzled, yawning, belly sprawling, nails on the long side and in need of some clipping.

She begins with the *downs*, fancying these 'encourage' him.

Now and again he lifts his head and looks up at her.

Eventually, he rocks himself to action, like a sea lion suddenly hungry on some foam-flecked American shore.

He lumbers to the centre of the park – his clear, green stage on which to perform – traces a circle, squats... and begins.

When he has finished and has gone for his wander, she walks over in brown shoes that are laced and flat.

She cleans up what has been left.

For this, she employs those parts of the paper that are useless to her: reviews of London plays, restaurants… articles on festivals in Andalucía.

Today, binning the bundle, she notices a survey: ski boots, rated out of ten.

Once, an officious man, walking with poles, stopped and told her off… before propelling himself on.

The mothers and others who use the park are, for the most part, tolerant: they remember the days when she used to bring her dog.

# Smoke House

HENRY Hoffman was walking on Main Street and his nose was on fire. This fact apart, he was proceeding quite normally. He smiled genially and nodded as he passed by Michael Maguire.

A straight-backed, silver-haired sixty-something, well-known as an attorney and council member in the small High Plains town of Fort Tinder, Hoffman appeared entirely unaware of his small but steady blaze. The seat of the flames, so it seemed, was the tip of his nose, or, possibly, the small briars of hair that – unless Maguire was mistaken – crackled audibly within it, the fire rising up the ridge of the rest of it as if through an incline of firs.

No other soul on the street or in any of the stores that fronted it seemed to notice that Mr Hoffman was aflame, or permitted this apparently clear fact to cause them to exhibit the slightest perturbation.

That Hoffman was transporting his own personal beacon, not unlike the orange flare of an oil stack, seemed evident and remarkable only to Maguire.

Slinging in his truck the items he supposed he might need
for the plumbing job to which he was headed at Mrs Minty
McTwain's, Maguire wondered about the hooch he'd drunk
the previous night.

The bartender had plucked it from under the counter,
eyes darting, with a whispered 'Get some of *this*' through his
bushy ginger beard.

As a relative newcomer in town, Maguire had felt obliged.
The moonshine's mule-kick had fair thrown him from his
stool. The barkeep offered a case, shorn of some bucks.
Maguire for his part had pleaded need of the men's room.

Aided by the gloom of the joint, he exited – fast as his
faltering legs could carry him.

On the sidewalk outside, he shook himself, like a dog
from a dream on a porch-front. He then headed back to the
house where he was lodging, throat burning like nothing he
could remember.

Heck, Maguire thought to himself, as he now climbed
into his truck, it sure had been some firewater.

'It's Mrs Root who *you* need,' said Minty McTwain, as Maguire
straightened with a wince from under the sink in her kitchen.

He'd been stuck in a lean-cum-crouch, fixing the sump:
stripping it out, unclogging the pipework of grinds and gunk,
screwing it all back for her. 'My! Just *look* at all that dirt!' Minty
McTwain had repeatedly exclaimed, as Maguire had gone
about his mining and dumping.

It was a small enough job, but – in an echo of the
moonshine the night before – not without its pain: a stab
somewhere in his lower spine that reminded Maguire (as if he
needed it) that he wasn't getting any younger.

'We call her place the Smoke House,' Minty McTwain
continued. 'It's in the woods further up the valley. Right near
the top. Where the hills horseshoe and it's nothing but trees
and brush. Hidden. Kinda like a lady's... Well, you know.
You won't see her actual place for all of the pines. But it's
there... smokin'. Often times you won't even make out the

smoke on account of the mist. But she's the one for your pain. She'll get to the… *bottom* of it, I promise you that.'

Maguire reddened a little, aware that, bent beneath the sink, under Minty McTwain's watchful supervision, he'd been exhibiting a fair acreage of cleavage between his shirt and his jeans.

'You won't get your truck up there,' Minty McTwain went on. 'Terrain's no good for that. There's a trail though and, if you stick to it, it'll take you right to her door. We all use her. Dexter, my husband, well, I just couldn't sleep for his snoring. But she did her thing on him and I've had peace at night ever since.'

'Her *thing*?' Maguire asked.

'With her hands,' said Minty McTwain. 'Laying them on, so to speak. She takes a hold of whatever it is that's at fault, or ailin', and then she makes a kind of mould with her ingredients. Like a potter, I guess. Then she puts it in… well, an oven, or burner, you'd probably call it. That's where the smoke comes from, through a stack. Like they do with that what's-it-called… some places… you know, with wood?'

'Charcoal?' offered Maguire.

'Yes, that's it,' said Minty McTwain. 'And she keeps that thing of yours in her oven for a while and smokes it right there, till all of the badness bleeds out. It's not something folks tend to talk about… a trip to Mrs Root's. But we've all used her at one time, like I said. Ears, eyes, teeth… tongues,' said Minty McTwain, drawing-out this last item on her list while fixing Maguire's eye. 'Ain't something we generally share with a stranger. But I figure it'd be a shame to see a man like you fall outta shape. Why, in your line, I expect you need that back of yours for all kinda things.'

Maguire began to tidy up and put his tools in his bag. He felt a fresh twinge in his back, but tried not to show it. A smile on Minty McTwain's not insubstantially made-up face signalled she had sensed it, all the same.

'I'm in need of some attention to something upstairs,' she continued casually. 'If you have the time.'

'I'm sorry, but I'm required elsewhere,' said Maguire. 'Other side of town.'

'In demand,' said Minty McTwain, her pink-painted nails planting more dollars than Maguire had asked for in the breast pocket of his shirt. 'Well, we all need a little plumbing now and again, don't we?'

Never mind that he was a blow-in of the drifter kind, Maguire found plenty of work that fall. In fact, as the only proper plumber in town since the death of the old-timer who'd previously taken care of things, he came to be regarded as something of a life-saver as far as the routine round of blockages, leaks and breakdowns in its homes and commercial premises was concerned.

After that business about Henry Hoffman's nose, he'd made a point of staying clear of any liquor whose source might have been some still in the backwoods.

Even so, Maguire continued to catch sight of bizarre scenes involving certain of the locals. Passing the front of Fort Tinder's principal funeral parlour one day, Maguire felt sure the beard of Carson Travers, the undertaker, was ablaze – albeit that this was something of which Travers, soberly studying some papers on his counter, seemed completely unaware. Once, as Maguire stood in line to be served at the grocery store, smoke seemed to curl from the fingers of Merle McAdam, the owner, as she cut at a cheese for a customer – an occurrence that caused neither the customer nor Mrs McAdam to bat an eye. Similarly, the orange and red flames that ate their way through Grismond Guthrie's eyebrows as if they were brushwood – in his booth at the post office – caused elderly Mr Guthrie not the slightest consternation. In fact, he raised his flaming arches (with some bemusement) and asked Maguire, who had obviously betrayed alarm, if he was feeling quite all right.

The outbreaks were by no means confined to the town's adults. A boy Maguire saw on a swing as he passed the park one day was burning, so it seemed, by the seat of his short pants: a trail of flame and smoke following him through the air. Meanwhile, a dog on a woman's leash bore a tail that sparked like a fuse on a firecracker. And the tabby cat that sat in the window of Walt Nash's hardware store sported whiskers that had little pears of bright light at the end of each stalk, like candles on a Christmas tree. As with everyone else in the town, the boy and the pets seemed entirely unconscious of these matters.

One burning prompted Maguire – out of what he felt what his Christian duty – to intervene. Passing by one of the town's several churches one morning, he saw that the leg of its minister, Pastor Smith, was aflame – fire entwining the pastor's pants, as if dancing on the trunk of a tree. Maguire jumped from his truck and ran towards the churchman as the pastor closed a white wicket gate.

'Yes?' said Pastor Smith, startled by Maguire's sudden appearance.

'Sir! I mean *Reverend*... I mean... I... I,' said Maguire, as Pastor Smith stood and smiled in a bemused manner – the flames at his left leg now licking his waist in a way that caused Maguire to step back.

'Yes?' repeated Pastor Smith, '... Mr?'

'Maguire,' said Maguire, adding quickly, 'You're on fire, sir... your leg.'

Pastor Smith, as if to humour him, looked down and appeared to see no more than the leg of his pants and his shoe, as everything *should* have been, on the sidewalk.

'Can't you see that?' asked Maguire.

Pastor Smith responded with a look that seemed to say he was non-plussed, if not bewildered, by the claims of this agitated man who was assailing him. And yet there was something in his eyes and in his lips that betrayed discomfort – things that suggested to Maguire that the pastor was *not* non-plussed and actually *knew* of his burning (even if, physically, it was not yet hurting him). For a second, doubt seemed to play upon the pastor's face, in the way that happens when men who've sought to pick a fight, in a bar or on the street, suddenly realise they're outgunned.

It was, Maguire knew, the flicker of fear.

Pastor Smith's countenance tightened. His eyes fixed Maguire's. 'I think I'd know if such a thing was happening to me, sir. I think I'd be *aware* of something like that.'

'But—'

'Good day to you, Mr Maguire,' said Pastor Smith, who was walking away now, his leg still very much on fire.

Even as a breeze fanned the flames that beset him, causing them to rise with an audible roar... so that he resembled some kind of burning bush, the churchman maintained his denial.

'If your eye causes you to stumble, pluck it out and throw it from you. It is better for you to enter life with one eye, than to have two eyes and be cast into the fiery hell...

'Book of Matthew, Mr Maguire. Chapter eighteen, verse nine, I think you'll find.

'I hope to see you in church sometime.'

As autumn gave way to winter, Maguire found himself settling in the town in a way that was unusual for him. His mind took a turn whereby it wanted the fires he'd seen on its citizens *not* to be there. And so he became dismissive of them and was no longer as startled as he had been when, for example, he now saw a senior whose scalp was aflame on a porch-front rocker of an evening, or was passed by a skateboarding teen with an arm like a lit flambeau. Nor even did he stare on catching sight of a young girl running to her mother in a back lane, her twin plaits of hair sparking brightly... the mother stroking her child with a blazing hand of her own.

Something that aided Maguire's ability to normalise these fires was the fact that, as well as seeming to be without physical pain, the burnings were oddly sporadic: the afflicted citizens and pets seeming to somehow have ways of suppressing them, perhaps hurrying home to use a yard hose, or sousing themselves in the shower or bath (though Maguire had seen no direct evidence of this).

They were strange, contained affairs – like fires in trash

cans, stoves or barbeques, that, until something caused them to reignite, seemed by and large to burn themselves out. Except, of course, that – here in Fort Tinder – the receptacles were humans.

Another thing – a personal thing – played heavily on Maguire's mind at this time, further serving to sideline the subject of the fires. And this was his lack of 'stirring' where there ought – at least now and again – to have been a stirring. In short, he had found himself in that state of manhood where precious little seemed to be happening – let alone firing – under his hood.

Although it may have made no sense to any other, Maguire connected his lack of spark with the fires that seemed to be burning in almost all humanity around him. At a deeper level, he connected it also with his rootlessness: the matter of being the wild rover (after a fashion), that had been his since his walkout from a tech firm in Silicon Valley some twenty years previously.

It seemed to Maguire that men like Henry Hoffman and Grismond Guthrie – small-town and small-time, as they undoubtedly were – had sown their seed, planted themselves, *belonged* – in their case, to Fort Tinder – in a way that had resonance and was meaningful.

Remembering the advice of Minty McTwain, he resolved to pay a visit to the woman she had spoken of.

He needed the wisdom of Mrs Root.

It was a mid-October afternoon when he found the trail. Something Maguire noticed as he walked was that, while the trees near the town in the lower valley had already shed most of their leaves (in the way that was to be expected of the time of year), the upper valley – which was the land of Mrs Root – was verdant and mantled.

Birdsong played in the trees and from time to time Maguire heard the fall of a stream or caught sight of a skittering deer, as he pursued the steepening way into the dense woods of the high valley.

Over time, the moon started its climb and, through the canopy of the trees, stars began to show, the sky losing its pronounced blueness to a paleness, and with it the cool of evening.

The sudden and harsh sound of a bird shooting off through the trees unnerved Maguire.

With no sign of any shack, he wondered if he had lost his way and ought to double back. He stopped and leant on a trunk.

Scanning the woods around him, his eyes fell upon a small square of yellow light through the dark limbs of the trees.

Maguire calculated this could be only one thing: the window of Mrs Root.

It was as if she knew he was out there and had lit her lantern for him.

Despite the dimness, Maguire could tell that the panels of the porch were green and soft, and he wondered if they would take his weight. He stepped gingerly to the shack's front door and saw that it stood ajar.

'Well come on in, if you're comin'!' a woman – her voice feisty and crisp – called from within.

'Coulda done with you last week,' Mrs Root continued, not lifting her eyes from the needle and thread with which, by the light of an oil lamp, she was working at some fabric. 'Trouble with my drains. Had a flood here like the Mississippi. Right through the house. Not that anyone would've given a damnation. Cause of it all some racoon, would you believe. Poor dumb critter. Drowned his-self in one of my gullies. Blocked everythin' real good. I fished him out and buried him. No one else to take care of it. That's what you get, livin' up here. Place like this. Not that I'm complainin'.'

Maguire looked around the room.

Fire was burning in a range of the kind not widely seen beyond museums and movies. Its light flickered on the glazing of samplers and old photographs of people –

mountain people – hung on the walls. Maguire took them for ancestors of Mrs Root. For a moment, he wondered if there was – or had ever been – a Mr Root: a casualty of the Civil War, perhaps… or even Independence.

'Now, Mister Plumber Man, what is it you're wanting from me?'

Mrs Root looked up at him.

She was a small, slight woman of senior years who had the dark, protuberant eyes of a squirrel (the pupil of her left somewhat skewed, as if keeping watch on something else, such as a clock – though Maguire was unaware of one – or a simmering pot on her stove). She wore a plain knitted woollen, unbuttoned over the top of what was either an apron or housecoat. Fine, silver hair scraped back in a bun contributed to Maguire's impression of one of the darting, bushy-tailed creatures that had crossed and re-crossed his path to her door. Her face was lined… worn, yet possessed, so it seemed to him, of a fierce intelligence, a *resistance*, more to the point, that he judged this old lady must have needed to survive, as she evidently had and did, in so remote a spot.

'Tongue in your head, dontcha?' she said abruptly, calling Maguire to order.

'Y-yes, ma'am,' Maguire stammered, thrown by her directness. He continued: 'I've been having a problem with my… back.'

'Back?!' she snorted. 'Hah! Don't give me any of *that*! No one ever came this far up the mountain with – what did you call it? – "trouble" with their back. Besides, if it *was* givin' you "trouble" you'd never have made it up here in the first place now, would you?'

Maguire gave an awkward look.

'Night's fallin', Mr Maguire. Winter's comin'… and neither you nor I is gettin' any younger. So, tell me, what's *really* troubled you to come up my mountain.'

'I… um…'

He glanced downward.

'Oh mercy. Do let's get on with it,' sighed Mrs Root,

putting aside her needlework and rising from her chair. 'Drop your pants!'

Startled by her directness, Maguire glanced at the brass buckle of his belt.

He didn't really know what he'd been expecting when setting out in search of Mrs Root. But he hadn't expected a parlour game quite like this.

Mrs Root continued: 'I don't know what you think you've got down there, mister. But it won't be anythin' these eyes haven't seen before, I can tell you that. Sure if I haven't seen half the men of that town up here at some point or other. Only reason most of 'em ever come up here is a problem with their peckers. So let's waste no more time and get on with it, while we can. Drop 'em, Mr Maguire. Or skedaddle back to town and leave me be.'

To Maguire's relief, Mrs Root turned away. He took this as a sign that, after her initial cussedness, the consultation that would follow would take place with some... sensitivity.

When Mrs Root turned back, he saw that she had pulled on gloves that rose up her forearms and looked as if they'd been stitched from some kind of animal skin. She lifted her oil lamp and advanced.

'Seen bigger,' said Mrs Root, bending. 'Smaller too, to be fair,' she added, moving the lamp across Maguire with a nearness that caused him to feel its glow. 'What's wrong with it?'

'It's... reluctant,' said Maguire, wondering how he'd come by the word.

'*Reluctant?*' replied Mrs Root.

'Uncooperative,' said Maguire – a word that also caused him to wonder.

Beyond the shack, a bird squawked – as if with derision – in the forest's sweet and endless dark.

'I think,' said Mrs Root, 'what you're *tryin'* to say is that it won't stand-to when you want it. And that, instead, it's all "at ease, soldier". Is *that* it?'

'Well, yes ma'am,' said Maguire. 'That's about the long and short.'

'Indeed,' said Mrs Root, straightening.

'Well, I can put your mind at rest on one thing,' she continued. 'That's nothin' I haven't seen before, or given a cure for. I think I oughtta be able to do somethin'.'

Imagining Mrs Root's 'something' to be a herbal remedy of a kind that she might grind in a bowl, or even a spell she might utter under a windchime in the woods, Maguire began to draw up his jeans.

'Hold on there, mister!' she interrupted, sharply. 'You can leave those buttons be! I ain't even *started* yet!'

And then Maguire remembered what Minty McTwain had said… about the laying-on of hands.

Mrs Root disappeared in the gloom behind a drape over a doorway. She re-appeared with a bucket of matter that was largely beyond discernment to Maguire, save that it looked dark and wet.

'Now you just stand there for a moment while I baste this thing as if it were Thanksgiving,' said Mrs Root, plunging her gloved hands into the tin pail.

'What *is* that?' asked Maguire, as she drew her arms from the pail, to the sound of a disconcerting *suck*.

'*This* is the body and spirit of the mountain,' said Mrs Root, with sudden reverence. 'The *real* land, the *sacred* land… away from your towns and your televisions, telegrams and whatever goddam else you have down there these days.'

'It looks like a lot of mud… and leaves,' said Maguire.

'That's about the gizzards of it,' replied Mrs Root, briskly. She continued: 'When I'm done I want you to get over and stand by the fire, so the mould can harden and give me somethin' to work with. When it has some rigidity – the mould, I mean – I'll take it off (that part of it may hurt a little, I warn you) and you can leave it with me. After that I'll do my thing and, with God's blessin', get rid of what's ailin' it. Now… try to keep still.'

Some while later, after Maguire had been standing by the fire of the range for what seemed an hour or more, Mrs Root uncorked him from the hardened mulch of his cocoon, chipping it loose with a hammer and chisel as Maguire averted his gaze.

With a wince, he felt the mould clunk free.

Mrs Root placed it on a plate in the glow of her oil lamp, where it sat, unceremoniously, like a large slug.

'What do you do with it now, exactly?' asked Maguire.

'Well,' said Mrs Root, 'first of all I work at whatever it is with my hands. Nowadays these old turkey claws look a little leathery, I'll grant. But my gran'ma told me my hands were special – that I had what she called "the gift". Anyway, you won't feel nothin' on your own person when I concern myself with that.'

Relieved to hear this, Maguire now felt himself breathe, having seemingly stopped doing so – beyond a few snatched gasps – at the earlier sight of Mrs Root's raised hammer.

'It's the *next* part where you may feel some pain,' continued Mrs Root.

'What's… "the next part"?' Maguire – his anxiety fast returning – enquired.

'That's when I put a hook in it,' responded Mrs Root.

'Hook?' said Maguire.

'To hang it,' she went on, '… for the smokin'. From time to time, dependin' on the case, the hookin' may cause some pain and even a few drops of blood. But it generally passes, in a day or two.'

'What then?' asked Maguire.

'I smoke it,' said Mrs Root. 'For as long as the job may take. I generally get a sense of when it's done. Couple of days is the average, but it can take longer sometimes… if the problem's lyin' deep and stubborn to get out. You wanna look?' she asked. 'I've got it all out back. The whole anatomy of that itty-bitty town… hung up. Ears, arms, fingers. The moulds, I mean. Not the actual flesh 'n' blood, which of course is decayin' on the owners anyway. Butt cheeks…' said Mrs Root, continuing – seemingly at random – with her list. 'All hangin' quiet 'n' still. Just like sides of deer, skinned rabbits, you name it. Plucked carcasses of turkey cocks. Proper butcher's pantry back there. I'll show you if you're interested. It might sting your eyes, though – the smoke, I mean. I'll warn you of that. But you can see for yourself... if you think I'm makin' any of this up.'

Maguire declined, reasoning that, for his peace of mind, the less he knew about the inner workings of Mrs Root's smoke house the better.

'No thank you, ma'am,' he said. 'That'll be fine.'

'That's what they all say. Pretty much,' Mrs Root replied.

Without warning, she now threw over him a jug of cold water, causing further shrinkage of the object whose animation – or lack of – had been the purpose of his mission.

'Here!' Mrs Root said, flinging him a towel rough as redwood bark. 'Dry yourself!'

Pulling up and buttoning his jeans at last, Maguire asked what he owed.

'Only my independence,' Mrs Root said sternly, staring into his eyes. 'Up here... in my wilderness. That's what I want. That's what I cherish. I have no use for your dollar bills.'

Maguire put his wallet back in his jacket.

He havered for a moment, for there was that *other* thing that he wanted to raise and have Mrs Root put right (without making a bigger jackass of himself than he suspected he already had).

She cut in: 'Well, what is it? There's somethin' else troublin' you, I can tell. I don't normally do two-for-one, but who knows when you'll get the chance to come up here again. So, out with it. Spit.'

'Mrs Root, would you think I was crazy if I told you I keep seeing people who are on fire?' asked Maguire. 'People who don't seem to know that they're burning. And in front of other folks who also seem unaware of the fact.'

She stilled for a moment, her cussedness retreating, her squirrel eyes taking on a thoughtful, pensive look.

'So, the smoulderin's begun down there,' she said, finally.

'Smouldering?' asked Maguire.

She put her hand on the back of a chair tucked under her table… eyed Maguire. 'I told 'em just as I told you Mr Maguire: all I've ever wanted was to be left alone, up here, in these hills. And they've always given me their word, each and every one. "Yes ma'am, Mrs Root" they've stood here under my own roof and said. "You have my pledge on that." But the truth is those sons of bitches want me out. Off of this mountain and someplace else. All the while they've been comin' up here they've been schemin', like snakes, the lot of 'em. But Ol' Ma Root, as they call me, why – livin' up here with Nature, as I do – I had wind of it, see. I smelt their deceit sourin' the breeze, saw it comin' in the curl of the leaves on the trees, heard it – and I scarce give a damn whether anyone believes me or not – in the hootin' of the owls. And now the tables are turnin', Mr Maguire. Believe you me!'

'How do you mean, "scheming"?' asked Maguire.

'Big hydra-lectric dam. That's what I mean,' said Mrs Root. 'Floodin' this here valley, my valley, with water. Drownin' my very house.'

The truth was that Maguire had heard of the plan, but it was not something with which he had sought to over concern himself, figuring that by the time they started building he'd have long drifted on, anyhow.

He judged it best to withhold this from Mrs Root.

'I can see why that would upset you,' said Maguire. 'But the burning?'

'No fire without smoke, is there Mr Maguire?' responded Mrs Root. 'Tell me,' she continued, 'what do you think beats a lake of water, Mr Maguire, you being a plumber 'n' all?'

'I'm not sure I—'

'I'll tell you,' Mrs Root cut in on him. 'A lake of fire. *That's* what. They all think that dam's gonna make 'em rich: money, jobs, contracts. But I'll see them burn in Hell, before they shift me.' Her small frame shook with anger. 'They think it'll be easy: uprootin' Ol' Ma Root. But they're forgettin': I have their secrets. I have their dirt. All smoked outta them and kept

118

right here. And I can rain their cheatin' 'n' fornicatin' down on 'em – fire 'n' brimstone, Mr Maguire, like it says in the Good Book – from up here, in *my* valley, any time I like.'

As she talked, Maguire saw that Mrs Root's eyes were no longer merely dark but had a certain determined sheen, like the sweated side of a horse hard-ridden; also that her hands, clasping the top of her chair, had on their backs veins that surged like mountain rivers – powerful and green. Her knuckles, meanwhile, flared white and prominent, like a chain of snow-capped peaks.

'That Hoffman fella for one,' said Mrs Root. 'Calls his-self an attorney. Why he's nothin' more than a Peeping Tom. I know all about his nosy nose, Mr Maguire. I'm the one who put paid to his perversion, smoked it out of him with my own hands. His dirt's right here in my smoke house. I can show you, if you don't believe me. Oh, I can singe that big beak of his whenever I want. Merle McAdam, cheatin' with her cheese-cutter. She's another. Woman can't help herself. Likewise, Grismond Guthrie, son of a bitch: readin' people's mail at the post office… riflin' it for whatever he could get. Ten dollars that devil took from a card for the Anderson boy who died of leukaemia last fall, sent with a letter from his aunt in Vermont.'

Mrs Root listed all of the people in the town who Maguire had seen burning one way or another, and then some. 'Carson Travers? That bald eagle with the beard? Sheriff Hooper… Pastor Smith… Miss O'Dowd at the elementary school. They've got it comin',' said Mrs Root. 'And as for that frigid witch Lettie Larson at the library. Well, let me tell you, I've so much of her dirt jarred-up out back it practically fills a shelf!'

Mrs Root paused, breathed deeply.

'You're new in the town, aintcha?' she began again.

Maguire nodded.

'Which explains how you can see the smoke they're ignorant of. Well, if you'll take my advice, you'll move on, Mr Maguire – and be quick about it.'

She stared at him, coldly; not so much a squirrel now as a hawk, eyeing its prey, atop a telegraph post or pine tree.

'Stick around Mr Maguire and you're liable to get singed.' Maguire said he'd bear her advice in mind.

'You do that,' replied Mrs Root, adding solemnly: 'It may all seem small – even innocent – now. But *this* is just the smoulderin'. You wait till it's taken root.'

Glancing again, with some embarrassment, at the mould on the plate, he asked (his voice having an audible note of disbelief) how long it would be till he was cured.

'That depends on how long it takes me to smoke out the badness. You'll know the answer to that better than me, Mr Maguire. Especially if you've been a sinner.'

They eyed each other for a moment, saying nothing.

Outside, on Mrs Root's front porch, Maguire reflected on the weirdness of what had passed and, in particular, her warning of what was to come.

Regardless of what his own eyes seemed to have seen in the town, Mrs Root's injunction about a lake of fire seemed to Maguire a step too far for the imagination: the crowning craziness of an evening few would believe if he ever recounted it.

At the same time, though, he noted how the hoots of the owls in the woods seemed to chide him for his scepticism; issuing their calls as if to underline the seriousness of what Mrs Root had said – that all of her words were *t-rooo… t-rooo.* That everything she had said would, eventually, come *t-roo.*

He buttoned his coat and pulled on a hat, then followed the trail back to the town in the moonlight.

In the days that followed, Maguire thought about the smoke that might be curling from Mrs Root's stack, and waited for a sign.

One night, after the best of a day up to his waist in the foul water of a blocked drain on a farm on the edge of town, Maguire went down with a fever. In his bed, he dreamt he was in Mrs Root's smoke house having been chased there through the upper valley by an awful glowing airborne *thing…*

a kind of outsize incandescent caterpillar that hurtled through the trees with squirrel-like speed. The voice of Minty McTwain reverberated with the leaps of the blazing bug – which contracted then elongated as it flew. 'Tongues!' Minty McTwain's cry echoed through the woods. 'Tongues!'

Next, Maguire was in Mrs Root's inner sanctum, where all of the moulds taken by her from the townspeople were hanging and swinging against him. The awful specimens resembled remnants of marionettes that might have been mutilated by some mad puppeteer. Hands and feet seemed to twitch and eyes to wink at Maguire. The larger, fatter items, meanwhile, had the look of heavy hams and round cheeses.

Although he could not figure how she had got there, Merle McAdam, from the grocery store, was drawing down her cheese-wire through one of the latter, with a grin that ran from ear to ear.

'Enough?' she was asking Grismond Guthrie, from the post office, who was positively drooling at her shoulder.

'More! More!!' he demanded as blood bubbled from whatever it was that she was cutting. On closer inspection, it had the look of human buttocks.

His cry was taken up by a crowd of townspeople who were also now there. 'We want more!' they chanted.

Maguire caught sight of the figure of Mrs Root, busy in one corner, stoking the hot coals of a brazier.

Slowly, the whole gallery grew thin and ghostly, till their figures were mere wisps.

Grinding his teeth and muttering the same incantation – about wanting more – Maguire came-to from the nightmare.

He sat up and shook himself in his bed.

Realising where he was, he fell back and slept.

Eventually, two days later, he woke with the sense that his health was restored.

After some while of being back in his normal routine, and when it seemed that nothing had changed in him in the bodily sense, Maguire stopped thinking about his expedition to the home of Mrs Root, and simply filed it as one of the weirder things he'd done in his life.

Something else to which he gave no more thought – and which, in truth, he'd pretty much dismissed on exiting her woods – was Mrs Root's warning to quit town.

The community wasn't such a bad place, he told himself, especially when the strange fires of its citizens seemed to burn themselves out and not re-ignite. Work was plentiful and the pay was good. The lack of another proper plumber in the town meant Maguire could price his jobs as high as he liked. And he did (while in all other respects remaining polite and professional). And no one seemed to mind, even for a task as trivial as a dripping tap, possibly on account of the financial killings they felt sure would soon come their way with the construction of the dam.

'Why,' Minty McTwain remarked to Maguire during one of Maguire's regular call-outs to fix her sump, 'you're practically one of us now.'

After the passing of spring and the onset of what had the look of being a long, dry summer in Fort Tinder, Maguire, who'd never stayed anywhere much more than a year, began to grow restless.

One warm night, with dollars aplenty in his pockets, he packed up his things and left, to the chirp of tree crickets and a cloud of mountain-road dust.

He drove his pickup three thousand miles, sleeping at pull-ins and parked-up at gas stations: the town and everything of it receding in the way that he liked, mentally as well as physically, the further he went.

As he clocked up the miles and the sunsets, Fort Tinder's strange beacon dimmed in his memory until it became to no more than a scorch-mark. This, he fully expected, would, in time be buried for good by the gunk and the grinds that he'd be called on to excavate from other blocked sumps in other small towns… anywhere in America.

One evening, as he continued to travel, the neon sign of a roadhouse caught Maguire's eye, and he stopped and signed-in at The Homely Hearth motel.

Having cleaned up in his room and put on a fresh shirt, he entered the establishment's diner and, directed by the waitress, took a seat at a table.

While he waited for his order of eggs ('fried easy') and steak ('juicy and not too charred') from the grill, a woman approached and asked if she might join him.

Maguire saw that the restaurant had grown busy, and, with a civil smile, agreed to her request.

She chose a chicken dish she described to Maguire as 'spicy', with a salad of green leaves and red peppers on the side.

As they ate, Maguire chewed thoughtfully, being struck by two things.

First, and above all, he grew aware that the part of him which had lain so long dormant was now, finally, stirring.

The second, smaller but still striking thing, was how the woman – who was tall and willowy with nails and lips that matched the red of her hair – detached her chicken from its breastbone so very precisely, so that the meat came away on her plate almost perfectly whole.

By the end of their meals, he and the woman were talking easily, and he accepted her offer when she asked if he would care to join her for a cup of something in her room.

Some while later, the woman took herself from on top of Maguire and lay beside him on the bed.

'I've never... not like *that* before,' she said, breathing quickly.

'Are you *always* that hard?' she continued after a moment. 'I thought I was going to have to hose you down.'

Maguire leaned to where his jeans hung on a chair and took a pack of cigarettes from the pocket other than the one that was heavy with his wallet.

'Reckon they junked the mould after they made you,' she added, her breath now beginning to steady.

Maguire smiled inwardly.

They each lay there for a time, smoking, without speaking.

After a while, the woman rose and went and turned on the TV, which was chained to a shelf at the end of the bed.

'Why, just look at that!' she said, as the set's picture formed.

And she wandered back to the bed.

A newscast showed an inferno laying waste a town. Higher up from the settlement, in what seemed the same valley, firefighters and various helicopters and planes had saved the home and life of an old woman in a remote shack, who was now being interviewed by a reporter.

Maguire didn't see or hear the name of Mrs Root... the cussed Mrs Root who always got to the bottom of things in her smoke house in the hills. For his attention was fixed on the woman who was climbing back into bed beside him and the flames that were crackling in the blood-red bush below her belly... now setting alight the sheets of the bed.

Red and orange tongues rose around them as if closing on a forest glade

The woman reached out an arm through the curtain of fire and drew back the TV's remote from the top of a chest, to better hear the words of the little, skew-eyed mountain lady who was smiling at the camera with great glee.

'I prayed for those pilots to do their thing with their cargoes of water and whatever else they carry. And Thank the Lord they did.'

The face of Mrs Root, the Mrs Root who could be relied on to smoke out badness – wherever it lay – filled the screen.

'"Drop 'em!" I said,' she crowed, throwing back her head, as if ready to fling herself into some fiddler's reel.

And, for an instant, Maguire saw her dancing with all of the flaming people and animals of the town, who were burning brightly and fiercely, flames beautifully flaying both fur and skin, all of them wheeling in rings of fire around Mrs Root, like the teeth of some great turning turbine or darkly magical timepiece, to which Mrs Root – the little lady who from her great mountain height got to the bottom of everything – possessed the one, and only, key.

# The Glass

IT was late in the year and the days were short and the snow was already thick on the land when Grigor Grigoriev arrived in the remote village of Krasyansk to repair the stained glass windows of its small cathedral.

No one met him at the railway halt: the locomotive resting there, in the immense Russian whiteness, gasping like some breathless beast, before re-gathering itself and dragging its dark tail of carriages on.

Under the icicled canopy of the shack that passed for the station house, Grigoriev found a sled angled on its runners against a corrugated iron wall. On this he placed his materials and his tools. He drew the sled's leather reins around him and pulled down his hat so that it was low on his brow. He then began to haul it over the plain of snow that stretched before him, the horizon all but indecipherable beneath a sky that seemed to darken with his every forward stride.

Krasyansk, it should be said, is no longer really a village. For some time it has been a scattered, depleted settlement at best: home to no more than a handful of loggers, farmers, rail workers and their families. Occasionally, as he walked, Grigoriev passed their houses, lit weakly by oil lamps and generators, recessed amid the birches and pines.

After almost an hour of walking and pulling the sled, Grigoriev came upon the cathedral, silhouetted on a slight rise, beyond which lay an expanse of dense, black firs.

He stopped and let the reins fall.

For several moments, he rested his gloved hands on his hips and breathed-in the cold, clear air. In the near-darkness, he then skirted the walls of the cathedral until he came to its door.

Inside the cathedral, its gold-painted murals and icons shone dully in the gloom.

Grigoriev stared at a huge haloed head he took to be that of Christ. Although by no means devout, he dropped to one knee and crossed himself.

With the light of his phone, which he realised in all other respects would now be useless (given the isolation of the village), he found his way to the vestry. There, on a small chest, he lit a candle. Having done so, he saw the stove, the pile of wood intended as its fuel and, against a wall, the couch that would be his bed.

Grigoriev laid a fire in the stove and lit it. Then he went back outside to the sled.

For several minutes, he stood looking at the stars, more aware now of the land and the sky than he had been when hauling the sled. In particular, his eyes and mind dwelt on the moon: it occurred to him that he could not remember when, in the city, he had seen it last. The smell of wood-smoke from the stove distracted him, and he set about unpacking the sled.

Having taken all of his things inside, Grigoriev stood over the stove in the candle-lit vestry. He did this so that his face and head might feel the benefit of its heat. During the walk from the railway lumps of ice had amassed in his beard and his eyebrows. He now leaned there and waited for the draughts of warmth to thaw them. Droplets and pieces of ice fell from his head to the stove's flat top, hissing as they did so.

After this, he slept.

In the morning, Grigoriev surveyed the damage that had been done to the windows of the cathedral. The details he had received were that a fierce storm had assailed the district in the late summer – bringing down trees, flooding land and drowning animals – during which much of the cathedral's old and fragile glazing had been lost.

As Grigoriev made his inspection, white beams of light lanced the cathedral through its missing panes. One gathering of saints, with Christ at their centre, was so riven that at first glance it seemed to Grigoriev as if it had been the victim of some shelling or similar martial assault.

He fetched a small ladder from the vestry and, having climbed it, felt the glass that remained. He assessed its age and its thickness, ran his fingers over the lead ridges and put their tips through the gaps. At one point, he placed his hand through a hole in Christ's white, right breast.

He climbed down, went back to the vestry and replenished the potbelly stove.

He boiled water on it for tea and ate herrings from a tin.

The priest, when he came, went about his business – praying and kissing the cathedral's modest icons – without acknowledging Grigor Grigoriev.

As the priest walked away through the snow, in his black kamilavka and cape, Grigoriev peered from his ladder through a hole in the glazing where the eye of Saint Andrey should have been.

Throughout that morning, Grigoriev traced the frames of the missing glass onto rolls of heavy paper. When necessary, he rested the ladder on a trunk of vestments and another case, containing candles, incense and a censer, to reach the required heights. He recorded the lines of the lost panes in thick black pencil on the cream-coloured rolls by running the pencil's tip along their ridged *cames* of lead: the various diamonds, petals, ribbons and wings accumulating until his paper was almost full.

Around each he made notes as to the nature and colour of the adjacent panes that remained. In those shadowed parts of the cathedral where he did this, his breath hung in the air, like forest mist.

At what he judged to be midday, Grigoriev stopped working and went outside with his mug.

He filled it with snow and then put it to melt on the stove.

He stood in the arched doorway of the cathedral and studied the plain in front of him and the forests at its sides.

His eyes made out where the priest seemed to have stepped through the snow.

As Grigoriev stood there, an icicle suspended from an eave dripped melt to his forehead. In its glassy trunk, Grigoriev saw what seemed to be himself – pendulous, blurred... a streak. Carmine and golden light flared upon it in the sun.

Grigoriev returned to the vestry where, never mind its stove, the temperature was colder than in the sunlight of the doorway.

He drank black tea as he flexed his fingers and stamped his feet, finishing the tin of herrings that he had opened for his breakfast.

He then ate three squares of baklava, having laid these to warm on the stove.

The fine pastry and crystallized honey melted within him.

Afterwards, calculating that there was relatively little light left in the day and that he had made good progress that morning, he left the cathedral and walked out into the white plain.

As he stepped through the snow, *waded* at times, he felt as if he were crossing not land, but an ocean, or a great lake, like Baikal. In the shallows, the snow sprayed from his shins. In the concealed dips, it cloyed at his thighs and, at times, his waist.

He could no longer see the trail left by the priest.

He wondered if it had snowed afresh while he had been

taking his lunch, but then he dismissed this, deciding instead that the priest's footprints must have melted in the sun.

Grigoriev turned and looked at the cathedral, topped with its black onion domes. He thought about what life, there, at Krasyansk, must have been like: its sawyers, their heavy horses pulling timber, strong-armed peasant women scything the meadows (quite possibly the land under his very feet).

Ghosts now – all of them – of course.

At the edge of the treeline of the forest that he'd kept on his right while walking from the railway, Grigoriev's eyes detected movement.

He turned for a better view and looked across the snow to the trees.

An elk raised its antlered head and stared back at him before retreating, slowly, into the forest.

Grigoriev walked back to the cathedral, sensing, as he did so, the sun sinking behind him.

Later, as he slept, Grigoriev dreamed of the elk he had seen: that he was riding on its back... through the forest... holding its huge antlers, that rose and curved like branches, in his fists. In various glades, people he had encountered but had not seen for years – among them a teacher from his schooldays, a cousin with whom he had danced at a wedding, a uniformed attendant who had once sold him a ticket for the Metro and an elderly woman whose creased face he remembered from behind a chained door – emerged from the trees to pat the elk's side and feel its snorts of warm breath.

After this, they stepped backwards, into the velvet darkness of the forest.

Eventually, the elk returned him to the cathedral (from where it had first roused him by knocking with its antlers on the door).

In the morning, Grigoriev set to work early. He took the thin mattress from his bed and, on the wooden slats beneath, unrolled the sheets of paper on which he had recorded the shapes of the lost and broken panes. On these he next placed the glass panels he had brought with him on the sled: rectangular sheets of yellow, green, blue and red. Then, kneeling at the bedframe, he began to trace the outlines of the panes with his cutter, all the while watching the revolutions of the cutter's little, oiled wheel. Griogriev angled his head to the glass, the spectacles he wore for the task frequently steaming.

As with the previous day, the priest arrived.

Grigoriev heard him praying and moving about in the cathedral.

His spiritual duties done, the priest entered the vestry. He looked in a chest, leafed through a ledger, whispered to himself and walked out – without, so it seemed to Grigoriev, even registering that he, Grigoriev, was there.

After grozing the edges of the new panes with an iron, and stacking them, Grigoriev made tea and ate two cubes of sugar.

He felt colder than the previous day and wondered if, in the night, he had caught a chill.

Momentarily, he remembered his dream-ride through the forest on the elk's back.

He considered going outside, but, observing the greyness of the sky through the high vestry window, he thought the better of it, and he continued with his work.

Cross-checking with the notes he had made, Grigoriev prepared his brushes, solutions and paints. He then set about illustrating the newly-cut pieces with the features they required: occasionally some missing element of a tree, hill or lamb, but, for the most part, fingers, eyes, feet and ears – carefully stroking-in the pigments, and to-ing and fro-ing between the bedframe and the windows to ensure the worthiness of those matches he intended to make.

During one such inspection, he saw from his ladder – through a hole in a ruby cloak – that outside it was snowing, and thickly: the forest beyond the cathedral barely visible for the falling flakes and failing light.

In the vestry, Grigoriev stoked the fire in the stove and

added more wood, whilst noting how the supply of logs against the wall had dwindled.

He used the stove as his kiln, wedging inside its upper half a steel tray on which, in batches, he set his painted panes to glaze in the stove's significant heat.

Any sense of time that Grigoriev may still have had now deserted him as he waited for each fresh batch to harden, then cool.

Initially, he heard the snowflakes falling against the vestry window, which they did with the sound of a tiny, silting clasp.

In time, this stopped as the window was smothered: a white cloak of snow steadily covering the casement from the bottom to the top.

The cathedral became cocooned, Grigoriev inside it, dunes of snow drifting against its door and its walls.

All the while, the stained glass consumed him – Grigoriev hearing nothing now but the determined, low grind of his cutter and an occasional heavy spark in the stove.

He surrendered himself to the glass utterly: the hairs of his eyebrows and beard virtually entwining with those of his precisely stroking brush.

The last pane Grigoriev painted was for the eye of Saint Andrey through whose socket he had seen the priest disappear previously (though Grigoriev struggled now to make sense of when this had been).

The morning of the next day brought with it a cobweb of frost that spread itself over Grigoriev as he lay on his couch: the web's latticework of silver strands encasing him, from the ushanka hat on his head to the soles of his thickly-socked feet.

In time, Grigoriev heard voices in the cathedral, and he sat-up in his clinging filaments of frost.

The priest's voice he quickly recognised.

What surprised Grigoriev, however, were the voices of others, responding, and at times singing, in what he realised to be a mass of the kind to which his mother had taken him in their home village when he was young.

133

Stepping from the vestry, Grigoriev saw that, as well as the priest, who was ministering at the altar, the cathedral was almost full.

Not with people as he knew them in the city, but of the kind who had once lived in that district: sawyers, farmers, farriers, peasant women, itinerants... all standing for the mass, in their jerkins and other coarse clothes, their rude boots and their headscarves.

Grigoriev walked through these congregants now, carrying his pieces of glass.

He did this as if these were no longer mere products of his toil, but something more: offertories, of a kind.

He fixed the new panes in the 'wounded' windows.

As he did so, he had the curious sensation that, with every pane that he cemented, a part of him seemed to be lost.

So much so that, at the completion of his labours, Grigoriev felt no more substantial than the ashes in the bottom of the vestry's potbelly stove.

When the mass ended, the departed of the village departed once more, filing through the cathedral's arched doorway and into the wide, white plain.

In its depths, they became dots, like birds in a pale sky. And then they disappeared.

One who'd been present, however, remained... and will always remain: body and, possibly, soul.

Caught, it might be said, by the claw of Krasyansk.

Trapped.

Like an insect in amber.

# The
# Examination

BLAKE felt a tap on his shoulder.

For a second, he saw a fingernail – thick, yellow – that its owner withdrew.

'*Yours* are they?' came a voice from behind him.

'I'm… sorry?' said Blake, turning.

He looked at his fellow passenger, who leaned back in his seat.

The man was old… *very* old, but trim, neat… alert.

He wore a tweed flat cap. Blake noted the knot of a tie over the collar of the man's raincoat. His eyes were coal-black, but had a gleam. On his face, a smirk.

'Well, that's a start,' the man continued.

'What is?' said Blake.

'Being "sorry".'

For a moment, the man's stare shifted beyond Blake, then switched back.

Like an agitator delighting in a street fight, he nodded and grinned at the fresh fracas at the front of the bus.

The disorder in which Blake had reluctantly intervened

minutes earlier had resumed: a gang of lads – in school uniform of varying degrees of dishevelment – scuffling, swearing, shouting.

A boy's phone was snatched and hurled.

'Your… *products,*' continued the man, with a strange mixture of relish and disdain. '*Chris,* isn't it?' he added, folding his arms.

'Yes,' said Blake.

'Thought I heard them call you that.'

Disliking what he felt to be the man's mockery, Blake turned away. He looked through the window at the passing shops. He tried to calculate whether, in the morning, he could make it to the garage *before* school… and get his car back. That would make *this* trip the last. And he'd be back to *his* radio, *his* heater, *his*… space. No More Buses.

The boys in the front were no longer scuffling. They were fighting now. One – was it Tyler Pritchard? – was being pinned down and punched.

The chirp at Blake's back resumed.

'Been there long?'

Blake again turned.

'King Edward's?' the man continued. 'Have you been teaching there long? You're new on here… the 44.'

Before Blake could answer, a bell began dinging. Not the orderly, single ding made by a passenger requesting that the driver stop, but a dinging for the hell of it, over and over, that came from where the boys were.

The driver responded with a barrage of threats, muffled from his distant post downstairs at the wheel.

'Oh, I'm sorry, it's not called that now, is it?' the man behind Blake continued. 'Mount Pleasant *Community,*' he said, elongating the 'u'. 'Yes: *that's* its name now.'

The bus stopped heavily.

The boys at the front swung forward. They gripped bars and seat-backs, as if rocked by a bomb blast. They kept their feet though… beat the driver as his game.

The lads yelled, laughed.

'Ah!' announced the man. 'I'm here: my stop. Nearly missed it, chatting with you. Saved by the bell… thanks to the actions of *your* boys.'

Blake turned from him and looked through the window at the houses in the road. They were large, older. He knew the area a little from his boyhood. There'd been a parade of shops where he'd sometimes ventured on his bike. It wasn't his home patch – his parents' house had been in a neighbourhood that lay further away – but the newsagent at the parade sold football stickers, which had been the thing among boys back then.

The route taken by the bus wasn't one that Blake used in his car. It was quicker for him to get home via the link road. His house was on an estate of new-builds on the other side of the bypass. Its location meant he had to drive to get anywhere, but as a place to live it was okay: no 'character' admittedly, but it was quiet. Its relative remoteness meant there was never any 'trouble'.

Looking absently through the window, he wondered if it wasn't perhaps time he moved on… career-wise: a different school, one that was… *easier*, in another town. They existed. Nothing 'private' – he had his principles – but a comprehensive, or a grammar, in a 'good area', somewhere leafy, where parents fought to send their kids, where house prices meant it might just as well be 'private', where all you had to do was turn up and…

Suddenly, he sensed himself in the trajectory of something that was falling.

Beside Blake's seat – collapsing, crumpling, *crashing* from a height – came the figure of the old man. In his raincoat, he had the vague look of something winged, something avian, that had been shot in mid-air.

Blake thrust out a hand and half-caught the man by his elbow. He slid over the seat and helped the man stand.

'Thank you,' said the man – who swayed, took hold of a strap, straightened himself. 'I'm—'

'Come on. I'll help you off,' said Blake.

139

The boys at the front watched as he assisted the man down the steps.

Outside, in the bus shelter, the man leaned heavily on a panel sprayed with graffiti.

'I shall be all right now,' he said.

The bus belched smoke as it pulled away, and the man drew short, shallow breaths.

He continued: 'My home is… around… the corner. No dis… tance… at… all.'

'I'll see you there,' said Blake. 'Take your time.' After some moments he put the man's arm across his shoulders. 'Right. Let's go and get you in.'

The house was a large, old, detached property covered with thick, twisting vines whose leaves had mostly been shed. The vines gave the house a strange, tatty look. They reminded Blake of the anatomical charts that doctors displayed in consulting rooms – illustrations of the kind that showed the human body with its arteries and muscles exposed. One end of the property possessed the architectural flourish of a battlement.

The wooden front gate was green, soft and sagging on its hinges. It left a film of slime on Blake's palm as he pushed it open.

He walked with the man up a path between tangles of weed and wet, matted grass. About halfway, they encountered a condom that lay soiled and wrinkled, like some small and spineless sea creature, on the mossed clay tiles of the path.

The man prodded it with the toe of his polished brogue shoe. He turned and looked Blake in the face. 'The baboons do it *here*. In my garden. Can you believe it? I'll have them one night, though, I tell you.'

Blake changed the subject. 'Do you live here *with* anyone?'

'*With*?' the man came back at him. 'Oh no. Independent. That's me.' He took himself from Blake's shoulders.

At the front door, he dug out a key from a pocket in his coat.

Blake waited on the porch steps.

The man beckoned him and had Blake push open the door, which was warped and which rubbed the frame as it opened. The man withdrew the key and put his hand back in his coat pocket.

The smell from the hall made Blake think of an uncle's house – an elderly relative his family had called 'uncle' but, in fact, some distant cousin – to which his mother had taken him as a boy. Blake remembered flytraps of yellow-brown tape hanging, like tongues, from ceilings… mahogany tea made in pots with water from a kettle that boiled on a blue flame. The back garden had had rhubarb and a toilet in a shed with spiders and a cold wooden seat, from which he'd coming running – aghast – on those occasions when he had no option but to use it.

'Come in,' said the man.

'I'd like to,' said Blake, 'but, if you're feeling better, I really should—'

'No, come in,' said the man. 'You must.' He looked Blake in the face and smiled.

Blake felt something against the front of his jacket. Something *pressing*. Above his waist. Near his belly button. To one side of his jacket's zip.

He looked down and saw a metal blade.

It was long, thick, pointed.

'I've asked you nicely,' said the man. 'Now… Get in!'

Blake heard the door slam shut behind him.

'What the hell do you think you're doing?' he said.

The man drove home a bolt and removed his raincoat.

He was swift, dextrous now.

He swapped the blade he'd poked at Blake from one hand to the other, the gleam of his coal-black eyes restored.

'This is kidnap!' said Blake. 'Are you mad?'

'Mind your lip!' said the man. He tossed his cap to a hook on a stand, waved the blade at Blake's chest.

Blake stepped back. 'What the hell *is* that thing? Put it away!'

'This *thing*,' said the man, 'is a British Army bayonet. Infantry issue. World War One. It's seen service, and, if need be, it shall do so again.'

The two of them eyed each other, neither speaking. From a passage off the hall came the heavy ticking of a clock.

'Look,' Blake began, 'let me go – *right* now – and, as far the police are concerned I might *just* forget this.'

'Police?' said the man, cocking his head. 'What has *this* to do with *them*? This is a school matter.'

'What do you mean by that?' asked Blake.

The man gestured to a door. 'In there!'

Behind Blake, the man threw a switch. The room's darkness gave way to a sickly, under-powered light. 'Sit!' the man barked. Blake complied. 'Good,' said the man. 'Seems like you're learning how to behave yourself.'

Blake began to look around him. What he took to be the room's windows were curtained with heavy crimson drapes. In the middle of the room stood a large desk, behind which was a chair. Blake noticed how they were on a kind of podium, a rectangle covered with a patterned carpet, where the floor had somehow been raised. To one side of the desk, on an easel, was something that Blake had seen in old films and photographs but had never personally encountered: a blackboard. The man glanced at it and looked back at Blake.

'Tea?' his captor enquired.

'I'm sorry?' said Blake.

'So you keep saying,' said the man. 'Your *tea*, though… how do you take it? Milk? Sugar?'

'Milk, two sugars, please,' said Blake, wrong-footed by the incongruity of the enquiry.

'Right,' said the man. 'Coming up!' He spun away, spun back. 'Oh, before *that*, I just need to do… *this*.'

The handcuffs issued a faint snap as the man, with pickpocket speed and precision, shackled Blake where he sat. And where he *sat*, Blake now realised, was at a table and chair arranged very much like a school desk. Blake yanked at the cuff and chain that now joined his left wrist to the leg of the desk, which he saw had been bolted to the room's parquet floor.

'You won't get out of those,' said the man, watching Blake struggle. 'Made in the days of proper coppers. Built to last.'

'I advise you to let me go. Now!' Blake said. 'You could get ten years for this!'

'Oh not that again,' said the man. 'Who'd believe you? Think! An elderly chap like me? Doing a thing like this? Anyway, the world and his wife saw you helping me off the bus. You volunteered.'

'You planned this, didn't you? Your... *fall*. There was nothing wrong with you.' Blake pulled again at his shackle. 'Why me?'

'Oh, stop grizzling, man. Do you think that's what they whinged at Waterloo? Do you think that's what they sobbed at The Somme? "Why *me-e-e*?!",' he mocked. 'Just stay there and hold your tongue. Anyway, no one can hear you. We're back from the road. The barbarians may have over-run the grounds, but the walls are thick. The castle stands strong. And its keep. It's just you and me here, Sonny Jim. Now... I'll get the tea.'

'Who are you?' Blake asked.

In the doorway, the man turned.

'My name is Clyst,' he said, '... as in mist. But with a y rather than an i. You can call me "Mr Clyst", or, if you prefer it, "Sir".'

Clyst returned – with a tray of crockery and a teapot in a woolly lime-green cosy. He poured a cup, which Blake took.

Blake sipped, stopped. He flung the cup across the room.

'For Christ's sake, what the hell am I doing here?' he demanded. 'What the hell are you doing with me?'

Clyst drew back. '*That*... Christopher,' he said, 'is no way to conduct yourself. Any repetition of language of that kind in this class and—'

'And *what?*' shouted Blake.

'I advise you to keep your cool, young man… or you might very well find out. More of that behaviour, and you'll be here after hours.'

'*After hours? Class?* What the hell do you mean?'

'We have work, Christopher. Work. Or, rather, you do. Papers. Papers to sit – and pass. And when you *have* passed them you may go. No further action required. Easy as that,' Clyst smiled. 'Now, tell me, what is it that you teach?'

'Media studies,' said Blake, 'if it's any of your business… and international relations.'

'International relations! Heavens!' said Clyst, who was holding the bayonet again, tapping it in his palm. 'At Mount Pleasant Community! That *does* sound grand! And – what was it? – "media", too. Well, that must make you *very* busy: all of those newspapers to read, all of that… *telly* to watch.'

'Oh, spare me your sarcasm,' said Blake. 'The world's moved on from Latin, Wordsworth and the "Eton Boating Song" – in case you hadn't noticed.'

'Oh, I've noticed,' said Clyst. 'Believe you me, I've noticed.' He walked to the desk in the centre of the room. He set down the bayonet, pulled out a drawer. 'Very different in my day, Chris.'

'Your day?'

'Oh, I taught there: Mount Pleasant, as you call it. When it was King Edward's, of course. History. Medieval, for the most part. Thirty years.'

'Is that what this is about?' asked Blake.

'In part, I suppose… yes.'

'Well, for Christ's— I'm sorry. I mean, for *goodness* sake, schools are schools. What their names are, how they're run, what they teach… all of that's way above my pay grade. It's nothing to do with me. Try the politicians.'

'And I would dearly love to. But come now,' said Clyst, looking up. 'That's hardly the attitude.'

'I did you a favour. I helped you get home,' said Blake.

Clyst went back to looking through the drawer. He pulled out what looked like two pamphlets. 'I know,' he said. 'Your behaviour was honourable. Exemplary, in fact. Pass these and you may go. No protests from me.'

'What are they?'

'From my day,' said Clyst, putting on spectacles. 'Matriculation papers at Ordinary Level, for English language and mathematics. The Metropolitan Board, 1953. Originally set for boys of sixteen. We were – what do they call it? – *single-sex* back then. Should be within your range, Chris,' said Clyst, peering at Blake over his half-moon glasses, '… even if, admittedly, outside your fields of expertise. They didn't have anything quite as fancy as "media studies" and "international relations" back then. Shall we say ninety minutes for each?'

Clyst placed the papers on Blake's desk.

Blake looked at the covers.

'This is ridiculous!' said Blake. 'What if I refuse?'

'There are two ways in which we can deal with this,' said Clyst. 'This way, which is the easier way, or another, which I promise you will be much harder.' He glanced back at the bayonet on his desk. 'Which would you prefer?'

Blake said nothing.

'Now,' Clyst continued, 'if you've any means of assistance, I shall need to relieve you of them. Phones, calculators – I wasn't born yesterday, young man. Let's have them.'

With his free hand, Blake reached into his jacket and drew out his mobile. He cursed inwardly. Why had he not had the wit to use it? Called 999 before this lunatic could take it from him? He'd been such a zombie – worrying about his car, spoons of sugar in his tea… acting in the way people did before something horrible happened: trapped in the queasy slow-motion that preceded a car crash you could see coming. No one's life ever flashed before them. It was 'One lump or two?' and…

Blake shuddered at the thought.

Clyst saw the tremor in Blake's hand as he surrendered his phone.

The older man smiled. 'Exam nerves? Oh, you'll be fine. Nothing to worry about, I'm sure.'

He placed a pencil and sharpener on Blake's desk. 'Three hours, then. Hand in sooner, if you want to. Good luck.'

Walking back to his desk, he studied Blake's phone. 'My! This really is quite a... *thing*.'

Blake looked at the English paper, picked up the maths paper, went back to the English one. Christ, he thought, what sort of language were they even speaking in – when was it? – 1953? Adverbs, collective nouns, prepositions, conditional tenses? Oh, do shut up! Subordinate clauses? *Subordinate?* Since when had anyone used words like that?

Blake looked up. He told Clyst: 'None of this makes any sense.'

'I'm sure the instructions for that paper are perfectly clear,' Clyst responded. 'They were written at a time when people knew how to use the Queen's English. I suggest you get on with it.'

'I'm not talking about the paper,' said Blake. 'I'm talking about *this*. Me being here, *chained* to this desk!' He set down his pencil, leaned back in his chair (in so far as his handcuff would allow). 'You answer *my* question... and I *might* answer these.'

'And if I don't?'

'Simple. Kill me. And get on with it!'

The words seemed to startle Clyst. 'Kill? *Kill?* My goodness! The very idea! Oh, surely there's no need for that?' He paused, eyed Blake for a moment, began. 'Very well. Three nights ago, I was the victim of a robbery... on my way home from the shops at the parade... what few businesses remain there. A lad – school age by the look of him – pulled a knife on me in the underpass. High on something or other, I don't doubt. Had my wallet and my watch – the one that my father left me. The fact that I didn't have a phone seemed to annoy him. I told him that I read the newspapers at the library, listened to the wireless for entertainment (after a fashion) and, in any case, had no one to dial. That only served to make him worse. I received quite a mouthful for my pains, I can tell you.'

'I'm sorry,' said Blake.

'When *I* was that age, something like that, in this neighbourhood, to a man of my years... it would have been unthinkable. Not only that but the... *copulations* in my garden – you saw the evidence – my parents' garden, where, in summer, they took their tea... the graffiti on the bus shelter, the vomit on the pavements, the litter in the hedges. Don't tell me you didn't see it. Where has all of this come from? How did it happen? Who has allowed it? Not me... *Chris*. Not me!'

'Times have changed,' said Blake. 'The area has changed. Jobs have gone. Factories have shut. Things aren't what they were here.'

'You're damned right they aren't!'

'They aren't *all* bad kids,' Blake countered. 'Not by a long way. And neither's the school. But... outcomes... they won't, they *can't* be the same. So many of our students have... issues. It isn't easy for them, or us.'

Clyst shook his head. He waved a dismissive hand. 'Oh, don't give me that... *crap*. There have always been "issues". There will always *be* "issues". You lack any sense of history. That's your problem. That's society's *real* problem today.'

'I think we can do without "Victorian values", if those are what you've got in mind: kids up chimneys, workhouses, mudlarks. Is *that* the Memory Lane you'd like us to go back to?'

'It's all about *Me*. It's all about *Now*. That's the world for you these days,' interrupted Clyst. '*My* generation went without. I never saw an egg till I was nine. Thought they came from a tin. Rationing. Can you believe it? Who'd have thought we'd actually won the war? Do you know, there are children in Africa, attending lessons *right now*, not a shilling between them, who are doing better than youngsters here. I, personally, got thirteen boys into Oxbridge. Thirteen! Never mind Durham, Exeter, Birmingham – and the rest. Ordinary lads, for the most part. Sons of gas fitters, plumbers, postmen... mothers who were dinner ladies or had jobs in the local shops. Did great things, many of them: wrote books, taught, entered the professions. Tell me, what's the tally for Mount Pleasant Community *now*... Chris? Hey? Tell me that! Second thoughts, don't! I don't think I could bear it.'

'People are trying their best. We're *all* trying our best. And not just so that the odd glamour boy – or girl – can go and get a First somewhere and never come back. Everyone has a chance now. We're trying to build a community—'

'Build? *Build*?! Well you haven't done a very good job so far, have you? It looks more like a *ruin*, to me.'

'Oh, come on! What about all the years *you* were in charge? *You* were in the driving seat for decades. We're *your* grandchildren! Like it or not!'

'Oh, be quiet! I don't want to hear any more. In *my* judgment, something... some*one*... needs to be examined... held to account. And fate has selected you, Chris. Fate has selected you. Please, just get on with it now. The clock is ticking.'

In the weak light of the room, Blake struggled with the papers. Stopping amid an essay to sharpen his pencil, he saw that Clyst now wore a black gown – sleeves spilling on the desk as his captor went through books from a pile beneath the bayonet... pursing his lips, puckering his brow.

During the maths paper, they argued over a note – Blake read it aloud – that said the *candidate* might use a slide rule. Blake said that since he didn't *have* a slide rule and had never used one, he was *entitled* – Clist winced at the word – to have this taken into consideration during the marking.

'Well that's your *bally* fault!' said Clyst. 'Don't lecture me, boy! Where did you go to school, anyway?'

'Mount Pleasant Community,' said Blake, 'when it was still King Edward's... just.' Blake smiled.

'That's enough!' said Clyst. 'From now on there will be silence in this examination room!'

Blake went back to the paper: a question about an equation and the value of $x$. He began his answer earnestly, but it became a kind of hieroglyphic: a chaotic chain of characters that formed something that resembled a scaffold... and a hanging man.

A *rat-tat-tat* broke the quiet of the room. Clyst was writing with chalk on the blackboard. Blake couldn't make out the words because of the board's angle on the easel and the weakness of the ceiling light. Clyst finally struck the board with the tip of the chalk, as if administering a particularly pointed full stop.

'Time!' Clyst called suddenly. 'Stop writing! Put down your pencils and pens!'

He was speaking, thought Blake, as if addressing not merely him, but an entire hall of pupils. 'Make sure your names are written clearly at the top of each paper. We don't want any mix-ups.'

Clyst picked up Blake's sheets. 'Thank you...' – he looked at the top of the first page – '... Mr *Blake.*'

Clyst walked towards his desk... turned. A strange smile came over his face. He continued to his chair, took a pen from his jacket pocket, removed the cap, glanced at Blake... and began to mark the papers.

Blake watched as Clyst's head shifted, as his lips whispered... as his dark eyes narrowed and their brows arched and sank. Blake thought him like some marsh-dwelling bird that could sometimes be seen in the boggy fields near his estate, where the houses stopped, stalking its sodden, echoey acres, letting out harsh screeches in the chill, soaking air.

And then it started... the evisceration... the sharp nib of Clyst's pen jabbing, stabbing, sticking, scraping at Blake's work. It was as if the pen's precise, golden point were in fact some blood-soaked bill, busy in the gutting of a fish, or some other hapless creature, its innards unspooling on a slimed and water-logged trunk: Clyst, the great crested something-or-other, spearing and ripping, tutting with his tongue, sucking at his teeth, as he skewered and impaled, one after the other, the schoolboy errors that Blake had committed – holding his mistakes up, moreover, for the ridicule of a court of circling and shrilling smaller birds, whining flies and buzzing wasps. Finally, he, Clyst, consumed them... devoured them, in his oh-so-neat-and-necktied gullet, under the red setting sun in that desolate swamp where he, Clyst, was king.

Watching him, Blake rocked nervously in his seat. One clenched buttock to the other. He felt a desperate urge to pee. He wondered if he might wet himself... *there*, like some infant, too terrified to ask for permission to be excused. He *had* to get out of this. There *had* to be a way. He'd been too compliant. What had become of his old anger? His student rage? Had it ever really existed? Or had it all been hormonal... confected... a means to 'go with' girls? Think! he told himself. Think! You got a First, didn't you? When it still counted for something? Oh Christ... and now he was thinking like Clyst. Think for yourself! Use your brain!! Use it!!!

Suddenly, the fog cleared on the sulphurous marshland... the Clyst kingdom... that Blakes's mind had conjured – doing so as if blown – and scattered – by crosswinds of a lashing, unforgiving kind.

First – Blake now saw – there'd been Clyst's repetition of his name... the way he'd said it ('Mr Blake'), the way he'd looked.

On the heels of this, came Blake's memory of something... some*one* unworthy of resurrection... who'd been banished – like a school bully, predatory priest or other abuser – to the darker corners of his consciousness.

'I know who you are,' Blake said now, calmly.

Clyst looked up from his desk. 'Penny dropped, has it?'

'You taught my father, Bob—'

'Robert Blake. Yes,' Clyst interrupted. 'I can see the resemblance.'

'You... beat him.'

'A not *un*able student *when* he put his mind to it,' Clyst said, taking off his glasses and putting them on the desk.

'He hated you,' Blake continued. 'He spoke of you with contempt.'

'Wouldn't apply himself. Not really. That was his problem.'

'He was – *is* – clever.'

'He could have made it, but he wouldn't knuckle down.'

'And so you beat him, you bastard.'

'*Disciplined* is, I think, the word that you're struggling for.'

'He had a mind of his own.'

'Ended up driving a cab. Picked me up once. He didn't say a thing. Not a word. Quiet as a mouse... the whole journey. Shame. I put a lot into that boy.'

Blake spluttered, shook his head.

'He had a rhyme for you. All the boys did. Want to hear it?'

'Not particularly.'

'Thrasher Clyst... never known to miss... blub and bawl... and he'll—'

'"Give you six more" ... Yes, I'm aware of that. Doesn't really scan, does it? Anyway, I'm not sure that you've got it quite right – rather like your papers. Still... better times, happier days. Seldom a week passes when I don't wish that I could turn back the clock. But that's not the matter before us now. The matter before us now is your examin—'

'You went too far, didn't you? They forced you out. You were beating lads black and blue... till their arses bled. Get something out of it, did you?'

'That's enough. Be quiet.'

'You clung on. But they threw you out... in the end.'

'I said, "Be quiet"!'

Clyst rose behind his desk.

'That or the police, wasn't it?' Blake continued. 'Did they let you keep your pension? Or did they take that, too? Is that why you're such a bitter old loon? Thirty years you say you were there. But I've got news for you. You've been excised, erased. *Exorcised*, in fact. It's as if you never existed. You're not even history… *Clyst*.' Blake spat his name with disdain.

Clyst seized the bayonet, slammed the blade on the desk. 'I said, "That's enough"!'

He shook with rage. Blake stopped.

Clyst re-took his seat, shuffled Blake's papers. 'The issue here, my boy,' he began, 'is your work, which, to use a lame but in your case *accurate* phrase… is not good enough.'

'I passed though, didn't I?' said Blake. 'That was the deal. That's all I had to do.'

'Forty per cent in mathematics,' said Clyst, looking over the top of the papers.

'Forty per cent? That's a pass then,' said Blake.

'What do you mean, "That's a pass"? Since when has forty per cent ever been a pass for anything?'

''Tis now, old man. That's official. And achieved *without* the slide rule. I'm entitled to an upgrade. Let's call it fifty. What about the English?'

Clyst said nothing, glanced at what he'd written. He looked up. 'Forty-one per cent.'

Blake went to raise his hands in triumph. The handcuff pulled him back. He grimaced. 'Now,' he told Clyst, 'you *get* here and take this *thing* off!'

Clyst remained seated behind his desk. An air of solemnity fell over him.

He pulled open a drawer.

He took from it a tasselled mortarboard (of the kind Blake had once hired for his university graduation but had never seen since) and placed it on his head.

'Mr Blake, I have to tell you,' Clyst began at last, 'that, in terms of *my* standards and the standards of *this* classroom, you have fallen far short.'

'What do you mean?' Blake demanded, jerking at the cuff.

Clyst rose and swept to the door.

He turned out the light as he left.

For some long minutes, Blake heard the sounds of shunting

and rummaging and doors being opened and shut. The noises seemed to come at first from downstairs in the house and then its upper storeys. Blake called out more than once but received no answer.

Eventually, the disturbances ceased, and the house fell silent, save for the sound of a clock ticking in a passage or room somewhere…

And then the footsteps began.

With each creak and crack of the staircase came a whisper – 'Thrasher Clyst…' – that rose to a murmur – 'Never known to… *desist*'.

The sibilants snaked through the gloom to the room where Blake sat shackled in the blackness.

'Blub and bawl…'

It was no longer a whisper, nor a murmur, but a full-throated incantation now.

'And he'll give you six more!'

The door to Blake's dark 'classroom' suddenly swung open.

The tall, gowned, mortarboarded figure of Clyst loomed in its frame, silhouetted against the yellow light of the hall.

Like the lifting of a raptor's dark wing, an arm rose slowly in his gown's black drapes, and then descended – swiftly.

Chained to his desk, Blake's body tautened at the awful sound of the scything *swish*.

Summoned from the dock to the witness stand to give evidence at his trial, Humphrey Clyst, M.A., held forth for the best of a day on the merits of corporal punishment. At the end of the proceedings, his sentence (although not insubstantial) was a suspended one, which meant that, rather than going to jail, he walked free – the judge stating that he was bearing in mind the defendant's age, public service and previous good character, together with the fact that, although an unacceptable level of coercion had been involved, the victim – 'beyond some bruising' – appeared to have suffered 'no lasting harm'.

To some, Clyst became a folk hero, appearing on radio, television and in podcasts (the nature of which had to be explained to him) to answer questions about what the programme hosts called his 'One-Man War'. There were appearances on chat and quiz shows with 'celebrities' he'd never heard of who laughed and clapped when he fielded their queries by quoting some episode of history or an epigram in Latin.

Certain broadcasters offered him large sums to appear on air in his mortarboard and gown and demonstrate his 'technique'. He turned down these requests, telling the young researchers who telephoned and turned up at his door that he had no desire to become 'end of the pier… the next Rector of Stiffkey' (a reference – lost on them – to a notorious English clergyman defrocked in the previous century).

After a while, though, the chauffeured rides to the studios stopped, and he resumed his seat on the upper deck of the 44.

Blake, for his part, moved away, feeling the need to be somewhere that he might never be found. He stopped teaching and took a job as a stockman on a poultry farm in a coastal county on the opposite side of England.

One night, in a village pub, he saw Clyst's face on the television news. There was a shot of the outside of Clyst's house: creeper-clad, with its battlement… as Blake remembered it.

The set's volume had been turned down. The subtitles of a report said that Clyst had been found dead after apparently disturbing *intruders* in his garden – the 'controversial teacher-turned-personality' had been 'stabbed repeatedly with' – there was a delay for a second or so before the white letters appeared on the screen – 'an unspecified weapon'.

The absence of sound gave the report a ghostly air: Clyst's smiling face – he was pictured in his tie and tweed cap – strangely at odds with the silent facts of his violent demise.

After barely a minute, he was gone – displaced by another news item.

To Blake, though, it was as if his ex-captor had issued a calling card and was, in fact, as alive ever. As if he'd been at Blake's table... drinking – some antiquated brew that now came only in bottles. As if he'd simply got up to go to the gents (where he was doubtless tutting about something, such as an absence of soap) – and that he would, above all, return.

As he walked home to his caravan on the farm, Blake thought about those things that he had *not* told the police... that he had not told anyone. How, when he had finished with his cane and before he had released him, Clyst had held him, hugged him, kissed him on his forehead, tears streaming the old monster's cheeks.

*My product.* That's what Clyst had called him.

With a mile or more left of his walk, the weather around Blake grew stormy. A stinging wind threatened to tear the telegraph wires from their poles beside the empty lanes.

The cables flew outwards and then inwards... to breaking point and back – whipping the bitter, black night into which Blake journeyed, with a *whoosh... whoosh... whoosh.*

# Thirteen

EVEN when he was forced to sell Fferm Ty Gwyn in consequence of his compulsion, Tomos Tomos's strange desire burned within him, smouldering in the twisted timber of his skeleton... bubbling in the hot, tarry oil of his blood.

As with those odd, black acres seen always smoking on awkward tracts of angular hills, the perverse insistence that hissed and sparked within the farmer – who was no longer a farmer – could be dampened, but never truly put out.

So it was that he managed to exclude from the sale of Fferm Ty Gwyn, in that notably rural corner of Wales, his collection of twelve tractors, and, furthermore, to persuade Ty Gwyn's new owners, David and Anna Haviland, to allow him to keep his fleet in the farm's old red barn, while he sorted his 'affairs'.

The Havilands smiled benevolently and said they knew that he'd 'been through a lot'. And it was true, Tomos Tomos *had* been through a lot. An awful lot. And it was also true that almost all of what he had been through had been due to the matter of his feelings for tractors.

Tractor Number Four, a fine pre-War Fordson, had cost him his marriage: Tanwen Tomos throwing off her apron and packing her bags on sight of its orange glow coming down the bryn, Tomos Tomos seated regally, as if lord and master of the valley, bringing home a new bride – his flesh-and-blood spouse foreseeing, rightly, no end to her husband's peculiar hunger.

The price of Tractor Number Eight, a red and – to Tomos Tomos – irresistible Allis-Chalmers that first rolled over the earth in 1926, was Ty Gwyn's finest field by far.

The consequence of Number 12, an ancient and skeletal Hart-Parr, was the loss of the farm itself: the tyre-less, bare-metal Parr proving more than Tomos Tomos's bank manager, Elfyn Thomas (no *close* relation), could bear – a wag at the bank writing on his files of Tomos Tomos's 'intractable' affliction.

But in *his* mind, Tomos Tomos's purchases had only ever been entirely normal. What man could not be drawn by horse power, fly wheels and differential lock?

There were aesthetic considerations, too. The pocka-pocka-pocka of the Duncan Brown in full flight was to him as sweet as the song of any choir or skylark; the aroma of diesel from a snub-nosed War-era Case, as fragrant as the scent of any elegant female of London or Paris.

And there was another thing… one that he told no other (though shrewd observers may not have needed the telling). And the strange truth was this: that, for Tomos Tomos, tractors had about them something shapely, something comely, something *alluring*. Long after he had lost any capacity for arousal by a pretty woman fetchingly dressed, or even a healthy heifer well-bred, there was for him in a tractor something… *stirring*. At markets and shows, there were knowing nods and winks about the 'queer old goat' of Ty Gwyn: one story having that a girl, employed to 'do' after the departure of his wife, had seen him naked, atop one of his tractors in the dark of his red barn: bony rump and thin ribs – white as chalk – rocking in that shady place, and all the while him a-cock-a-doodle-doing to its slates and its rafters, lustier than any sickle-tailed bird of beady eye and scarlet comb.

When the formalities of Ty Gwyn's sale were done, after his bank's possession of it through their procedure of foreclosure, Tomos Tomos showed David Haviland around its buildings and acres. Haviland then offered Tomos a lift back to the town. This the latter declined, asserting his wish to walk the lanes on his own, as he had in his youth. And so he set off amid evening birdsong and the sun's sinking yolk, his hand clasped to an old crook stick that had been his grandfather's, and, beneath a flap of his best (and only) tweed jacket – put on for the benefit of the Havilands – a pocket of Ty Gwyn's distinctive dark earth.

As Tomos walked, his mind turned to his tractors: all lined up in the cool shade of the red barn. He savoured the fact that, while in the dead words of a legal deed the Havilands were now the owners of Ty Gwyn, he, Tomos Tomos, had his tractors – 'Pob un o'r deuddeg,' he said to himself as he walked, '… all twelve' – their lamps like eyes in the red barn's gloom… watching, knowing.

To Tomos Tomos, the tractors were the guardians of the soul of Ty Gwyn. In his riding of them and – together – their riding of Ty Gywn, the tractors had become Ty Gwyn, so the farm lay – no, *lived* – within them: in their coats of paint, their flakes of rust (God forbid) and their clods of sea-green grease. Their oil was the farm's blood, their wires her sinews, their engines, pumps and carburettors her beating heart, breathing lungs and other vital organs.

The tractors *were* the farm and the farm *was* the tractors. To Tomos Tomos, it was as simple – and secret – as that.

No mere solicitor's pen and paper could contain her.

Foolish to think.

For several weeks after the sale, Tomos Tomos sat in his new 'house' in the town – small part of the pebbledashed property that was his – waiting for the Havilands to call… calculating, in the gloom of his room, how many of his tractors they would want.

Logically-speaking, it would be two, he told himself. And, when that request came, as he was convinced it surely would, he, Tomos Tomos, true heir of Ty Gwyn, would tell the soft-handed money man, Haviland, from Cardiff, London (or wherever it was), that, *Oh no* (and with a lilt in his voice which he hoped would not betray *too* much satisfaction)… *no, no*. He was sorry but he could not *possibly* sell his tractors. *Oh goodness, no*. Well, it would be like selling a daughter. And no father could ever bring himself to do such a thing.

Tomos pictured himself lowering the receiver (heroic, unswayed) on the city man's sweet-breathed overtures. He imagined Haviland continuing with desperate pleas ('Hello? Are you still there?') that he, Tomos Tomos, should just name his price.

Such were the words Tomos Tomos rehearsed in the dimness, in his chair by his gas fire that he knew not how to light; on the fire's tiled mantle, an old photo of Ty Gywn with his father – also Tomos Tomos – astride a Massey-Harris newly-delivered, all steel-and-rubber wonder, *shining* in the yard… the black-and-white image pin-holed at its corners, its curling paper cracked.

Haviland's call came one evening as Tomos was heating a cod fillet in parsley sauce whose carton he'd found stuck to the base of a freezer at the corner shop (which now called itself a *Pryce-Slasher*, or some such). He'd had to scrape away frost to see the photograph that made the small square of fish look huge. The girl on the till, who wore a badge with the words *Jade: Happy to Help*, had said the cod portion's price, without a thank you, or please, or offer of a bag, and, when he asked if the cod portion came with peas (as were shown in the photograph), gave him a queer look.

On the telephone, Haviland went through some pleasantries about how it felt good to be getting his hands dirty on the farm, to which Tomos Tomos made no response.

Haviland then paused and adopted a tone shorn of its heartiness. This, Tomos discerned as the voice men like Haviland – city men – used when it came to the discussion of serious things, like money, business, and the price of tractors.

He gripped the phone tightly and readied himself.

'I was wondering… Anna and I were wondering… about the tractors,' said Haviland. 'We've got some plans for the place and to be honest we could do with…'

Tomos felt a flush, rising in his neck.

*Now* was his moment. *Now* was his time.

He seized it, as if planting a standard… raising his colours, at the side of some great warrior prince – Owain Glyndwr, or Llywelyn ap Gruffudd.

'I'm sorry Mr Haviland…' he began.

'David… please… please call me David,' Haviland said. 'Or "Dai", if you prefer. My mother wouldn't like it. But, well… This is the land of our fathers – yours *and* mine – after all.'

And all of this wrong-footed Tomos, who had not planned for such interjections. Thrown as he was, he now found himself thinking, in his confusion, of cooking times and temperatures for the fillet of cod in parsley sauce… its carton's small print about 'fan' and 'non-fan' ovens – part of which had been left behind when he tore if from the base of the freezer at the *Pryce-Slasher*.

A lorry rumbled past his house, startling him. At Ty Gwyn, nothing of that kind had ever been heard. At night, from the fields and copses, there had only ever been the calls of birds; the occasional snort or whinny of a beast in the otherwise peaceful dark; the bark of a chained dog or roving fox, on some distant farm or hill.

Tomos gathered himself, however, and re-found his furrow.

'Yes, I'm sorry,' he said at last, 'but I could never part with my tractors.'

This last word galvanised him, so that, suddenly, he was working the gears, beginning to roll.

'You won't be the first to tell me to name my price, Mr Haviland. But I never shall. I am them and they are me. And that is how it is between us, you see.'

Tomos now thought of his beauties – all listening quietly, as he imagined them to be, in the blackness of the red barn: Aeronwy, the pretty little Austin with the company's name in a vermillion flourish that flew like a ribbon across the navy panels of her engine housing... Monty, his doughty Field Marshall with the stove pipe chimney that phut-phutted smoke over the fields of Ty Gwyn... and, if his neighbours, including Arwel Davies (whose mere five tractors could never hope to compare with his) missed Monty, then there was always Nerys, the Nuffield, bright as a Belisha beacon, whose beautiful coat could be seen from miles. And then, of course, there was Taran ('Thunder', if Tomos Tomos happened to use the English), the moody, bull-black old Oliver, possessor of the power of the most terrible cumulonimbus cloud, in whose way *nothing* would stand. And...

'I appreciate what you're saying,' Haviland broke in. 'And they *are* beautiful...'

The spine of Tomos Tomos tingled, as if warmed by summer sun.

'But it's not the tractors we want,' said Haviland. 'It's the space. You see, Anna and I have a small enterprise in mind, and we could...'

The tingle in Tomos's spine suddenly ceased.

'Enterprise?' he said, puzzlement – not to say shock – audible in his response.

'Pine. That's what we're thinking of,' said Haviland. 'In the barn. Kitchen tables, wardrobes, chairs, that kind of thing. Maybe some rattan, too. It's all a question of... *space*, really,' he said.

*Rattan?* wondered Tomos Tomos.

He heard a woman's voice behind Haviland, a scuffling sound with the phone (as if a hand was being moved over the mouthpiece, then taken from it).

He pictured Haviland's wife in those boots of hers that

weren't farm boots: hands on her hips... telling Haviland what to say and do.

'What about Ty Gwyn?' said Tomos, eventually.

'Well, we crunched the numbers on that before we came down. And Tom, you're right...'

*Tom* now was it? thought Tomos. Who was this 'Tom' that this stranger, this tractor-less man was bringing into this? It was not him: *he* was Twm, Tomos, Tomos Tomos Twelve Tractors, or even Mr Tomos of Ty Gwyn. Everyone knew that. Except this Mr... *No* Tractors.

Haviland was still talking. 'I can see why you got out, Tom. But then, you're a cleverer man than me.' He seemed to wait for Tomos to say something, but Tomos said nothing.

'So,' said Haviland, 'we're leasing the ground to Arwel Davies...'

'Arwel Davies?' said Tomos (quickly and with a catch in his voice, which he wished had not been there).

'We're keeping the house, obviously...'

Was that *all* he could call it... 'the house'... Ty Gwyn?

'...and we're going to do this, uh, pine. You know. Maybe with a few house plants, candles, cards... Anna's good at that kind of thing.'

'I see,' said Tomos (though he did not see).

Another scuffle came down the phone. '... in the barn,' added Haviland, as if prodded, '... like I said.'

'Well thank you for letting me know. Thank you very much,' Tomos said.

He lowered the phone.

Haviland was still speaking: tinny, remote.

To Tomos Tomos, the other man was like a pilot in films, or even an astronaut, radioing faintly to an airfield... mission control.

Suddenly, Tomos heard in Haviland's crackle something that alarmed him. '... and they were here again yesterday,' Haviland was saying, 'but, of course, I told them the tractors were yours.'

Tomos quickly put the phone back to his ear.

Haviland paused.

'It looked... formal, Tom. They had papers. Anyway, we thought maybe, um, you know... you'd want them... back?'

Next morning, Tomos caught the bus that went once a day every other day from the town in the direction of Ty Gwyn. The bus was empty save for him and the driver.

As it wound through the narrow lanes, Tomos fell into a reverie. He imagined places he'd ride his tractors, given the chance: on the palaces of the politicians in Cardiff and London (for a start): through their very doors and into their chambers and their fancy debates. More easefully, he also saw himself navigating an immense plain occupied by buffalo, under an infinite American sky – nothing in the distance but snow-capped mountains (which he thought he might also scale). Finally, he pictured himself alone, journeying across a mysterious sea of the Moon... his tyres embedding their cross-ply tracks in the soft silver of the lunar surface.

*Oof!!*

The brakes of the bus slammed through him: hurling him forward, throwing him back.

'Iesu!' said Tomos, steadying himself and remembering where he was.

The driver pulled to one side and made way for oncoming traffic.

And then Tomos saw them: one after another of his tractors... passing the bus and ascending the bryn (down which Tomos and the coach had just come).

Monty, the phut-phutting Field Marshall, was leading them in convoy in the lane from Ty Gwyn. At their steering wheels, a squadron of sullen, thick-set men.

The driver pulled the bus in tighter, its door hard against the hedge.

Tomos ran up and down the aisle. He threw his trembling hands to his head, slapped them against the windows, cried out as each tractor passed the bus... as his *loves* passed the bus... as his *life* passed it.

He watched from the back window, face against the glass, as the pert rear of the last – Siani, his sixty-year-old green and yellow John Deere (with bespoke Touch-O-Matic hydraulics) – disappeared over the brow of the bryn.

Skulking on the edge of the auction ring at the beast market and, at other times, sitting alone at tables in cafés frequented by farmers calling into the town, Tomos Tomos heard talk in the weeks that followed about the fate of his 'flock'. One wounding tale held that Taran had been bought by a council in the Eastern Valleys and was now harnessed for the pulling of tar by a road gang, his black thundercloud coat having been overpainted with a grim civic grey the colour of lead. Meanwhile, Monty, the Field Marshall, had been taken to England, or so it was said, and pulled apart for scrap. For her part, Siani, so the whispers went, was in servitude with a travelling fair, tugging the tents, boards and rails of a Ghost Train and the coconut shy that stood next to it. Tomos even heard stomach-churning stories that Arwel Davies, his old neighbour, had bought Nerys, his Nuffield, and had been seen parading her through the streets of the town.

Come evening, he could not sleep for nightmares in which Davies mounted his purchase – in ways that only a mind such as that of Tomos Tomos could possibly imagine.

Some months later, Anna Haviland, having brushed her hair and moisturised her face with an eco-friendly cream, was sitting up in bed one night studying a catalogue.

She lowered its pages and, without looking at him, said to her husband, 'Did you hear that?'

David Haviland had been trying to sleep through his wife's comments about expanding their business into cane sofas and sun-loungers suitable for conservatories.

'*What?*' he now said, irritably.

'*That*,' said Anna Haviland, who, like her husband, had grown used to the quiet that cloaked their farmhouse at night, particularly since the conversion of the beast houses that abutted it into showrooms and stores for the furniture and soft furnishings that their 'farm' now stocked.

They strained their ears to the darkness outside Ty Gwyn.

'It's getting nearer,' Anna Haviland said.

'It sounds like…' David Haviland began.

Ahead of Tomos Tomos, Ty Gywn, the farmhouse that had been his family's for three hundred years, lay white and sepulchral, like some fallen moon on the land.

As it advanced through the night, the ancient arms of the Ferguson Black that he drove were aloft in front of it, so that, seen from the heavens, the tractor resembled a stag beetle – antlers to the sky – as it roared down the silver lane that threaded the bryn.

'Tri ar ddeg!' Tomos Tomos called out to any who would hear him, from his shuddering seat beneath the stars.

'Tri ar ddeg!!'

Above the churning of his engine and the turning of his wheels, his word seemed to hold the still land spellbound.

Rabbits heard him in their holes; foxes halted on the sides of hills.

'Tri ar ddeg!!!' Tomos Tomos cried again, his neck stretched and his head strangely uplifted, as if he were no human now but an old farmyard cockerel gone mad: a glaring-eyed bird of bedlam that crowed and flapped its flea-feather wings *not* for the coming of the dawn, but for the coming of the dark.

('Thirteen!... Thirteen!!... Thirteen!!!')

# The Brass

LATE afternoon sun cast a jewelled light through the ancient stained glass. The rays burnished the breastplate of Sir Dylan Penrhys with ruby, sapphire and emerald pools that flared and waned as clouds passed over the old church of Saint Tathana. Apart from my own absorbed and solitary labours, its tall-grassed yard and cool interior stood stock-still on its yewed and lichened tump, the silence of the summer day unbroken by so much as a rook-caw or bee-murmur.

I had been kneeling there, in that tranquil temple of the Welsh borderland, since morning, delineating and shading on my stretched and weighted paper the form of my subject: his helmet, his face, his body, legs and sword. Then – finally – his feet, and the curious small hound that curled there.

Quite suddenly, I had the strangest sense of a *growl*... being issued by the animal no less (and even the feeling of its head lifting slightly, towards me, as if irritated by my disturbance of its slumbers).

For a moment, I drew back my fingers: fearful, I confess, of a bite.

*Foolishness*, I said to myself, regaining my composure and attributing my fancy to the intensity of my immersion in my task, which was now almost complete.

Steadily, the sun and its gemstone pools drew back from the transept where I toiled, leaving both it and the rest of Saint Tathana's in a deepening gloom that grew chill.

I rose stiffly, stamping my feet to restore in my limbs some circulation of my blood, and ate the last of a sandwich I'd bitten at earlier in the day.

Part of whatever I had absent-mindedly filled it with that morning fell from my hand. A morsel, perhaps, for a church mouse? Anxious, however, to leave no litter, I bent to retrieve it.

In the dim light, I ran my hands over the Godwin tiles and prehistoric flagstones, but found no trace: my fingertips touching only the floor and the rubbing that I had made of Penrhys and his canine companion. Finally, I dismissed the idea that I had dropped anything at all, putting the notion down to my fatigue after the best of a day copying Sir Dylan – moony eyes, sad mouth, slim thighs – who had died 'yonge' of '*ficknesse*', so his memorial said.

As the sun's last embers expired, I collected my weights, scrolled-up my paper and, with Penrhys and his hound under my arm, made my way to the thick and aged north door.

Unfettered darkness fell over Saint Tathana's now: her rood screen, lectern and pews, her venerable stone font, the monuments to the great and good of her seemingly vanished parish – all utterly eclipsed, as I dropped the heavy latch.

That night I slept badly. Of itself this was nothing unusual. I had for some time been having trouble at work. I was 'a creative' at a firm specialising in *image consultancy* – 'public relations' to give it its more workaday term – in a brash part of London full of plate glass and brutal steel. The tipping point had been a meeting at which our boss, Gabriella, told us we'd have to *strive harder* if we and our firm were to achieve our *joint goals* in a *highly-competitive marketplace*. The *bottom line* was 'brass', she said. At the end (already turning on her heel) she asked if there were any questions. For reasons of which I was not wholly aware (then or afterwards), I found myself rising and reciting Rupert Brooke, asking, 'And is there honey still for tea?'

Gabriella and I stared at one another across the pods and pot-plants of our open-plan office. Applause broke out among some, then more, then almost all of my colleagues, who appeared to take my words as a protest (though I wasn't sure I had actually intended them as that). Gabriella headed to the lift followed by some flunkeys. Later, I was seen off the premises by 'security'.

The rubbing was something my doctor recommended. 'One a day,' he said, 'with charcoal or wax. It'll take your mind off things.'

I started with the churches of my neighbourhood, then fanned further afield, shading in earnest in places of worship, grand and small. Chapels, priories, abbeys, cathedrals – I did them all. I was calmer, yes, but I was also increasingly detached from the world: functioning, but like a kind of hermit within it. Returning to my flat, I'd store the various squires, ladies, bishops and abbesses scrolled-up beneath my bed.

*That* night, though – the one that followed my visit to Saint Tathana's – proved strange indeed.

My normal nightmare was one in which Gabriella, in flowing robes, rode the back of a huge and bristled boar, itself cloaked with heraldry in the manner of a medieval horse. The monstrous animal snouted for truffles in a forest where I cowered. Invariably, I revealed myself – to its dripping nostrils, scimitar tusks and foul, yellow teeth – by way of some part of my anatomy that I was unable to conceal (a finger that beckoned to my burial place in leaf litter, a toe that protruded from a hole in a mossed and hollow trunk). But, that night, I saw something different and – in its way – even *stranger*: a thing… a presence… that seemed to have been conjured *not* by any nightmare, but in a curious, waking dream.

I was stirred from my slumbers by an awkward, metallic sound. Drawing myself up on my pillows, my eyes discerned in the darkness a greyish figure, sitting on the end of my bed. His back was to me and he had the attitude of one who was immersed in great thought. Around his form hovered an emanation, a kind of aura or glow. I couldn't see his face, but his pose suggested that his chin was in his palm.

With a chafing sound – the same metallic noise that had awoken me – the figure lifted one leg over the other.

I rubbed my eyes and looked again.

Whether from fatigue or fright on my part – or his – the form melted, like a phantom, from my view. Within a matter of moments, I saw nothing, merely the vague end of my bed and the blackness beyond.

Next morning I went to the park. Since my lay-off from work I'd taken to making a circuit of the lake when not in search of a church and a rubbing. Returning to the block where I lived, I found myself cornered in the lobby by Mrs Khan (from the landing below mine) who, not for the first time, suggested my need of a 'good woman'.

Lowering her voice – our concierge, Jakub, was at his desk (albeit playing some game on his phone) – she asked if I hadn't in fact acquired a 'little friend'. In response to my evident puzzlement, she added that she had heard (while lying in bed beside Mr Khan) a certain 'yelping' in the night. She had not *minded*, she said: she was not the jealous type. And Mr Khan had snored throughout. However, while *she* was open-minded about such matters, *he* was more – she paused to find the right word – *conservative* when it came to such 'things'. It would therefore be wise of me to be 'discreet' lest he should complain to the management about the 'activities' – she seemed to wink – of non-residents in my flat.

A cab drew up outside and she exited (a certain swing, so it seemed to me, in her hips).

In my flat, I lifted the blinds and sprinkled some feed in my fish tank. Its water looked low and I checked for a leak but could find nothing. A siren in the street distracted me, and I thought no more of it.

That night, as usual, I struggled for sleep. The slavering boar made its customary appearance, as Gabriella cracked a whip. Now, however, the three of us weren't in a wood but were circling the lake in the park: countless laps through all kinds of weather: thunderstorms, droughts, snow. Eventually, I fell to my knees at the kiosk that sold coffee and knickknacks.

A door in its wall flew open and I staggered inside. Mrs Khan, who had no logical reason to be there, drew down a shutter as, outside our little castle, Gabriella's steaming, tail-tossing beast snorted wildly and speared footballs with its tusks (between biting at bunting and upturning bins).

Suddenly – in my bed – I sensed something damp, like a snout, nuzzle my face. And I came-to, from my terror.

I sat up on my pillows, and saw him again: the strange, silvery figure from the night before, this time not sitting but standing, fully upright, at the foot of my bed.

'Who are y-you?' I stammered.

He gazed downwards, not really listening – preoccupied, it seemed.

I began again. 'I asked you—'

And now he looked up, interrupted me.

'You really don't look well,' he said. 'Are you ill?'

'A bad dream. That's all,' I answered. 'Anyway,' I added, a little affronted, 'you don't look so good yourself.'

'I've been dead for six hundred years,' he said. 'What's your excuse?'

I shifted on my pillows.

'There's no need for that,' I said. 'Besides, who do you think you are? Coming in here… talking to me like that. I've a good mind to—'

'What?' he said.

I stopped for a moment, swallowed. Adjusting themselves to the gloom, my eyes fell on the decidedly large sword sheathed at his side.

I began again, rather more humbly. 'Look, I don't know what you want,' I said, 'but if you mean to rob me then I can tell you that you've made a mistake. I am, by some margin, the poorest person in this block and I would be very grateful if you would just... go away.'

'Well that's rich!' he replied. 'Considering *you're* the one who brought me here.'

'What do you mean?' I said.

'Don't tell me you've forgotten already!' he shot back, pressing a palm to the pommel of his sword. 'The church! The rubbing! You took long enough. All day as I recall. Infernal charcoal everywhere. Precious little respect for *my* privacy.'

I pushed myself up on my pillows, rubbed my eyes, re-opened them. He was still there: suited and booted in armour plate, his form suffused with a silvery glow, as if lit by its own private moonbeam.

'You're... Sir Dylan Penrhys,' I uttered.

'Thank goodness for that!' he said. 'The ducat drops at last.'

'What are you... *doing*?' I asked.

'Well, at the moment,' he replied, 'I'm exercising his highness.'

'His... *highness*?' I responded (worried as to his meaning).

A small, shining dog suddenly jumped onto my bed: the very hound, I knew immediately, that I had charcoaled in the church at the feet of Penrhys.

Mutt and master now stared at me, and I at them – my disbelief fast melting.

'What is it that you want?' I asked.

'Well, for a start, better living conditions,' said Penrhys. 'Thus far I've had to water Prince' (the hound gave me a haughty look) 'at your absurdly tiny stew pond.'

For a moment I wondered what he meant, before – to coin a phrase – the ducat dropped and I realised he was referring to my fish tank.

'I'm... sorry,' I said, albeit perhaps involuntarily.

'We'll talk about it in the morning,' Penrhys said. 'Now get some rest. You look like—'

'I've seen a ghost?' I broke in. 'Yes… rest,' I said to myself and slid down my pillows.

My eyelids lowered heavily, like a pair of portcullises.

'Don't mind us,' I seemed to hear him say. 'We'll make ourselves at home.'

The morning sun cast a bar of light across my face through a gap in my curtains. Its stripe gave me a strange sense of entombment, as if I were peeping out through a crack in a coffin. I lay in bed for some while, going over what I remembered of the night. Eventually, I pushed aside the duvet and drew out from under the bed the scrolled-up sheet on which I had charcoaled the image of Penrhys.

A weak outline, barely perceptible to my eye, was all that remained of my hours of rubbing.

After breakfast, I collected my car from the basement and drove into the country, determined to return to that church from which I had – according to my night visitors, at least – raised (in spirit) Sir Dylan Penrhys.

Finally, I found myself in Wales and at the lychgate of Saint Tathana's, on the ancient tump that stood like some lonely tor in an otherwise featureless landscape of copses and fields.

A breeze bent the tall, dry grass of the churchyard as I made my way between the lichened headstones and flaking tombs. Save for a slight whisper among the stalks, the setting was as soundless as it had been on my earlier exploration. The temple's interior reposed as previously: warm quarters where the sun shone through the stained glass, and, beyond the rays, gloomy, shadowed solitudes of sudden and intense chill.

I made for the transept where, those days earlier, I had found the memorial to Penrhys. Back then, it had – to my eyes, at least – beckoned me. Now, I struggled to find it. I wondered whether it had in fact been somewhere else: a side chapel or perhaps – in my confusion – even some other church.

To my dismay, I then began to experience the dizziness and the feeling of being light-headed that had affected me intermittently for some while (a condition which had begun prior to my forced leave from work).

My ears seemed to hear a snort of derision. I sensed the tickle of warm breath on my neck.

I fell to my knees, my palms pressing on the indentations of letters, the shallow valleys of vowels, details of dates, that had been polished almost smooth by the passage of centuries.

Focusing my eyes on what my hands had detected, I now saw the memorial to Penrhys: I was right on top of it.

On my previous visit, its brass had been bright: a beacon amid the dark wood, dull stone and dim light of the church. Now, its oblong plate was tarnished, barely decipherable, indistinguishable from the great flagstones that flanked it – with whose boulders it seemed to be melding before me, as I stared.

Had anyone seen me at that moment, head bowed towards Saint Tathana's altar, they might have taken me for some devout pilgrim, or theatrically repentant sinner.

Within my own mind, practically prostrate as I was on Penrhys's monument, I had the strange sense of seeing not *him* there, but... me.

I rose to my feet. I took from a pocket my copy of *Hare's*: the handbook I employed to plot my rubbings (which I always carried with me on my trips). 'A spirited example,' old Hare enthused. 'Fine face, striking sword (in scabbard) and interesting hound at feet.'

I remembered how the entry had caught my eye... then wondered – before dismissing the notion – if I had tumbled into some kind of trap.

I reminded myself that appearances could deceive. Hadn't my working life – making bad companies look good... 'knights in shining armour' – taught me exactly that? Penrhys's monument was *still* there, intact, I told myself. Its discolouration might have been caused by any number of things: a leak from the ceiling, some breakdown in the rota for cleaning (not that Saint Tathana's truly showed much evidence of such a thing).

And yet, even as I stood there and stared, the image on the rectangular plate – whoever it might have been – seemed to fade.

I gathered myself and made for the door.

As I lifted its latch, I heard something behind me... deep in the gloom.

The sound rose again from the stillness.

I willed it to be the sigh of the wind, the scurry of a squirrel, or even – somehow – the chirp of a bird... and I stepped out, into the yard.

But it was, quite clearly, a woman's voice.

As if calling after me, it softly repeated one word.

'Penrhys.'


That night, undressing for bed, I caught sight of him in my mirror: his pearl-grey head peering over my shoulder.

'What are you doing?' he asked.

'I'm getting ready for bed,' I said, '... if it's any business of yours.'

'My, you *are* a dull one,' he replied with a sneer. 'Am I really in the land of the living?'

'And what do you mean by that?' I asked, turning on him.

'Well,' he said, 'a man of your age, with only little fish for friends... Oughtn't you to be *out*?'

'Out where?' I said, buttoning the jacket of my pyjamas.

'Taverns! Playhouses! Quaffing mead! Singing songs! Carousing in the company of...' (he looked me up and down) '... ladies. Or, if you prefer—'

I stopped him. '*You* want to go out,' I said.

'Well, since you mention it,' he said.

He leant snootily on his sword.

I surveyed him.

It then occurred to me that if I did indeed take him somewhere I might, with luck, not bring him back: shrugging him off in a pub, or on a dance floor, or in a queue at a kebab shop. *Thank you and goodnight, good knight.*

'Very well,' I said *un*buttoning my pyjamas.

I looked at his armour.

'Don't suppose you've got something *else* you could wear?'

'Didn't have time to pack, did I?' he snapped. 'Given how a certain tomb-raider disturbed me! This suit *is* a little limiting,' he went on. 'Still, not to worry. Everyone else will see right through me. *You're* the only one who knows, you know.'

'What do you mean by that?' I asked.

'That's how it is between a spirit and his summoner. Didn't they teach you anything at college?'

'Image Management – if you even *know* what that it is,' I snapped back. 'Got a 2:1, actually.'

After two rounds at *The Angel* – sparkling water in my case (I wanted to have my wits about me), sweet cider in his – I suggested we ought to be going (rehearsing in my head suitable places where I might abandon him). Being still relatively early, the takeaways of the neighbourhood had few customers and therefore offered little scope for any move on my part. I settled on the idea of shoving him down the basement steps of one of the big houses in Crécy Road. With any luck he'd end up in a heap – bruised, buckled and unable to right himself in that stupid suit of his.

I was flexing my fingers and switching places on the dimly-lit pavement – to his sword-bearing side – when, suddenly, he stopped.

'Well look at this!' he said, pointing an armour-plated digit.

## HELLFIRE CLUB

The sign glowed red above some railings. A neon arrow throbbed in the downward direction of a cellar.

'Shall we?' asked my tormentor, already making his descent.

The place was… weird: a strange, bohemian underworld whose presence in my neighbourhood I could scarcely credit: velvet drapes, crimson banquettes, decidedly exotic murals, soft lights and even softer piano music. Not uncivilised in its way, yet…

People I half-recognised, and some I actually knew, performed cabaret acts on a small stage around which candle-lit tables clustered. In this bizarre karaoke, Mrs Khan, my neighbour, teased her way (with several winks in my direction, so it seemed) through a fan dance with ostrich feathers to the drumbeat and rasp of a small orchestra in a pit. Mr Khan, who I had (obviously quite wrongly) assumed to be the sternest of men, then appeared in a top hat and tails and went through an array of magic tricks, one of which saw him shoot floral bouquets from his cuffs, culminating in the appearance of a dove on the lacquered crown of his head.

Their turns and those of my other neighbours drew polite applause from the club's clientele. Dylan, as I had sometimes taken to calling him, was a hullaballoo of over-the-top bravoes and encores, which, fortunately, only I seemed to notice.

The most disturbing performance of the night, though, came from Gabriella, who strode onto the stage in the scarlet coat of a ring-mistress, gripping a highly worrisome whip. This she cracked not at lions or tigers but at the boar that I recognised all too readily from my nightmares. At her command, it pranced meekly between podiums, having on its hairy back a pair of silk wings. She ended her act with one final, firm crack of her instrument of obedience and a stare, so it seemed, at me.

'Zooks!' Dylan cried at my side. 'That lady can handle herself! And maybe she would like to handle a certain good knight. Get her over here!'

'Are you quite mad?' I asked.

I shoved him from his seat as Jakub, our concierge, lumbered onto the stage what seemed to be some kind of flugelhorn. 'Come on,' I said, 'we're going!'

At the exit, a goon with a neck rather wider than a side of roast beef refused to let us leave.

'The show's just begun,' he said. (Jakub's purple-faced horn-puffing seemingly the sign that the whole ghastly business was about to repeat.)

'But we've seen it,' I protested.

'That's not the point,' he said, pointing us back to our seats.

'Look! We're leaving!' I said.

'No one's leaving,' he said, 'while the show goes on. Rules of the house.'

I turned to Dylan. 'How about giving me a hand here?' I asked. 'You've got a sword, haven't you? Well... *waggle* it! What sort of damned no-good knight are you?'

I turned back to the heavy, who gave me an odd look. To my surprise, he stepped aside and pushed open the exit door. I brushed past him, Penrhys (timid as a mouse) somewhere in tow, the tip of his scabbard scraping up the steps as we left.

We shuffled home, in drizzling rain, his armour clunking on the pavement, splashing through its puddles.

As – finally – I undressed for bed, there was a curious coda to our very strange evening. I couldn't tell whether it was the light, my tiredness, or due to some other cause, but when I stood in front of my bedroom mirror, and looked in the glass, I was nowhere to be seen.

Penrhys, however, looked back at me... quite clearly.

Bold as brass, it might be said.

In the days that followed, Penrhys pestered me increasingly. 'Entertainment!' he demanded. 'Music! Japes! Jousts!'

Finally, I took him and his mutt over the road to the park.

Was there not a horse he might mount? he wanted to know as we waited at the pelican crossing. I pointed to one in the children's playground that had rubber handles for ears. And where was the deer herd? he continued. Where ran and rutted the boars (the word caused me to wince) and the harts?

'Your attitude is positively medieval,' I told him.

He responded with a puzzled, wounded look (which made me feel faintly guilty).

At the lake, his eyes lit up. 'A veritable feast of fowls!' he declared of its suburban ducks and swans, his gauntlets gripping the waterside railings.

Before I knew it, he'd whistled-up that hound of his and the creature was airborne: flying over the fencing amid mothers and children busily feeding corn and bread crusts to an appreciative flock.

In the next second, Prince, legs splayed fore and aft, was crashing wildly into the lake's green water.

A frightful commotion ensued: snarling, yelping and a thrashing of wings and webbed feet that sprayed a soup of algae over stunned parents and screaming toddlers. Feathers flew amid a cacophony of quacks from flapping and darting ducks, and lunges and hisses from seething swans and furious geese. And, through it all, came Penrhys's insane commentary – 'Good sport! Bravo! Well done, sir!' – ringing in my ears.

Suddenly, I felt weak.

Penrhys's cries were the last words I heard as I had the strange sense of being... submerged.

The entire, disagreeable scene melted to a blur.

When I came-to, I was near the gates, the whole of me soaked, dripping: the debris of black leaves in my hair, a film of foul-smelling slime on my cheeks and my chin.

It was as if I – like some madman – had entered the lake, never mind the devilry of Penrhys and Prince.

Neither showed up at the flat till several hours later. Each as dry as the old psalm and hymn books at Saint Tathana's.

Needless to say, both acted as if nothing had occurred.

My – *our* – lives continued in much the same vein: the strangeness of it all giving way to a kind of normality.

As the days and weeks went on, I came to see little of anyone but them. Given their realness to me, their actuality (or otherwise) to others was something I lost sight of. On the bus or at the cinema, I'd ask for two and-a-half tickets, generally finding that paying-up quickly was the way of ensuring least fuss.

After a while, however, Dylan re-began his nightly moping at the foot of my bed.

Weary of his intrusions, I snapped at him to tell me his problem, or leave me in peace.

He announced, in his flouncy fashion, that he was a knight and, although he could see that *my* existence was rather monkish (save perhaps for a woman's name he claimed I called out in my sleep), that, as a knight, he had knightly needs.

I told him to make himself plain or to clear off and find someone else to haunt. Whereupon he began (with characteristic disregard for my yawns and my repeated glances at my alarm clock) a long and moany harangue about how I had taken him – *seized* him, in fact – from his lawful resting place, in flagrant breach of all codes of chivalry… detaining him in a 'dungeon' that lacked the comforts of even the farmhouse of a malodorous rustic squire… *hostage*, it might be said, in a manner that drove an ox cart through all courtly rules of ransom. (Prince, at this point, leapt onto my covers and eyed me accusingly.) And *if*, Penrhys prattled on, I was determined to keep him there then the least I should do was ensure that, as a gentleman, he was henceforth kept in the manner to which he was accustomed and, specifically, that his *needs* were met.

Given the lateness of the hour and the creeping feverishness I had felt since the episode at the lake, I decided to ignore most of his comments and came instead to what seemed to be his point.

'Needs?' I said.

'A woman!' he responded, sharply.

I paused, swallowed, looked at his breastplate… his sword.

I thought about (although I did not want to think about them) his doubtless fortified nethers.

'That won't be easy… in this day and age,' I said. (I couldn't see him being taken by a dating agency. Knights in shining armour? Strictly imaginary, weren't they? And he'd surely look just that little bit odd at a singles' night. Something *might* be done on the internet. But his photograph? The visor of his helmet? Up… or down?)

'There are, I believe, places men can… go. Not that I've ever used them, of course. *If* they're desperate,' I said.

'I don't mean *any* woman, you fool!' he rebuked me, now openly angry. (Prince by this time was astride me and baring his silvery fangs in my face.) 'I mean *the* woman!'

'And who might that be?' I asked, somewhat timidly.

'Why, the Lady Aneira! Who else?'

'Yes, of course,' I said. 'And where might I find—'

'In the church! Whence you took me!'

'And you want me to?'

'Raise her also! As you raised me! So that, *together*, that sweet maiden and I may… be.'

Weary after Penrhys's intrusions, I dispensed with the idea of driving to Wales. A failure of the trains meant it was late in the day when I finally arrived at Saint Tathana's. Small bats danced around its squat tower in the dusk. Inside the church, I followed the directions Penrhys had given. These took me to a Lady Chapel I had previously overlooked. Aneira's memorial – a beautiful brass – lay near its altar.

I carefully weighted my paper over her, noticing, as I did so, how the small stone chamber seemed sweeter-smelling than the rest of the church.

Kneeling beside her, I began to take her likeness.

I had made only the most tentative first strokes when I felt, through the tips of my charcoal and fingers, the beating of her heart in her breast.

As I worked on – tracing and shading – I sensed warmth radiating upwards through the shroud of white paper.

Soon her eyes came to life: her pupils watching me as I continued to capture her. This I did, I'm not ashamed to say, with some tenderness: blowing fragments of charcoal from her face and her neck. Unless my eyes were deceiving me, her silk scarf at times lifted lightly – as if in a breeze – before re-settling on her shoulders.

As my impression took shape, darkening and extending, I had the sense that she was guiding my hand, encouraging me, rising to me, *leaving* that plate of cold brass.

In a shuddered exhalation, a word seemed to sound from her lips (as if she had recognised and was speaking the name of her saviour). It was the voice that I had heard on my previous departure.

'Penrhys.'

Finally, I felt her take my hand, her cool fingers locking with mine, as she and I raised-up the rest of her.

We stepped from the church hand in hand, the small hound from her pretty feet joining us at her heels.

Together, in the moonlight, we walked the deserted lanes that led from St Tathana's.

The hoots of owls and the calls of other birds sounded lyrically across the hedges and the fields, as if singing a special nocturne they had composed for us.

When, the next day, Penrhys clamped his armoured self around Aneira, I felt some jealousy, I confess. The two of them made little attempt to conceal their feeling that I was surplus to requirements. I felt wronged, I must say, particularly in view of the closeness – intimacy, even – that Aneira and I seemed to have shared in the Lady Chapel. Difficult as it was, I put these sentiments to one side, hoping that now – at last – Penrhys would grant me some peace.

From that time forwards, they carried on like love-struck teens: out at all hours, never telling me when they'd be home. I tried to live my own life, even contemplating a return to work (if my superiors would lower the drawbridge to their castle).

Our domestic 'arrangements' wore me down. Three adults and two dogs in a flat as small as mine just didn't 'go'.

Prince and Duchess (Aneira's pet hound), scampered and barked as they pleased. I feared it could only be a matter of time until there was a complaint from Mr Khan.

One evening, as my 'house guests' cooed and lounged on my sofa, I made a show of consulting my copy of *Hare's* (perched, irritably, on the wicker stool in the corner to which I'd once again been consigned).

My intention was to signal that, if so inclined, I could raise-up – with ease – an alternative knight and lady... indeed an entire court, if I so wished.

The pair ignored me, giggling instead at the way Prince and Duchess were running amok.

I pictured Mr Khan coming up in the lift, our concierge Jakub riding shotgun (with his flugelhorn).

Rather than finding any new brasses in *Hare's*, my eyes and fingers fell, once again, on the page relating to Penrhys.

I re-read the guide's warm appreciation of his image. But this time I also turned the page (something that – strangely – I had previously failed to do). Had they been stuck together? I wondered. Deliberately perhaps? In an act of concealment or 'airbrushing' of the kind in which we – I still thought of myself as being on the books of my former firm – specialised in our tower by the Thames?

I read the rest of *Hare's* notes with alarm – including the account of Penrhys's death – 'yonge' from '*ficknesse*'... and the part played by Aneira,

Hare disclosed that far from being the gallant knight of his own imaginings, Penrhys was, in fact, a penniless gadabout with nothing to his name save his title, inherited after the deaths of several better-placed siblings who'd perished on campaigns that he had flunked. Aneira had been his betrothed in a piece of Machiavellian manoeuvring the precise intent of which had been lost with time, but which might well, Hare commented, have had its roots in some attempted monopoly over mutton or wool. She, Hare went on, was something of a schemer (and clearly far removed from the romantic figure my mind had naively conjured).

Their betrothal had ended in high drama. Learning of the romps of rakish Penrhys with a rival maiden of their parish, Aneira (her name a derivation of 'snow' – and clearly the possessor of a very cold heart) gave her husband-to-be hemlock in an assignation in her bedchamber – a deed which, in due course, earned her a date with the executioner's axe.

Aneira's brass was pictured beneath this account of her times and crimes – all tousled locks, darkly ringed eyes and a mouth corrupted by the cruellest of curls – like an antique *Wanted* poster from the American West.

This image – far more moll than maiden – was utterly at odds with that of the innocent I had encountered in the Lady Chapel at St Tathana's. But it was as nothing to the shock that came next. For, studying the picture more closely, I saw – putting to one side her look of having passed a rough night in the cells – how closely she resembled a woman I knew all too well.

'The bottom line is brass!' the voice of Gabriella echoed in my ears.

My copy of *Hare's* almost fell from my hands.

I took a grip of it and, over the top of its pages, observed Penrhys and his wicked lady (Aneira or Gabriella – whichever of them it might be).

I was shocked – and frightened, let it be said – that they could be there... *larking*... in my lounge: the wastrel and his murderess. Not to mention their horrible hounds.

As I closed *Hare's* covers, the eyes of my 'guests' seemed to look at me – and narrow.

I needed to act, I told myself. My time was running out.

Next morning, I slipped from my flat quietly, nosing my car from the block's basement in the pewter-grey light of the dawn.

I set off for Saint Tathana's, determined to lay the whole matter to rest.

As my car threaded the narrow lanes of the deep country that enclosed the old church, a storm that had threatened for hours erupted at last. Black clouds, that had massed in the sky like great sea galleons, drilled down rain.

The road ahead of me became treacherous with ruts and pools, as if it were something from turnpike days – or earlier. I noticed that the thatched cottages that occasionally clung to its sides were now mere hovels at best.

It was as if I had crossed into an altogether older – and more primitive – time.

When I reached it, the yard of the church was no longer sweet and easeful, but restless and bleak. Its headstones seemed to bend themselves towards one another as if exchanging conspiratorial whispers; the windswept grass arching as if 'in' on the secret of the murmurous memorials and tombs.

The exposed roots of a tar-dark yew clawed one side of the tump on which the church sat. The tree did this as if seeking to withhold not only Saint Tathana's stones and beams, but something far uglier.

Having entered, I struggled to shut the great oaken door. A savage gust blasted it back at me. I fought to keep my feet. Finally, I heaved it to, and the heavy latch fell with a decisive smack.

At this, the old church gave out a sound that seemed like a gasp.

That apart, her marble monuments, dusty kneelers and threadbare banners all reposed as previously: silent and still.

I gathered myself, resting one hand on the ancient font, which stood burdensome and grey in the gloom.

I watched for a moment as the thick, crimson curtain over the vestry swayed in the draught from the storm.

The intense coldness of the font's stone caused me to snatch back my hand. Could any infant have survived baptism there? I wondered. Feverous death – 'yonge of *ficknesse*' – would surely have ensued.

As I advanced into the aisle, the gale's ferocity grew. Rain squalled against Tathana's stained glass, as if determined to drain all colour from the panes. For an instant, I seemed to see water streaming the pale cheeks of martyrs and saints, like so many tears.

Wind all the while whistled and surged and sucked at the church's old stones, so that, as I walked between them, one word seemed to taunt me from its darkly ranked pews.

The serpent-like hiss came again and again.

'Penrhys... Penrhys... Penrhy*sssss.*'

I refused to let this invocation distract me.

I found the brass of Penrhys.

And in the dim light I knelt beside it.

Its form was now even blacker than before. No face or limbs could be seen. It was more like the mouth to some pitch-dark pit than a memorial in appreciation of one who was missed.

I weighted my paper over it, and began.

My face and, in time, the rest of me, I recognised, of course.

How could I not?

There, it – *I* – appeared, on the paper in front of me.

I had found myself, at last.

What was more was that after all of my solitude – my countless rubbings in so many empty temples – I was now no longer alone.

At my side, stood the Lady... Gabriella, whose cup I took, drank and gave thanks for, as I charcoaled on – and shaded – into the dark.

'Brass,' I heard her say above me, as my worldly self withdrew.

'The bottom line is bra*sssss.*'

# The Gate

WILLIAMS was walking the path that ran behind the houses which backed onto the playing fields. It was late afternoon. Sunlight was streaking through the gaps between the properties and glancing in white flashes from the tops of the walls that curtained the right side of the way.

Every so often, the brightness dazzled him. The houses formed a jagged line on a ridge and were old, big and gloomy. Many had seen better days and were now flats occupied by singletons of the less well-off kind, students and shift workers. Their gardens fell away in long plots that were largely overgrown. Apart from the bursts of sun, the path – caught between the mossy walls and the line of sycamore trees that skirted the fields – lay in cool, dark shade. Tall, dying grass leaned into Williams, seeding itself on his trousers and his shoes as he walked.

Suddenly, a nettle stung his right hand. He stopped, put the skin to his mouth and sucked. The hairiness of his skin against his lips surprised him. He looked at the small mark below his wrist. The sting, together with a shard of sunlight stabbing between the houses, disorientated him.

For a moment, he stood there, wavered. He looked at the nettle that rose insolently at his hip: the biggest in a clump that climbed from some blackened bricks in the wall beside him. A wasp now buzzed near his face. He stepped back, twisted, batted it away. As he did so, he noticed a shaft of light behind him. It shone through a gate that stood open in the wall. A butterfly fluttered in the beam. Williams wondered why he hadn't noticed this when walking past only a moment earlier. He walked back to the wooden gateway, and through it.

The garden, unlike most of those that could be seen from the far side of the fields, was cultivated, but not neat. Williams stepped along a rough border that ran between beds of vegetables. On one side were green beans strung around canes, some of which had collapsed. On the other, potato plants wandered scruffily towards a wall that sprouted foxgloves and which was overhung with elderflower from the garden next door. His eyes fell on a small stone donkey standing in some weeds. What seemed like the smashed shells of snails littered the low plateau of its saddle.

'Can I help you?' a voice asked.

Williams looked up, swung around.

For an instant, his eyes fixed on a rind of fat – dark, leathery – dangling from a bird-table. The table leaned in the angled manner of a headstone in a churchyard. Williams hadn't noticed the man. Nor the fire that he'd been tending behind the bean canes, which now sent up sparks and milky-coloured smoke.

'I said, "Can I help you?"' the man repeated. He stepped from behind the fire.

The man was old and held a stick. He was tall and almost skeletally thin. Drab skin the colour of the bean canes clasped itself tightly on his pinched face and prominent nose. Grey-white hair fell in heavy licks over his forehead. His clothes hung from him, as if taken from someone larger: tan trousers that looked to be corduroy, a white shirt that showed his neck (which was long and thin), a cardigan that was rust-coloured.

'I've been stung,' Williams said.

'Stung? What by?' said the man.

'A nettle,' said Williams.

'A nettle?' said the man, tilting his head, as if to fix his right eye on Williams, as if that eye were better than his left.

'Yes,' said Williams, '… on the path… in your wall.'

The man seemed to tense, to tighten his hold on the stick. 'And now you're threatening me?' he said. 'Is that it?'

'No—' Williams began.

'That path is *officially* closed,' said the man. 'Any use is at *your* risk. I've no liability. As far as the law is concerned, *you* are trespassing.'

The man's face, which had been bloodless, took on a raspberry flush.

Williams looked at the stick, how the man was holding it, as if it were a weapon, drawn.

'I didn't know. I'm sorry,' he said.

The man saw how Williams was looking at the stick. He lowered it but kept it at his side. 'So why *are* you here?' he asked.

'I'm looking for something,' said Williams.

As he spoke, a heap of brambles on top of the man's fire caught light. The brambles fizzed as the flames went through them.

The man stepped away from the blaze. 'What?' he said.

'I said "I'm looking… for something",' Williams said.

'I heard that,' said the man. '*What* are you looking for?'

'A kite,' said Williams, calmly. 'My boy was flying it.'

'When?' said the man.

'Yesterday,' said Williams, '… on the fields. It came down. It might have—'

'A kite?' the man interrupted. 'I think I'd have seen that. I think I'd have remembered that. Nothing wrong with *my* eyes. From the house, I can see clean over the fields, and beyond. I can see right over the bay.'

Williams looked at the house. It was tall, end of a terrace. A fascia the colour of dishwater had come away in places to expose the brickwork beneath. Some laundry hung from a line across a small yard. A TV aerial of the kind no one installed any more clung to the black stack of a chimney.

The man saw how Williams was looking at the house. 'Is that *it*?' he asked.

'Yes,' said Williams.

'Well, I'm sure I haven't seen a kite. What colour was it?'

'Red,' said Williams. And then he added, 'In the shape of a diamond.'

'Well, as I say, I haven't seen it, but I'll look out for it,' said the man.

They stared at each other for a moment.

'Thank you,' said Williams. He turned to leave.

'How old is your boy?' the man called after him.

Williams turned back.

'Eight,' said Williams.

Suddenly, the man hunched himself and began to cough. The flames of the fire had given way to thick, slate-coloured smoke which a breeze was now blowing across the garden so that the man stood in a dense bank of it.

'Are you all right?' Williams asked.

'Perfectly,' said the man, straightening.

Williams continued down to the gate.

As he drew it behind him, he looked for a moment at the man, who was still watching him – erect now... even haughty – amid the drifting clouds of smoke.

That night, Williams was troubled by a dream. He was a boy again. He was in the back seat of his parents' car and they were on a touring holiday in France. His father announced they were low on petrol and that they would need to find a filling station where they could stop. At the filling station, his father got out and spoke to the attendant. Williams watched through the side window, his nostrils and lips against the trim of the car door. He saw his father enter the shop at the station even though his father seemed to be wearing no trousers. Meanwhile, his mother was saying words that he could not hear correctly from her seat in the front. It was as if she were speaking to him through the radio and doing this from a place far away, her signal dropping in… fading out.

In a cage beside the doorway to the shop was a bird. It was black, about the size of a jackdaw, and it stared at Williams, who returned its look. For a moment, he caught sight of his father who was inside the shop, asking for something. Then he looked back at the bird. And now the creature was different. On its neck was the head of the man from the house by the fields. The bars of its cage had been replaced with the metal forks of the TV aerial from his chimney. Meanwhile, the attendant, all pitted nose and pocked cheeks, pressed the nozzle of the petrol pump hard into the car. The birdman hopped about in his cage, cocking his head, eyeing Williams, who backed away from the window. The numbers on the old-style pump whirled around in a blur. The attendant yanked out the nozzle with a leer, and Williams slid back to the window.

His father came out of the shop, now with his trousers on. Tom Williams saw his son staring at the cage from the back of the car. He stopped beside it and looked at the bird. Williams heard it call out, the sound entering the car through his mother's wound-down window.

'*You* are trespassing!' the birdman trilled irritably between hops.

'Look Bobby!' Williams's mother was saying in her drifting voice. 'That bird is talking French.'

His father stood by the cage, smiling. 'Can you hear it, Bobby?' he was saying. 'Can you hear it?'

They drove off, the attendant grinning from the step of the shop; beside him the birdman, poking his neck – head tilted, eye glaring – through the bars of the cage.

In almost next to no time Williams's father was announcing – on a road lined with poplar trees – that they were low on petrol and that he would have to stop to fill up again. And they pulled in at what only Williams seemed to recognise as the same filling station.

Everything that had been gone through played out in the same way again… and again… and again.

A rectangle of light brightened around the blind in Williams's bedroom.

He threw off his bedclothes and went to the window. He opened the slats of the blind just enough so that he could see onto the road outside his block. Even so, the light bruised his eyes. And, again, he remembered…

He and his parents were now past the avenue of poplar trees and approaching a crossroads. Williams was behind his father: seated in the back, head leaning against the door, staring into the distance beyond the car's wing mirror. They passed a stall selling big green watermelons and yellow and red fruit in trays angled to the road, half-in, half-out of the shade of a shack.

'This one sounds nice,' his mother said, reading aloud a description of a guesthouse from a book she was holding. The guesthouse was in a village with a river and an old abbey that was open to the public.

'Do the rooms have baths?' Williams's father asked. 'That's what I want: a nice, long soak.'

And then his mother's voice changed from her reading one to one that was high and quick. 'Oh Tom! Did you see that stall? We could do with some fruit. Can we go back?' She turned in her seat to Williams. 'Would you like some fruit, Bobby?'

Although he heard her, Williams kept his eyes on the strip of dusty verge that separated the road ahead from the fields of maize at its side.

'I can probably turn around up there,' Williams's father said, looking at the crossroads ahead of them.

'What do you fancy?' his mother asked his father.

'I'd like some peaches,' he said. 'I'd like to sink my teeth into a nice, juicy peach.'

'Anything else?'

'No, just peaches.'

They were nearing the crossroads now. The sky was cloudless: a blanket of blue that occupied his sight in a way that made Williams think of the sea, except that everything was upside down.

A breeze stirred the tassel-tops of the maize.

Williams heard the car's indicator *tick-tock*.

'Where did I put my bag?' Williams's mother asked.

'It's under your seat,' said his father.

'Under my *seat?*'

'You left it on the seat – in plain sight. Anyone could have taken it. So I put it under there. You need to be more careful with that bag. It's got our passports. It's got everything in it.'

Williams's mother bent forward and felt with her hands under the seat.

'I can't find it.' she said.

'It's there. I put it there,' his father said.

He was slowing, pulling into the crossroads now, swinging the car around. 'I put it there this morning.' He let the car idle, leaned over, began to feel under his wife's seat with one hand.

'Oh, *I've* got it,' she said, brushing his hand away.

'Thank heaven for that,' said his father. 'You know, sometimes—'

Only Williams saw the oncoming truck.

It was two days later when a farmer found him, still sitting on the back seat: the only part of the car – crushed metal and smashed glass apart – that had survived: he and it flying deep into the maize field beside the highway. The farmer took him to the police. At the counter at the gendarmerie, the farmer held Williams's hand. 'Il y a un garçon,' the farmer said.

Williams now washed, left his flat and went into town. He ate breakfast at a café and afterwards sat on a bench in a precinct where he looked at a girl with green hair who was busking on a guitar. He remained there during a rain shower, long after the girl had gone. Later he walked to the playing fields. He watched a woman calling a dog which was big and loose and chasing some Canada geese.

He walked from the fields to the path at the back of the houses and started to make his way down it. He remembered the nettles. He raised his arms and hands so that they were level with his ribs. He felt the warm wetness of his T-shirt after the rain, the heaviness of his jeans.

The man was in the gateway, head sticking out, eyes inspecting the path. 'I wondered if you'd come,' he said. 'I've got something for you.' He turned back into the garden. Williams stepped through the gate and followed him.

The falling sun filled the plot with a purple-pink wash, silhouetting its canes and other ramshackle fixtures. Williams and the man picked their way between its heaps and its bushes and beds.

'Wait here,' the man said.

He left Williams on a rough turf path and went into a shed that Williams had seen the day before. It listed and looked like it had been nailed together from old doors and bookcases.

The man came out carrying something: the object and his own figure unclear in the tinted, failing light.

'Here,' he said, passing what had been in his hands to Williams. 'One red kite.'

The diamond of nylon, taut on its balsa crucifix, was feather-light on Williams's fingers.

'I made it,' said the man, 'for your boy... in case you didn't find his.'

They each looked at the kite.

'Have you?' the man asked.

'What?' said Williams.

'Found it?'

'No,' said Williams.

The man seemed pleased. 'It's red,' he said.

'Yes,' said Williams.

'I make things,' said the man. 'It's what I like to do...

now. I had this sheet. Well, it was no good to me. Scarlet. Like something from a bordello. Never slept a wink on it. Don't really know how it came to be there.'

'Where?' said Williams.

'The airing cupboard,' said the man, as if surprised.

'Here, you'll need this.' He handed Williams a large ball of twine. 'I've made a hole in the wood. Run it through there, tie it tight and your boy will be fine.'

'Thank you,' said Williams.

The man nodded. His eyes seemed to shine.

'Will he fly it?'

'Yes.'

'When?'

'Soon,' said Williams.

'On the fields?' asked the man.

'Yes.'

'I'll look out for it then,' he said, '… from the house.'

The man noticed Williams's clothes: the fact that they were wet, almost sodden.

'Get caught in the rain, did you?'

Williams said nothing.

'Well, you can stop your searching now,' the man went on. 'It may not be the greatest kite in the world, but at least you'll have one: your boy, I mean.'

'Thank you,' said Williams.

'Anything could have happened to yours,' said the man. He made a flick with his head. 'Seen some of these gardens? People round here! Bloody students! Save A Whale? They don't give a damn! Could be anywhere, your kite. In one of their jungles, I expect.'

The man moved towards Williams, as if in some effort to see – closely – what Williams was thinking. As he did so, Williams smelt the man, his odour. In doing this, he felt that – somehow – he knew the man: the stained linoleum on his kitchen floor, the pantry in which butter (and little else) sat melting in a dish, the sharp sliver of soap – grained with dirt – on a small, pimpled mat between taps that were old and stiff.

'Well, I've got to get on,' said the man. He turned and headed up the garden.

Williams made for the gate: the kite and coarse twine in his hands.

Suddenly, the man's voice came after him.

'What's his name?'

Williams turned. In the shadow cast by the house, he could barely see the man. He wondered if the man was still there. Then, in a small pool of light, Williams saw him, or at least what seemed to be his head: angled, looking down.

'Bobby,' said Williams.

'Bring him,' the man's voice called back, 'when you fly the kite. I'd like to meet him.' The man's head had moved from the light now and Williams struggled to see him. The voice continued, 'You'll bring him... yes?'

'Yes,' said Williams, and he turned and stepped through the gate.

That night, Williams did not dream, or sleep. He lay on his bed and listened to the cars on the road as they passed his block. He thought about whales and wondered why the man was so opposed to saving them.

In the morning, he caught a bus and stayed on it for two hours. He sat upstairs, the kite beside him, on the seat at the back. The bus ran from the railway station to a depot on the other side of town and then back to the railway station in a continuous shuttle. Williams had previously discovered that, as long as he bought a ticket to get on, no one ever asked him to get off. One time, having ridden it for the best of a day, he'd shouted at the driver to open the door. Having leapt off, Williams then urinated against the wall along the seafront, as the bus pulled away. Some of the passengers watched.

Now the bus passed the harbour and the scruffy strip of beach. The tide was out and the shoreline was empty. Williams wondered if the man had ever seen a whale... if a whale had somehow given him offence: slighted him, soaked him with its spout. He thought of the man... sitting in the window at the top of the house, looking over the bay – from his crow's nest – scanning the sea... tutting.

Williams picked up the kite and got off the bus.

He walked with it to the centre circle of one of the football pitches on the playing fields, then stood there and waited. Before long, he felt a breeze from the beach. Slackening the ball of twine, he let the wind take the kite. He reeled out the line and the kite rose into the sky, the wind scudding it in a ripple-rattle of sound.

In his high window, the man's heart quickened and his thin lips moved as if he were speaking to someone who was near. The kite soared, looped and traced figures of eight. The man cocked his head excitedly: first this way, then that. He smiled... laughed... roared... *sang* – the kite seemingly exceeding every possible hope he might have had: its climbing and diving diamond lacerating the grey-blue dusk with spectacular scarlet streaks.

When Williams opened the gate, the man was standing at the top of the garden.

'That was wonderful!' the man called out. 'I loved every minute. It made me feel... young!'

Even in the dim light, Williams could see how the man was looking – expectantly – beyond him, head to one side, a bulging eye on the open gate.

The man stepped forwards.

'And the boy?' he asked. 'Where is the maestro? The magical one?'

The man moved nearer. He swung his head from left to right, surveying the garden in front of him for any presence that he might have missed.

'Bobby!' he called out. 'Are you there?'

The man was now at the very edge of the part of the garden that lay in shadow. Williams stood motionless in the last of the light. He and the man were within touching distance.

He felt the man's breath – warm... sour – on his cheeks.

The man stared at him in silence.

'There *is* no boy, is there?' the man said eventually. 'There never was any... *son.*'

Williams said nothing. He stared back at the man. And now he held the kite before him in a way that made it look not like a toy, but a shield.

The man bent towards Williams.

'You're just the same, aren't you?' he said. 'Here to steal. I knew it the minute I saw you – barging in. You'd have it all, wouldn't you? Peaches! Melons! You'd take the lot! Forbidden fruit!'

Williams felt the man's spit.

'Should I take you to the police?' the man continued. 'Or deal with you myself? Admit it! Whoever you are! There is no boy! There is no... BOBBY!'

Suddenly, from out of the shade, the man's stick scythed down on Williams.

He gripped it, stopped it – an inch from his temple – snatched it from the man.

'There *is* a boy!' Williams shouted, his hand tightening on the stick, wrenching it from the man. 'There is!'

The man slipped. He fell so that his shoes and, above them, his long, thin legs flailed in the faint light. He tried to scrabble up the slope... on his buttocks... into the shadow: feet kicking, palms pushing at the garden's cold turf.

Williams went down to the open gate. He swung it shut, dropped the latch, bolted it.

Then he walked back up the slope and into the darkness.

From its blackness, came a grotesque squawking and rustling.

As he advanced, Williams held up what were no longer his kite and the stick that he'd seized from the man, but his sword and his shield.

'Can you hear it, Bobby?' his father – somewhere – was saying.

# Clippings

IN what they both knew to be her twilight years, Harry Blench began to ask his employer Miss Cannington-Dew about his future at Minchbury Manor, where he'd been the gardener for close on half a century.

His early enquiries were made obliquely with comments such as 'I suppose I shan't be needed here very much longer' and 'I dare say the new squire will be taking charge of all of that'. Near the end though, while Miss Cannington-Dew still had the strength of limb and mind to attend to the details of the manor and its sizeable estate, Blench raised the matter of his position rather more directly.

Finding her at some papers in her study one morning, he asked simply, 'Will I still be wanted?'

Appreciating his concern, Miss Cannington-Dew replied that there would always be a place for him at Minchbury Manor.

After that, Blench didn't raise the matter anymore, holding that he, Miss Cannington-Dew and the garden (for that matter) had what was then – and perhaps is still – spoken of in England as 'an understanding'.

When Miss Cannington-Dew's end finally came, her departure was sudden but peaceful – in her bed after a walk through Minchbury's gardens, to the song of a blackbird one still and perfumed dusk. It was, thought Blench, as if his employer had engaged in a last act of communion… absorbing Minchbury and ensuring that everything was as it should be, before nodding to herself with quiet satisfaction and taking her leave.

Prior to her passing, Blench did, however, inform his mistress of one particular thing. And this was the state of his shears. The blades were becoming blunt, he said. Never mind his grinding of them in the potting shed, they seemed incapable of delivering their true, sharp cut of old.

When Miss Cannington-Dew's will was read he was pleased to find she had remembered him and his worry – a provision in her will stating: *'And to Minchbury's loyal gardener and guardian, Mr Henry Blench, one new – and sharp – pair of shears.'*

The gesture meant a great deal to Blench, who received the shining blades from her solicitor at Minchbury one morning, their keen edges and steely tips glinting in the sun: confirmation, Blench considered, that his work at ancient Minchbury was indeed not yet done.

Even so, when Oliver Luston inherited his deceased aunt's estate, as Blench had long known Luston surely would, the veteran groundsman, who'd never gardened anywhere else (save for the small plot at his cottage), grew uneasy for his tenure.

Relations between the men had been awkward since Luston's boyhood. Once, when Luston had been six or seven, Blench had put him over his knee and given him a spanking, having caught the wayward youngster hurling windfall apples at the topiaries of the manor's yew hedges.

The hedge carvings were Blench's pride, albeit perhaps not his joy: there was for him something more important in them than a quality as trite as that. For one thing, they had begun their lives under his grandfather who, along with Blench's father, had served Miss Cannington-Dew's parents and grandparents as gardeners at Minchbury for their entire careers. Blench had dutifully maintained the creations, which included a tusked elephant and an impressive castle, as well as a cupid complete with bow and arrow, while adding numerous works of his own.

Over the decades, Minchbury's many topiaries grew to a remarkable gallery of garden monuments. They included Father Time with his scythe and hourglass; a fine pheasant and a salmon, in a nod to the shooting and fishing that had taken place on the estate in times past; a large pipe in the form of a traditional briar with its own coil of 'smoke' (a memorial to Miss Cannington-Dew's father), and a magnificent penny-farthing bicycle (this being the particular interest of her grandmother). As far as Blench was concerned, the sculptures embodied the estate and were the protectors of its spirit. He had the sense that, rather like the ravens of the Tower of London and the Barbary apes on the Rock of Gibraltar, as long as they were there – manning the battlements – all would be well.

In the evenings, by his fireside in his cottage in the village, he often thought of them: keeping watch, vigilant, in the gloaming.

Upon his arrival to take up residence as Minchbury, Oliver Luston set about inspecting his new property. He spent several highly satisfactory hours fingering his aunt's former possessions, scrutinising the hallmarks of her silver and peering into the corners of paintings – blowing away dust, where necessary – for the artists' signatures (whose names – and prices at auction – he checked keenly on his smartphone). Having roamed proprietorially through the rooms and cellars of the house, his eyes came to rest on the garden.

Standing in the window of what had been his aunt's study, Luston surveyed Minchbury's lawns, borders, bowers and hedges. Yes, he noted, *they* – the topiaries – were *still* there: the windmill with its sails, the aeroplane that everyone thought so clever, the motorcar, the hot air balloon 'lifting off' with its basket... and all the rest. And to Luston they were as dislikeable as ever: mock full of life, intense with restraint, verdant yet dead, intolerably hemming the house, the grounds... him. He would have them out, root and branch. *And* that old bugger Blench: he hadn't forgotten that spanking.

Through the glass of the window, Luston heard a sound – a soft, scraping sound – that was irritating – to *his* ears at least – for its determined irregularity (as if the perpetrator were pruning something – and pruning with particular care). In the manner of some distinctive smell, or a memento discovered in a drawer, the noise transported Luston to his boyhood. And he was immediately certain of its source.

Blench appeared from behind one of the hedges, carrying a stepladder.

Unchanged by the decades – at a distance, at least – save for a slight stoop and the thinning of his hair, the gardener wore the same clothes that Luston remembered: a leather apron and a white shirt with the sleeves rolled up, as might have been seen on a ship's surgeon in the days of Nelson.

Luston watched as Blench climbed the stepladder to a topiary of a swan that had been one of Miss Cannington-Dew's favourites. Near the top of the ladder, Blench turned and looked back at the house.

For a moment, the two men saw each other across the garden. And from all of those years earlier, the smack of Blench's hand on Luston's backside renewed its reverberation – sounding, clearly, in the ears and minds of both men, and hanging between them, or so it seemed, in the heavy air of the afternoon – all birdsong and buzzing of insects giving way to its echo.

Each man looked away, Luston seeming to sense – even now – the sting in his buttocks.

Blench paused, then raised his shears to the swan's neck... to clip some new and unwanted growth.

That night, in his aunt's four-poster bed, Luston slept badly. The topiaries of the manor's garden came to life in a dream that disturbed him. The large wheel of the penny-farthing, the sails of the windmill and the propeller of the aeroplane all began to turn, the latter taxiing busily along the top of its tall hedge. Smoke curled from the briar pipe, and the salmon swished its tail. The hot air balloon rose from its mooring and blotted out the sun. The cupid's arrow meanwhile flew at him, not singly but in a horrible hail that arced across the garden in a sky-blackening swarm. Conscious of his nightmare, Luston vowed in his sleep to 'deal' with the creations. 'Off with your heads,' he muttered in his sheets. 'Off with your heads, the lot of you!'

Suddenly, Luston came-to in the dark.

The cause of his awakening was a painful sensation at the side of his head: a sharp stinging that ran the length of his left ear.

He sat up in the curtained womb of his aunt's four-poster, wondering what on earth the awful smarting could be.

As he pondered the possibilities – a blockage of wax, an ache from a tooth, some kind of sciatica or chill (there were plenty of queer 'cold spots' at Minchbury) – his discomfort seemed to ease.

And, in time, he fell back to his pillow… and shallow, fitful sleep.

Next morning, in a mood even less charitable than normal, owing to his disturbed night, Luston began to formulate his 'vision' for Minchbury and, in particular, its grounds.

The hedges and topiaries would go; of that, he was certain. And, out with them, much of the lawn. In their place, he would have a swimming pool – Beverly Hills blue: that was the hue he was looking for – with loungers on terraces and awnings against the sun. (One of the several odd things about Minchbury, as far as Luston was concerned, was that, never mind its mildewed 'feel' and the mouldering presence of Blench, the place somehow caught more than its fair share of sun; it was really quite a trap.)

There would be a barbecue and a bar (naturally), thought

Luston, his mind still plotting, and pretty things down from town for weekends; longer, if they wished.

His mind then turned to Blench, who – stubborn taproot that he was – wouldn't like any of it, of course. Once again, Luston remembered the gardener putting him over his knee and Blench's growl (his voice had always possessed one, even when young). 'I'm going to give you a clip you won't forget.'

Well, now Blench would suffer some punishment, Luston nodded to himself. For *he* was lord of the manor now, and he would do with Minchbury whatever he damned well pleased.

Luston recalled with a shudder his failures, the travails he'd suffered, the humiliation and depth of his fall: City financier to 'sales executive' at a small-fry estate agency: a showroom by a bus shelter, under the seediest 'sauna' imaginable.

He'd served his time as heir. Now, he meant to enjoy himself. There'd be no going back.

That afternoon, Blench went to the house, thinking it best to show some courtesy to his new employer. He rang the bell at the door to the kitchen garden at the rear of the manor. After some moments, Luston opened it.

'Mr Oliver,' said Blench, removing his hat and attempting a smile.

'Blench,' said Luston, coolly, returning the greeting.

'Beggin' your pardon, sir…'

Blench told Luston some expenditure was needed. His stepladder was wormed and distinctly rickety: it had been there since the days of Miss Cannington-Dew's parents, and nobody wanted an accident.

Luston, standing firmly on the step above Blench, brushed the enquiry aside. There would be no need, he said. He had plans for Minchbury. What he actually wanted to know, he continued, were Blench's own intentions. 'At your time of life,' said Luston, 'I expect what you *really* want is a cut in your hours.'

He told Blench to go away and come up with 'a spot of self-pruning, some ideas for scaling back'. There was no huge rush, Luston said, but really and truly the sooner the better. Neither of them was getting any younger. If he wanted to pack things in completely... to 'cut loose' for a well-earned retirement, said Luston (enjoying the concern that seemed to come over the gardener's face), he would entirely understand.

That night, pleased with his vision for Minchbury and how he'd dealt with his old adversary Blench, sleep came sweetly to Luston on the pillows of his aunt's four-poster. Until, that is, a pain – similar to that of the previous night, albeit several degrees greater – caused him once more to awake in the small hours: the affliction this time running the length of his right earlobe.

Luston rose from the bed and paced around his room, holding one hand to his aching ear. He wandered to the chamber's mullioned window and looked out on the moonlit garden.

To his surprise, he thought he saw a shape, perhaps even a figure.

He could not be sure, for his eyes were watering with the awful pain and his head was cocked at an awkward angle, but the form, if that's what it was, seemed to retreat over the lawn beyond the fishpond and sundial, and to then slip away and disappear.

Some while after this, Luston's agony ebbed and, in time, he returned to the four-poster, and slept.

Next morning, Luston welcomed the first of what he hoped would be many pretty things as a guest of the manor.

After lunching on the contents of a hamper brought by his visitor, he and the pretty thing whiled away the afternoon, frolicking in Minchbury's grounds.

At one point, the pretty thing became separated from an item of underwear – the airborne latter coming to rest on the topiary tip of Father Time's scythe.

Blench, who'd been weeding a nearby border, rose

soberly on his ladder and removed the offending garment, delivering a determined cut through the crotch.

That night, Luston (his vigour and rigour boosted by various potent powders that the pretty thing had brought) romped wildly with his guest in Miss Cannington-Dew's four-poster.

Sated at last, the two of them slept.

In the small hours, however, Luston awoke suddenly, gripped by a terrible pain in his mouth. The source of the agony seemed to be his tongue. Except that, bizarrely, his tongue didn't seem to be… *there*.

When he tried to utter a sound – goodness how he wished to howl – the only noise that came forth was a kind of gargle.

His mounting panic roused the pretty thing beside him.

Together – Luston's eyes bulging and his nostrils flaring, like those of some mad bull – they forced their fingers down his throat, and drew out the disappeared organ, which, it seemed, had sunk in his gullet, as if detached.

The shocked Luston poked forth the grey and greasy thing, patting and prodding it, in terror and disbelief – sitting, for the next hour, bolt upright in bed until certain it was there, connected to the rest of him. This it seemed to be, though tasting very odd and having the scent of something *untonguely*: like damp grass newly-cut, or even a compost heap of scraps and peelings.

In the coming days, Luston summoned architects, master builders and pleasure pool designers to Minchbury.

Their quotations, samples and ideas all fed his fevered 'vision'.

Yet, as his plans gathered pace, so did his nightly torments.

His strange lancing, stabbing and cutting pains were now really quite savage.

There were other sensations too. As he lay in his bed, his ears seemed to hear *rustles*. And at times he felt as if his ankles and wrists were being bound.

In his mind, it was as if the manor's hedge was in the

habit of entering the house after dark. Insane as he knew the thought to be, he imagined it climbing the carpeted stairs and snaking its way on top of him through the curtains of the four-poster, grotesquely coiling itself around his torso.

More than once, he'd seen himself horribly embowered in a dark-green bed of yew: his nose and lips protruding from its awful depths, his eyes staring out in fear.

Worse still, were the visions he had of Blench.

In these, the grey-faced gardener towered over Luston on a stepladder, opening and closing his shining shears. Those same words Blench had uttered in Luston's boyhood – 'I'm going to give you a clip you won't forget!' – taunted the squire as he cowered in terror.

In the nightmares, the wormed ladder wobbled as Luston looked up, with pleading eyes.

'There could be an accident. Didn't I warn you?' the grizzled gardener on his swaying scaffold growled, as he held up his shears in a great, glistening V.

Even when Blench melted into the blackness, Luston seemed to hear the dreadful scrape of their blades, opening and shutting.

One moonlit night, Luston rose in agony and staggered from his bed. So many were the points of pain on his tortured body that he knew not where to reach to comfort himself.

He dragged himself to what had been Miss Cannington-Dew's dressing table.

There, in its mirrors, he seemed to detect a form.

Closing in on their glass, his eyes fell on the most astonishing thing: an ear-less, nose-less, hand-less man who, those and *other* ghastly omissions apart, bore an awful resemblance to... him.

On the morning of the arrival of the appointed contractors at Minchbury, no sign of Luston, or any form of life (beyond the watchful topiaries), could be found. The tradesmen, who never so much as unpacked their things, returned home the same way they had come. The grand scheme of Oliver Luston lay in ruins before it had even begun, his shimmering 'vision' of Minchbury – as an oasis of his own making – evaporated to nothing, like a desert mirage.

Oliver Luston's brief interregnum as squire of Minchbury Manor has long passed. To this day, mystery shrouds his fate. Some say that a jail cell in South America was – and may still be – his. Another story holds that – having involved himself in something characteristically foolish – he was received by appreciative sharks in the South China Sea. Suggestions of a stranger kind speak of something darker and even more macabre, much closer to home....

The rather more substantial era of Harry Blench, keeper of Minchbury's grounds, has also reached its end – on the walked earth at least. On one of its yew hedges, the topiary form of a gardener, that some think not unlike him, can be observed, wheeling a brimming barrow on its neat and level brow.

Certain visitors who've seen this green man at his labours have been troubled by what they think they have perceived, particularly in the last sunlight of the day.

At such times, the sun's sinking rays have a tendency to redden that quiet part of the country, and the temperature at Minchbury can hasten to a chill.

To these onlookers, the spilling contents of the barrow have seemed not weeds or garden clippings being carted off, but *other* lopped things.

Either way, the monument (for those who know the story) recalls the pledge of spirited Miss Cannington-Dew that – regardless of inheritances rooted in family trees – her trusted gardener, Harry Blench, would always have a place at Minchbury.

Like the rest of the manor's topiaries and its carefully trimmed and thrush-crossed lawns, the sculpture is certainly worth seeing, should you ever find yourself wandering that way.

It may, however, be best not to tarry at the old house and, in particular, in its gardens, at too late an hour in the day.

# A Shining Beacon

THE small town of Skelmere Junction isn't easily come upon in its backwater of the English North Country, particularly since the closure of the railway connection from which it took its name.

In its heyday it was a hub of the wool trade: a packing station for fleeces sent to mills, the home also of a noted sheep market, not to mention a horse fair and a summer show in a bustling field of brass bands, bunting and white marquees.

The yellow York stone of its huddle of houses and shops has darkened considerably since then. And it is, by all accounts, a much quieter place now: erased from timetables for buses as well as trains, vanished from all modern maps; forgotten in its frost pocket, it might be said.

On some nights, it is said to lie quite silent in its ancient fold. Soundless, save for the soft clink of bulbs on various wire-strung lights, swayed by the wind that cuts over the nearby mere (the word for 'lake' that the locals have traditionally preferred).

Improbable as it seems, its Christmas illuminations are now Skelmere's claim to fame – *if* that's the word. Some might favour another.

Should yours be a wandering nature, it's possible that, one evening, you might find yourself entering Skelmere's still-pretty squares, straying down its narrow ways, and witnessing – in person – the aura of those rather peculiar lanterns.

For the present, what follows, as far as the events are known, is an account of how those lights – 'curious' is an adjective some have used – came into being.

Or maybe that last word should be… *beings*.

You, dear readers and perhaps rovers, can be the judges of that.

'NOW, Harold, don't go taking any of what I'm about to say *personally*,' Walter Wheeler began – shuffling some papers while seated at his desk in the mayor's parlour.

Harold Watts didn't like the sound of that. If ever a word was loaded it was *personally*. It was a stab in the back and a punch on the nose at the same time. That's the kind of word it was.

'… but you and me need to have a conversation…'

*Conversation*. There was another. A wheedling, weaselly word. Typical from the tongue of a politician like Walter Wheeler (even if he was only mayor of Skelmere Junction). *Not* having a conversation was what it really meant. Being *told* was an appropriate translation.

'… about the lights,' Wheeler said and looked up.

Up to that point Skelmere's first citizen had avoided his visitor's gaze. Now he studied Watts keenly, to see how his words had sunk in, if indeed they had.

'The lights?' said Watts, nonplussed. 'What about them?'

Harold Watts hadn't expected this. When Rosie Dawes rang to ask him to come to the town hall – for 'a bit of official business' in the mayor's parlour – he'd formed an entirely different impression. In his mind, the receipt of some award had loomed large: a scroll signed by Wheeler, a glass of sherry and a sandwich afterwards, maybe even an alderpersonship (if that was the term).

He'd been up a ladder, angled rather awkwardly, against the spire of St Hilda's. Right beside the weathercock. Installing a new lightning rod (which now poked up, behind the bird's back, in a way that made it seem, to Harold at least, like the shiny old rooster had been skewered for a spit-roast).

Reaching into a pocket for his mobile, he'd almost slipped.

Weirdest thing was that, despite the height, the signal had been terrible: Rosie's voice somehow scrambled: a strange, throaty, furry sound, lisping and clicking in Harold's right ear.

'Yes!' Watts had said loudly before ending the call. 'YES!'

'What *about* the lights?' he now repeated to Wheeler while tusking and tutting in his head. The Christmas lights? Was that *it*? Blumin eck! The money he'd paid to dry-clean his suit! Cheek for his pains from the girl on the counter.

'"Fibro-synthetic blend"?' she'd said, looking at the label. 'Are you *sure* you want it dry-cleaned?'

And how it now reeked. Like the purple bergs in the urinals at *The Swan*. He'd seen Wheeler back off as he walked in. The bloody pen and ink.

'Well,' his host continued, 'there are some in the community who think it's time for... a change.'

Watts leaned forward in his seat. 'A change?'

'And as mayor it's my job to listen to what folk are saying. And, frankly Harold, folk are saying rather a lot.'

Wheeler put on some specs, took a sheet from the pile in front of him, began to read aloud.

'"Dear Mayor, I'm asking you for pity's sake to put a stop to our town's annual humiliation in the form of its so-called Christmas lights. To say that the illuminations..."' (Wheeler negotiated the word syllable by syllable, as if communicating by wireless to a listener at the North Pole) '"... of Skelmere Junction have seen better days would be a gross..."' Wheeler mumbled for a moment, and moved on. '"The Santa and sleigh, which has been strung across High Street these past twenty years, is now so lacking in bulbs that on its last outing it resembled nothing so much as a scarecrow on water-skis. It's time you pulled the plug on the whole…"'

He stopped, looked up, gave Watts an embarrassed half-smile.

'Well, perhaps that one *does* go a little far. Native of these parts if ever there were. But that's the tenor. And I have to tell you Harold, the writer's not alone.'

Wheeler picked up another letter.

'"Mr Mayor, The near blacked-out state of the snowman in Bridge Lane last year was obscene. His flashing carrot nose…" And I think I can safely leave that one there. Marjorie Potts, the wool shop,' Wheeler indicated. 'Needless, I'm sure.'

Watts heard Wheeler in stunned silence. So *this* was their game was it? Not a thank you, a handshake and the right to graze sheep on Scraggby Road roundabout, but a stab in the back – cuts, multiple wounds – with poisoned pens. Just like Julius Caesar. Skelmere folk! Nothing but—

'Ay now, Walter…' Watts reared.

But Wheeler was off again with another moanful missive. '"The reindeer on the lamp standard outside my shop has been leaping there so long the animal must be positively arthritic…"' (This last word the mayor pronounced as if invoking the name of an ancient king.) '"Any humane electrician would have had the thing put down be now."'

Watts could contain himself no longer. 'You don't have to tell me who that's from. Clive Ashton! The swine! Been after my contract for years!'

'But he's a butcher,' said Wheeler, looking up. 'What's he know about electrics?'

'Exactly!' said Harold, eyes swelling in their sockets (rather like lightbulbs, Walter Wheeler thought).

'Not for him!' Watts followed-up smartly. 'For his brother-in-law. Over at Scraggby Sands. Does lights ont seafront… after a fashion.'

'Now don't go blowing a fuse, Harold. I told you not to take it personally.'

There it was again, thought Watts – that word. Oh, he'd bloody well take things personally with Clive Ashton all right. There'd be no more pork sausages from *his* shop. Or chops on a Saturday. Harold Watts would be up the supermarket from now on, like every bugger else. 'Shop Skelmere'? Be damned!

Wheeler was reading again. 'Reverend Wilson. "I'd like to put on record my appreciation of the work done over the years with regard to our Christmas lights by Mr Harold Watts."'

Ah! Now that was more like it, thought Harold. At least the vicar knew which side *his* bread was buttered. Quite right too. A respectable note went on St Hilda's collection plate every Sunday. Same in his father's time, and his grandfather's.

'"But the angels on the clock tower might now perhaps be described as shabby rather than seraphim,"' continued Wheeler. 'Whatever that means,' he said, glancing at Harold. 'Sounds like a medicine, dunt it?' Wheeler went back to the letter: '"And (for several years now) we've had two wise men rather than three in the nativity on the railings. I don't wish to sound ungrateful but…"' He let the letter peter.

'Is that it?' Watts asked.

'Need I go on?' Wheeler replied.

Watts saw the look of a man whose mind was already on his haddock supper. And doubtless there was a grumble in his pile from Stanley Sugden about the state of some illumination outside his fish bar: a wild exaggeration about bulbs that were battered or burnt-out.

Watts wondered for a moment if it was Sugden who'd cooked-up the whole thing. He and Wheeler were committee men: the Loyal Order of the Skels. The town's 'friendly society', or so it styled itself. It met upstairs once a month at *The Swan*. Men only. Watts had at best been an infrequent attendee. He tried to remember if he'd renewed his subs.

'May *I* now speak?' he began.

'Of course,' said Wheeler, knowing full well what was to come.

'My family has been doing the Christmas lights in this town since 1901,' said Watts.

'I know that,' said Wheeler.

'And it was my great-grandfather who brought electricity to Skelmere Junction in 1898.'

'I know that also,' said Wheeler, with a sigh. 'Appen it's a fact you've acquainted me with on more than one occasion.'

'You could actually say that, in so far as Skelmere Junction exists on any map, it's because *we*, the Watts family, bloody well put it there! Electricity is in our blood! It's in our name!' Harold's eyes were blazing now. 'It was the Wattses, it might be said, who took Skelmere out from the Dark Ages. A fact some folk round here seem to have forgotten. Perhaps they need reminding, Mr Mayor!'

Wheeler didn't care for the colour that Watts, in his anger, was turning: a kind of electric blue.

'Ay! Come on! Calm down! There's no need for any of that Mr Mayor stuff tween thee and me.'

Wheeler sought to soothe things. 'Glass of water?' he asked.

'No!' Harold snapped. 'Water and electrics don't mix. Everybody knows that!'

'Well you're the expert,' said Wheeler. 'It's all double Dutch to me. Fret about changing a lightbulb, meself. First thing the wife says is "Call Harold – he'll know".'

Wheeler sensed Watts brighten, the mood lighten (a little).

'What I'm wondering,' he began, 'is whether – not for this year (too late for that, I'll warrant) but the Christmas after – there might be… another way – a middle way, so to speak.'

'Middle way?' asked Harold.

'I've had a letter,' he picked up a lavender-coloured sheet (one that Harold fancied Wheeler had clearly set aside) 'from Lavinia Bloom. Runs that shop int square – boutique, I think she calls it – *Guiding Light*. Candles, smelly stuff, that kind of thing.'

'I know it,' said Harold. 'Only been there five minutes.'

'Two years, actually,' Wheeler continued. 'And in my opinion the kind of forward-looking business this town needs (albeit some folk seem keen enough for it to die on its feet). Ask me, that lady's planted something here.' He paused, searched for a phrase. 'Sown a seed.'

'What?' cried Harold. 'Cheesecloth blouses! Tank tops crow-shetted by kiddies in some ruddy sweatshop! Water bottled from backyard tap! That's our future, is it? Give over Walter!'

'Don't knock it, Harold. Tourists love it. The wife swears by her bath salts. Reckons they've done wonders for her lumbago. Nepalese, or summat.'

Wheeler went back to the letter.

'Anyway, *she* says "Dear Walter" – Wheeler coughed – 'I mean, "Mr Mayor... Although relatively new to Skelmere I hope you won't mind me pointing out that the Christmas lights are a little jaded."'

'Jaded!?' Harold exclaimed.

Wheeler continued: '"Could I possibly suggest the creation of something more in keeping with our times that would also establish Skelmere as a shining beacon"' – Wheeler repeated this last description (with evident relish) – '"for the whole district. I am happy to offer my services in support of same. Yours truly, Lavinia Bloom. PS If your wife..." Oh—' Wheeler cut himself short. 'No need to bother ourselves with that last part.'

Harold said nothing, sat in silence.

'So, all I'm asking,' Wheeler began, 'is that you call on Lavinia' – he corrected himself – 'Ms Bloom, and talk about what *might* be done next year. Too late for us to do owt this Christmas, as I've said. No doubts you'll be busy anyroad – sorting out spare bulbs for your reindeers and snowmen, and whatnot.'

Wheeler stared at Watts.

Eventually, Harold spoke. 'So what you're saying is: this Christmas is my last.'

'Well, yes. I mean, no. No. I mean… maybe,' Wheeler said.

With this, Harold rose and made for the door. As he did so, he sensed that the eyes of the portraits on the walls were upon him, including the glower of his heavily-whiskered great-grandfather Augustus, who had himself once worn the mayor's chain; all of them, so it seemed to Harold, judging him, contemptuous of him, angry at this incontrovertible evidence of his incompetence, the fact that he had shamed their town.

'Go see Lavinia! I mean, Ms Bloom!' Wheeler called after him. 'As for this Christmas… well, just go out with a bang!'

The door slammed shut.

The letters on Wheeler's desk blizzarded against him, the links of his chain rising and falling in a soft, plinking shuffle.

The voice of Rosie Dawes, at her desk in an anteroom, came through the intercom. (At least, Wheeler *thought* it was her voice. The line was weighty with fuzz… static. More a growl than her usual trill.)

'How'd 'e take it?'

'Personally,' Wheeler said.

That night, in the heavy, gloomy lounge of the hillside villa built by his great-grandfather (a property undeniably imposing though always having a certain chill at odds with its pioneering place in the history of electricity), Harold Watts looked down at the community of Skelmere Junction, lit-up below.

Was it not now, at hours such as this, that Skelmere – on the shores of the still and darkened water – was at its most beautiful?

He gazed on the lights of the little town, with awe.

Yes, in the day it still wasn't half-bad compared with many places – even allowing for some of the fangled stuff and ways that had come in. But at night, nestling there… *twinkling*, as it did. It was like… Bethlehem.

'And all the work of the Wattses,' he whispered, in the drawing-room's cold air.

He drew away from the window and took from a shelf one of several albums relating to his forebears. As he often did, he began to turn the leaves, lingering over certain of its contents: Josiah Watts, brother of his great-grandfather, illuminating a paddle steamer that plied the mere, 'gay bulbs burning brightly from bow to stern', according to a yellowed front page from the *Skelmere Shuttle* that promised a 'Full Photographic Report Inside'... a picture of wild-haired Julian Watts, a cousin – his very name a nod to the family's obsession with energy – who'd apparently been mad as a hatter but had supplied the engineering nous for everything in Skelmere from the signals on the steam railway to the circuit board for the town's first road traffic light *and* staged a spectacular *son et lumière* – The Snow Queen – against the walls of the town hall, to which farmers and hill-folk from miles had come... Harold's grandmother Augustina – another great Watts – pivotal in the introduction of telephony to Skelmere (at a time when interest was switching from the wool trade to charabancs of trippers). 'The lady who connected Skelmere Junction to the world,' proclaimed the heading of an obituary printed in a magazine...

Suddenly, the page in Harold's hands went dark, flashed back to visibility, dulled again, then reappeared as, above him, the ceiling light flickered.

Its bulb began to dim in an all too familiar way. For, although the Watts family had worked wonders for little Skelmere, the wiring of their own residence had been their private shame. As the last of their line, Harold, unmarried and heirless, had felt little compulsion to act beyond a never-ending series of patch-ups and solderings, with nightly descents to the cellar and its rust-crusted fuse box, always undertaken to the same incantation. 'Cobblers and shoes, cobblers and shoes, cobblers...'

Now though, still holding the album (and in a faintly liturgical way), he wandered back to the bay window of the drawing-room and again surveyed Skelmere Junction. He recalled his words with Walter Wheeler. About how his family – the Watts family – had *single-handedly* taken the town from the Dark Ages.

'And, *if* we wanted to,' Watts thought to himself, looking down on the little, glinting town, 'we could just as easily send it back.'

Moonlight appeared on the waters of the mere. In Harold's mind the silver beam seemed to signal a path... a *way*, to use Wheeler's word.

'With a bang,' Watts whispered, absently.

In the morning, Harold stepped inside what he had to confess was the pretty frontage of *Guiding Light* in Skelmere's square.

A chime over the door summoned Lavinia Bloom from invisibility at the back of the shop, a weighty cloud of scent wafting with her (noticeable even above the several burning sticks discharging clouds of incense-like smoke that assailed Harold's eyes and throat).

'I've come about making Skelmere a beacon,' he said.

'A *shining* beacon!' Lavinia Bloom corrected him. 'And you are Mr Watts. Good! I've been expecting you.'

Watts looked at her. She was a largish woman, dark-haired, made-up and wearing something, thought Harold, like the smocks boatmen on the mere had once donned (only hers was patterned with a pattern that wasn't quite a pattern... of lines and blobs). Across her forehead, strapping in place her straight, centre-parted hair, was a mauve bandana.

The slappity sound that had accompanied her advance came from the sandals that Harold registered on her (otherwise bare) feet.

By now his eyes were watering and he began to cough.

'May I offer you something?' Lavinia Bloom asked. 'A glass of water, perhaps?'

'Water would be nice,' Harold said. He drew a handkerchief from his pocket, dabbed at his eyes, blew.

'Come on through,' said Lavinia Bloom, and she led him

– past various ornaments, carvings and candles – into the back of the shop, via a bead curtain.

In a small office that she called her *boudoir*, she told Watts to sit. She returned with a glass whose contents were scattered with what seemed to Watts to be petals, of a kind.

'There,' she said. 'Drink that. You men on your own… you need taking care of.'

Watts took a sip, put the glass down, wondered how she knew about him and his 'status'. Wasn't that the term nowadays?

'I was saying the same only the other day to Reverend Wilson,' Lavinia Bloom continued. She promptly began to work her way through the names of what seemed to Harold to be most of the membership of the Skelmere Skels. The sound quickly became a drone.

Harold fixed his eyes on a pendant – more a disc, in actual fact – of the sun, suspended on his hostess's chest. It lay there like the pendulum on a glass-cased clock: stuck in the valley between Lavinia Bloom's undeniably large breasts.

It had eyes and a mouth, and it seemed to draw Harold in.

He gathered his thoughts. 'About the shining beacon,' he began.

'Well,' said Lavinia Bloom, embarking on what seemed to Harold to be another endless ramble. A sharp ray of winter sun now pierced the room's small window, causing the disc of her pendant to emit a curious, flame-like glint.

As she continued, Watts found himself drifting drowsily in a world far removed from Skelmere Junction (with its telegraph poles, scuttles of coal that still kept many a home fire burning, washing lines and whist drives). This *other* world was a place of ancient rites… symbols… exotica… setting suns and rising moons (or was it rising suns and setting moons?). It was a warm, easeful, sun-drenched place of coconut palms and honeyed balms. Wonderful words floated about Watts, like falling leaves on an autumn breeze: 'Mayan temples', 'Egyptian pharaohs', 'Cathay', 'Araby' and 'Ancient

Greece'. All *utterly* unlike Skelmere and, in particular, his own chill villa, with its mildewed cellar and fiddlesome fuse box.

All that was required, Lavinia Bloom intoned, was a little... sacrifice.

*Sacrifice?*

Harold Watts didn't like the sound of that. It was rather like... *personally*. Hadn't he made enough sacrifices for the good of Skelmere Junction? Personal ones an' all?

He shook himself... came-to.

His sight was blurry.

Slowly, like the figurehead of an old ship, the heavy-chested form of Lavinia Bloom solidified out of the mist.

'Yes, yes, well I'll...' said Harold, rising from his seat a little unsteadily and making his way out.

'Bear it in mind?' Lavinia Bloom called after him.

'Yes, yes, I'll bear it in mind,' he said, nearing the door.

Its dangling chime drew over him as he hurried out – the cords and bells brushing the thinning hair of his crown. Their touch and jangle seemed to him like pawing and laughter of a sneering, sarcastic kind.

He shuddered as he moved quickly across the square, having been prompted to imagine some horrible, trailing creature – all fins and limbs – in the murky depths of the mere.

That night, Watts went up to his draughty bedroom early. The lights of the house had failed in their all too familiar fashion. Ordinarily, he would have traipsed down into the cellar and put things right. But that night, for some reason, he felt disinclined. He undressed (partially) and climbed into bed by the pewtery moonlight that fell through his curtainless windows.

The night was clear and from his pillows he was able to gaze out at the star-lit sky.

He found himself thinking about the house, its past and his ancestors. He imagined them devising things, in the way that he knew they had, in its various outbuildings, one of which had been known as 'the laboratory'. He thought about the state of the building now: gripped by ivy, its windows cracked, its clay-tiled roof caved-in.

He recalled a cutting from one of the albums downstairs. About a dinner one Christmas at *The Swan*. The whole town had been there – all the needy folk anyway – near enough. And all paid for by the Wattses.

He thought about Wheeler and the lights. Yes, things had… 'got away' from him. But there were reasons. Among them the fact that he wasn't the brightest bulb in the Watts tree. He knew that. He had the genes, but somehow lacked the drive, the energy. That was what happened – wasn't it? – come the end of the line, the last of the wick, the dying of the light. It was 'mend and make do', 'batten down the hatches'… conserve, not create.

He mulled over his meeting with Lavinia Bloom.

*Sacrifice?* What more did the town want from him? Blood?

As the night wore on, he found himself to be both hot and cold – and above all restless – under the bedclothes.

He wondered if he hadn't caught a chill while up the spire of St Hilda's. He also wondered about the petal-strewn water proffered by Lavinia Bloom. Hadn't Walter Wheeler-bloody-Dealer suggested some similar refreshment in his parlour?

On the walls of his bedroom the branches of trees that had turned wild in the villa's once neatly groomed gardens cast moving moon shadows that had the look of antlers and horns.

Suddenly, Watts saw himself upstairs in a room at *The Swan* – a meeting of The Skels. An extraordinary meeting, it had to be said. For there, on a huge silver platter, on top of the table in the centre of the room, was he – Harold Watts – *in flagrante* with Lavinia Bloom. The two of them bare as the day they were born, their mound of pale flesh looking like nothing so much as a Christmas turkey, plucked, stuffed and ready for the oven.

Around them rotated the entire male membership of the Loyal Order of Skels, who appeared to have removed the hotel's collection of antlered stag skulls from its walls so that they paraded with these same objects on their heads as they enacted their circular dance.

'Sow a seed!' called out Walter Wheeler – recognisable (as he pranced) by his mayoral chain.

'Bare me in mind!' cried out Lavinia Bloom as she clamped Watts to the salver in two powerful white thighs – naked save for her mauve bandana and the sun pendant that swung from her bosom.

Its disc spun hypnotically before Harold's eyes, the metal catching the light cast by the cut-glass chandelier above them (installed by Harold's great-great uncle Jeremiah, some ninety-nine years earlier).

'Shining beacon!' Watts heard someone call out.

'Guiding light!' answered another.

'Sacrifice!' the swirling, antler-skulled Skels demanded as one.

Suddenly, in the decorative mouldings of cherubs and vines that covered the ceiling, the face of Harold's grandmother – Augustina – appeared: her head squeezing from the mouth of a cherub's clarion, in a piece of madness visible only to Watts, pinned as he was on his platter by the legs and knees of Lavinia Bloom.

'You have the power, Harold! *You* have the power!' the black-bonneted head of Augustina Watts called down to him from her height.

'Sacrifice!' the Skels bellowed around the table below her.

'*You* have the power, Harold!' his grandmother called out one final time as her head squirmed back into the cherub's clarion, like a crab into a shell.

'Sacrifice!' the circling Skels once more snorted, their ceremony seeming to near its climax, the oak-panelled room appearing to pulsate around them.

Suddenly, seen only by Harold, the ceiling started to crack. The chandelier began to shake, slip and then shower the room with sparks. Smoke and dust engulfed Lavinia Bloom and the suited shoulders and antler-skulls of the Skels – who rocked and circled and chanted on regardless.

Next, the chandelier's great, shining bulk – it had been delivered to *The Swan* on a horse-drawn dray, such was its weight: Harold had the clipping in an album – was detaching – *falling* – from the white, splintering ceiling to the chaotic scene below.

'No!' Harold Watts screamed. 'No!!'

And then he sat up in his bed.

The next day, Watts busied himself with a series of small jobs around the town. His clients – the authors, or at least co-signatories, of those complaints to the council about his Christmas lights – were surprised to find him cheerfully knocking their doors. In fact, they were taken aback. Not only by his chirpy manner but his insistence on waving any fee. All part of his service, he told them. Wasn't Christmas a time for giving? A little sacrifice wouldn't hurt.

So it was that, among many other calls, he found himself re-wiring the pie-warmer at Stanley Sugden's fish bar ('Engineering update from supplier, Stan – this'll keep your steak and kidneys piping'), adjusting the drum speeds at Ena Allsopp's launderette ('That's a much more suitable spin for you, Ena'), fine-tuning the circuitry of Clive Ashton's bacon-slicer ('That'll give thee a far sharper cut, Clive – fittest rasher this side of Scraggby an' no mistake'), correcting the intercom at the town hall ('There you go, Walter – you and rest of council will be hanging on each other's every word') and sorting the burglar alarm at Marjorie Potts's wool shop ('Goodness your cables were a mess, Mrs P – I've tied you off good an' proper now').

The most taxing task was at St Hilda's. An alteration to the circuitry of the lightning conductor beside the weathercock.

The maker, Watts informed Reverend Wilson, had come up with an ingenious way of harnessing energy in the event of a lightning strike – a more or less failsafe way of warming the pews. Not to mention his lectern, of course.

Finally, for Lavinia Bloom at *Guiding Light*, a motion

sensor for when she was in the back of her shop, which, in place of her door chime, would play any tune or carol of her choosing, from *California Dreaming* to *Little Donkey*, whenever a soul came in. All downloadable from the internet at her *mere* – 'Pardon the pun,' said Harold – press of its red button.

'Just push on that when you're ready,' said Harold, indicating a scarlet pad, 'and it'll be all systems go,' he added, with a smile.

He stepped from her doorway into the square and relished a warming glow of winter sun. Inside him, the conviction bloomed that – never mind his recent travails – all would now be well with Skelmere... all would go on as it ought.

Making his way home, he seemed to see his grandparents and several more of his ancestors, standing on corners and the doorsteps of shops: Julian Watts – holding aloft a bowler hat; Harold's great-grandfather, Augustus, not scowling as in his portrait at the town hall, but nodding, as if with approval; his grandmother, Augustina, waving a lace handkerchief as he passed.

All of them signalling, so he felt: telling him that he was worthy. Telling him that *he* was a Watts.

Longer-standing inhabitants of outlying villages in that part of the North Country well recall the spectacle of a sudden bright light in the sky above Skelmere (an explosion, some took it to be, or even an asteroid), the white glow gradually giving way to a steady pink sheen.

More often than not, the precise date escapes them, other than it being a late afternoon not long before one Christmas.

In many respects, the chronology no longer matters. For the greater curiosity about Skelmere is this: those odd, haunting lights (their aura so imitative of a shepherd's delight and visible from afar when skies are clear) never, *ever* extinguish.

As those able to locate the lonely old wool town will attest, its peculiar lamps glow not just at Christmas, but on every night of the year.

It is the uncannily detailed and intensely life-like (if that is the term) nature of Skelmere's lanterns (of recent years at least) that has held wanderers rapt. *Shocked* it may even be said, in the case of certain inquisitive souls who've seen fit to brush from the bulbs their winter shrouds of frost and snow for the purpose of a closer inspection.

Those with some passing knowledge of the mere-side settlement have – though opting *not* to articulate the thought for fear of looking foolish – detected a certain similarity with former well-known figures in the town.

A glowing ass in the stable of a nativity on the churchyard railings has, for example, caused some to remember a particular past mayor: the sparkling 'rope' to its neck being thought in their eyes to resemble a chain of office. A flashing snowman, meanwhile, has recalled to others a Skelmerian once prominent in the butchery trade – this connection kindled by the frosty fellow's 'parts'. Among them (but not exclusively) his nose, eyes and the buttons on his coat... crafted, so it seems, with pork sausages, black pudding, faggots, rissoles and other unlikely products.

As far as the angels on the clock tower in the square are concerned, one – with a shock of upstanding hair – has been said to bear an uncanny likeness to a particular past vicar. A second angel, locked – or so it has appeared – in a rather unholy union with the first, has meanwhile been likened to a certain lady not known for her cheerfulness who once ran a wool shop (shuttered and closed these past several years).

And while 'holly' and 'ivy' would in any other town take the form of lights burning keenly in bright-green and berry-red, in Skelmere Junction's case these are the monikers apparently given to two electrified old ladies 'grumbling' sourly – so accounts have it – across a glowing garden gate.

Strangest of all though is the fairy that tops the town's tree.

Such figures are of course normally garbed prettily in silver and pink. But Skelmere's, at the pinnacle of a tall, bulb-decked fir, is said to be both a little large for the task and to wear – as far as vestments are concerned – nothing more than a mauve bandana.

Those are but a few of the oddities some believe that – in perhaps the way watchers see faces in a fire – they've witnessed in the lights of Skelmere Junction.

'More Old Nick than Saint Nick' is a comment that's been heard from travellers who've hastened – with a shiver – from this strange street theatre.

Not Bethlehem then, as Harold Watts once called it.

But 'a shining beacon'?

Well, yes, of a sort...

And what, when all is said and done, of Harold Watts, last in a line of great English illuminators, whose story, it could be said, this is?

Reliable reports to the rest of the world are rare from Skelmere Junction. But intelligence has it that, one late autumn evening, callers to his empty house on its melancholy hill came upon a cinder... beneath a blackened fuse box at the foot of the cellar steps.

The wiring of the damp, old villa was proclaimed to be – for the seat of such a luminary family in the field of electricity – in a truly shocking state.

# Thanks

Matthew G. Rees thanks Jon Gower, Sally Spedding, Gill Figg (for the use of her art, particularly), Simon Howells, Brian Manton and others for kind support in various ways during the creation of this collection; also Janna Liggan of *Lamplit Underground* for promoting his story Red Kite which later became The Gate.

Matthew G. Rees grew up in the border country between England and Wales known as the Marches. In his early career he was a newspaper journalist. Later he entered teaching, working for a period in Moscow. Diverse other employment has included time as a night-shift cab driver. His first story collection *Keyhole* was published by Three Impostors press in 2019. Two plays by Rees, *Dragonfly* and *Sand Dancer*, have been performed professionally.

Printed in Great Britain
by Amazon

54957617R00142